THE
FIRST VAMPIRE

A NOVEL OF SAMSON & DELILAH

ALICIA BENSON

A VIRTUAL TALES BOOK

The First Vampire—A Novel of Samson & Delilah

Copyright © 2008 Alicia Benson (www.aliciabenson.com)

Cover Art © 2008 Michael Grills (www.michaelgrills.ca)

Edited by P. June Diehl (www.angelfire.com/biz7/iwriteforyou)

A Virtual Tales Book
PO Box 822674
Vancouver, WA 98682 USA

www.VirtualTales.com

ISBN 0-9801506-8-X

First Edition: October 2008

Printed in the United States of America

9 7 8 0 9 8 0 1 5 0 6 8 1

This book is dedicated to Robert,
who is my rudder and my inspiration

and also to everyone who read the first draft
and told me that the aliens had to go.

Coming Soon From Alicia Benson:

Fool Me Twice
(Another Novel of Samson & Delilah)

www.AliciaBenson.com

PROLOGUE

Samson lay buried in a tomb of his own making. As the collapsed building stabilized, a thick layer of dust settled around him. In his blindness, he couldn't see it, but he could feel its gritty weight upon his skin. It gathered near his nostrils, making it harder for him to breathe. He forced himself to be calm, to lie still as the grinding screech of stone against stone faded.

As the noise of the collapse lessened, it was replaced by the aggrieved shrieks of the Philistines. Only moments ago they had been enjoying a public feast day. Flags had fluttered in the sunshine, and the citizens of the city had milled about the square sampling the various temptations and entertainments on offer from the local merchants.

He was supposed to be part of the entertainment as well—chained to the center pillars of their temple, a conquered captive on display for them to mock and spit on. Now those who had been inside the temple were dead, and those who loved them were screaming and scurrying about on top of the fallen slabs looking for hope.

Samson knew they would find little. Even from beneath feet of fallen marble, he could hear everything. And almost no living sounds came from beneath the ruined temple—just his own ragged breathing, that of a few others. Of the thousands buried with him, all were dead or dying.

He would die soon too, he knew. A great hunk of marble, uprooted from its centuries-old footings, weighed heavily on his chest, making him struggle for every breath. Very soon, he would lie forever with his enemies. Even in his fevered state, the irony was not lost on him. *God and Delilah must both be laughing at me now*, he thought.

A flicker of remorse flared within Samson. They had captured him, blinded him, and tortured him without mercy, but the Philistines were not his true enemy. She was. Delilah. The one who had betrayed him, who had wormed his secret out of him and then delivered him into the hands of his enemies.

Only he wasn't dead, he reminded himself. He was buried, but not dead. A crack sounded from just above him, and Samson looked up to see the marble slab that formed the roof of his narrow tomb slip several inches and come to rest even closer to his face. Alarm and adrenaline shot through him, followed swiftly by shock that he could see anything at all.

The Philistines had put out his eyes, but now he could see. How fitting for God to have restored his sight so the last thing he saw would be the inside of his own tomb, he thought.

But that wasn't all he could see. Down the ragged sides of the marble slabs, tiny rivulets of blood coursed toward him. He watched their progress transfixed; something in his raging brain told him those drops were all that mattered. He struggled toward them, but the blocks held him pinned from the neck down, forcing him to lay there, trapped, waiting for what seemed like an eternity before the first drop of blood splashed down onto his upturned face. Still warm, it ran into his eyes and nose, clearing a shiny path through the dust. Samson strained forward, tongue extended, needing to know the taste of Philistine blood more than he needed air in his burning lungs. The next drop hit his open mouth, and the strange restless need he'd been feeling all day suddenly had form.

He stayed there for hours sucking blood from the stones, until the sun went down and the rescuers departed. Then he pushed away the blocks that had covered him and crawled out of the rubble.

⚜

CHAPTER 1

She answered the phone without looking up on the second ring. "Ariana Chambers."

"Hi, it's me," said a voice she knew too well, yet apparently not well enough.

"James," she responded, "Hi."

"I'm sorry to call you at work, but..."

Ariana looked at her watch. It was after 10:00 p.m. "That's okay," she said wistfully. "Is something the matter?" She knew why he was calling.

James hesitated. "You haven't signed the papers."

No more pretending. "I know, James," she said. "I'm sorry. I've been... busy. I promise I'll read them this weekend, and your lawyer will have them by Tuesday."

James sighed. "Thank you, Ariana. I'm sorry it's come to this, but now that it has, I just want to get it over with."

Their life together. Their marriage. *Yep, best just to get it over with.* She wanted to cry or scream, but did neither.

"I'll let you get back to work, then," James was saying. "Goodnight, Ariana."

"Goodnight. I..." Ariana forced herself not to say *I love you.* It was a habit she had to break. "I'll sign the papers."

James put the phone back in the cradle. If Ariana said he would have the papers by Tuesday, he knew that's when it would be. His wife was a person of her word. And part of him hated her for it. People trusted Ariana. She was beautiful and brilliant and had a gift for finance, but it took more than smarts to persuade investors to let you manage hundreds of millions of dollars of their money. It took something extraordinary. And that's why he had asked for the divorce—

because Ariana wasn't content to be ordinary. Over the last six years, James had come to realize he didn't want an extraordinary life. He just wanted the usual things—a home, a family, maybe a dog.

Realizing he was still staring at the phone, James forced himself to put it down and trudge into the kitchen. The linoleum glared back at him. He pulled open two of the particle board cabinet doors and stared for a moment at the rows of tin cans. Nothing looked likely to calm the slight queasiness that beset him whenever he thought about the huge mistake he could be making.

Two steps brought him back into his tiny entryway, and his neglected running shoes caught his eye. He hadn't been running all week. He quickly exchanged his khakis for a pair of shorts, threw on his shoes, and headed downstairs. Leaving his apartment was always the same. Stale air hit him in the face as soon as he stepped outside. There was no breeze in mid-town. The apartment he had shared with Ariana faced the Hudson. It always had a breeze.

Killing off the familiar litany of doubt, James focused instead on the flow of the sidewalk beneath his feet. His usual route took him through the southern portion of Central Park, but he looked at his watch as he neared the stone wall along the park's western edge. A nagging voice in his head reminded him of the lateness of the hour, but he passed through the entryway with a shrug. His route wasn't too far off the main thoroughfares and lanterns dotted the path at regular intervals. He told himself it was as safe as any other Manhattan street at night.

Inside the park, the green of summer still lingered despite the chill in the air, and the fluorescent lamps cast everything in their radius as a strange, bright blue-green. The deeper shadows faded into pure black, and James kept his eyes on the path illuminated before him.

About 20 minutes later, he topped the hill that marked the half-way point in his five-mile course. The walls to the right and left of the path got taller in this section, and he could no longer see over them.

James rounded the bend at the bottom of the hill and shivered, despite his exertion, as a sudden cool breeze stirred behind him. Before he could wonder at it, something hooked around his neck, pulling him backward. He struggled, but before he could get a handhold or land a blow, his attacker jerked him off his feet and vaulted them both back over the top of the wall.

CHAPTER 2

Toria drained a few more drops from the runner she had pinned against a tree, her black-clad body a stain against the man's white flesh. From Ash's vantage point, she might have been an otherworldly ballerina, cradling her petite form against her partner.

"I didn't know this was a dinner meeting," Ash quipped from across an expanse of dark grass.

Toria turned, giving a last, longing look at her victim. Reluctantly, she let him drop to the ground, where he landed with a thud and a weak groan.

"I'll never understand your fascination with joggers," Ash said, taking a step toward his old friend.

Toria licked the blood from her lips and ran a hand through her thick, dark ringlets. "It's because they never see it coming," she said, sounding almost wistful. "Out here running alone," she gestured at the fake wilderness of Central Park and snickered, "they feel immortal." Licking a trail of blood from the back of her hand, she stole a surreptitious glance at the fading runner.

Ash rolled his dark eyes. "Come on," he said, indicating a spot farther up the hill. "I can't talk to you with your leftovers staring at me."

As they passed the heap of flesh at the base of the tree, he couldn't stop the beginning of his usual sermon. "You take too many risks, Toria," he said, shifting his gaze back to her.

A baleful glare was her only response.

"But we've had this discussion many times," he acknowledged, her expression reminding him of just how many.

"And you can be sure I didn't invite you here just to have it again," Toria snapped, stopping to put a hand on her slim hip in the same defiant stance Ash always thought of when she came to mind.

Ash studied her as she stood, not an inch over five feet, but defiant as always. When they first met, she had been a concubine of the great Kurdish warrior Saladin. Ash had fought with him as a mercenary when he retook Jerusalem from the Crusaders. With stratagems worthy of Saladin himself, Toria had clawed her way to the top of his harem and eventually into Saladin's confidence.

"Why did you ask *me* here?" Ash queried, suddenly not sure he wanted to know the answer. He fingered the cell phone in the pocket of his overcoat, resisting the temptation to dial for his car service. He was ready to get out of the park. The place gave him the creeps.

"Why do you always think I have an ulterior motive?" Toria asked, looking up at him with a deceptively sweet smile. "Can't I just want to see my old friend?"

Ash frowned. "Toria, in the thousand years I've known you, you've never once done anything without an ulterior motive." He studied her small form, clothed in her usual black attire. Even her fingernails were painted black, he noticed. She had worn bright colors when he first met her, but he thought the black suited her better. "So much ruthlessness in such a small package," he muttered, meeting Toria's gaze. "It's why I turned you, you know. I couldn't bear to see so much power and such dark loveliness crumble into dust."

Toria took a step toward him, her gaze warming, but Ash put out his hand. "Does the Council know you're here?" he asked softly.

Toria hesitated. "Yes," she said, "but I'm not here to spy on you, if that's what you're thinking."

Ash opened his mouth to deny it, but couldn't give voice to the lie.

"They're really not so bad, Ash," Toria said. "If you would deign to associate with them once in a while, they would get over their fascination with you."

Ash shook his head. "I think I prefer having them watch me from a distance."

"Unlike humans," she said in a pout, "with whom you freely associate every day."

Ash ran a tired hand through his dark hair. He knew his refusal to join the larger vampire society rankled Toria. Still, he couldn't do it. They were an abomination—an abomination that had started with him, every one of them a walking, talking reminder of his own failures and weaknesses.

"Why did you ask me here, Toria?" he repeated.

"There have been some disappearances," she explained, dropping the pouting coquette routine.

"What's that got to do with me?" he asked. "It's probably another feud or something equally stupid. Either way, it's strictly Council business."

Ash turned to go, but Toria grabbed him by the arm. "This is more than the usual violence, Ash. We don't know what's happening."

Ash heard runners approaching on the path below and lowered his voice to a whisper. "What do you mean? Have you investigated?"

Toria released his arm. "Of course," she retorted. "I'm looking into all of them myself. They're all young, and some appear to have died in the usual ways, but not all of them. The official explanation, of course, is that they killed themselves, but I don't believe it."

"So what do you think is happening?" he pressed.

Toria splayed her hands open. "I don't know yet," she said. "So far all I have is rumors."

"Why am I just hearing about this now?" Ash demanded.

"I didn't want to bother you," Toria said with a touch of what seemed like genuine hurt. "I know you don't like it when we intrude into your human life." She spat out the word human as if it was a bit of bad meat. "Besides, you haven't been in town for some time now."

Another pair of runners trudged past on the path below. Ash shook his head. "We can't talk properly here," he said. "I'm going to be in New York on business for at least a few weeks. Come by my townhouse when you've got more information, and I'll see if there's anything I can do."

Toria nodded, murmured an all but inaudible word of thanks, and backed away into the darkness.

Ash turned in the opposite direction and retraced his steps back down the hill. Halfway down, a strangled grunt forced him to turn back.

Toria's discarded jogger lay awkwardly at the base of the tree. The sweat on his skin hadn't even dried, but he was pale and unmoving. Ash knelt and put two fingers to the man's throat, detecting a very weak pulse. The poor man wouldn't last much longer. Suddenly, the man's eyes opened, and Ash drew back, startled.

"My wife," the man pleaded. He drew in a breath as if to say more, but no words came.

He stared at Ash for another moment before his gaze went blank, and Ash was shocked to find that the man's emotion had touched him, reaching a place in him he thought long hardened. Whoever he was, the man bore real love for his wife. Ash remembered the feeling, and was surprised he still could. When he thought of Delilah it was usually hate and recrimination that rose to the fore.

Putting her out of his mind, Ash looked into the man's slowly closing eyes and decided to do something he had not done in many lifetimes—something he'd thought never to do again. He flexed his tongue against his palette to expose his fangs.

There was no need to drain any more blood from the man; only the final step remained. With one fang Ash opened a vein in his own wrist and pressed it to the man's lips, ignoring the flicker of doubt coalescing at the back of his mind. As the first and strongest vampire, the ones he created were very powerful. Ash hoped he was not making a mistake with this man. Perhaps nostalgia had gotten the better of him, but he thought the time might have finally come when his progeny need not be killers.

Ash let the man drink his fill. The effort weakened him, but he immediately pulled out his phone and called his driver. They needed to get out of the park.

He waited just a moment as his strength returned, then stood and dragged the semi-conscious runner to his feet. He couldn't stand, but Ash slung one of his arms across his shoulders and braced the man's body against his own. Then he carried him, feet dangling just above the ground, to the edge of the park

A short car ride later, Ash slung the now completely unconscious man over his shoulder and carried him in through the garage entrance of his townhouse. After three flights of stairs, he opened the door to one of the spare bedrooms and deposited the man onto the bed.

CHAPTER 3

Except for the wooden chair in which she sat and the bouquet of Number 2 pencils on Detective Simmons' desk, every other surface in the Midtown North police precinct seemed to have taken refuge under innumerable coats of medium blue paint. Blue stretched out before her in every direction.

"And that was the last time you heard from him?" Detective Simmons asked.

Ariana nodded, the motion increasing the strange sense she had of being at sea. She looked back at the detective and caught his cloudy eyes roving over her figure, so she returned the favor. Neither tall nor short, with just the beginnings of a comb-over, Detective Simmons was as plain as his name.

"So the two of you no longer live together, is that right?" the detective asked.

"Yes. James moved out just over a month ago," Ariana explained, "but he wouldn't go away without telling me."

Detective Simmons' viewed her with skepticism. "So, you think he's been missing for three days?" he asked.

"Yes," Ariana confirmed. "We spoke on Friday night, and I haven't been able to reach him since."

The detective made a half-hearted notation on his yellow pad. "And what time was it when you got this call on Friday?"

"Around ten."

"You were working?" The detective asked, looking away from her to scribble something else onto the pad.

"Yes," Ariana repeated, wondering if he was really writing anything down.

"And did your husband sound unusual in any way?"

Ariana hesitated. "No, he just wanted to see if I'd signed the divorce papers."

The detective lowered his pen. "Is it possible your husband just doesn't want to talk to you?" he asked. "Or maybe he's off rethinking the divorce?"

His voice had grown patronizing, but Ariana thought he was trying to be nice. "No," she said slowly, shaking her head. "He'd made up his mind." An errant lock of blonde hair slipped into her field of view; she hastily tucked it behind her ear.

Detective Simmons' skeptical look resurfaced. "You're sure he couldn't just be holed up in a bar somewhere?"

"My husband doesn't drink, officer," Ariana said through tight lips. "He was in his apartment on Friday night, and now he's nowhere to be found. If you knew James, you'd know that something must have happened. Please tell me you'll help me."

The officer drew back in his chair. "Look, lady, don't worry," he said, pushing his yellow pad in her direction. "Put down his full name and address, and if you know where he likes to go, put that down too. We'll put someone on it tonight. We'll check his apartment, hospitals… and we'll let you know what we find."

Ariana carefully wrote down the address of James' apartment, his office, and the words CENTRAL PARK in giant letters, and slid the pad back across the desk. Detective Simmons read it and gave her a questioning look.

"He jogs there at least four times a week," she explained.

The detective slid the pad to one side. "That's very helpful, Mrs. Chambers. That will give the boys somewhere to start."

Ariana stood and pulled one of her business cards from her wallet. "Please take this, Detective," she said. "I understand it may not seem urgent to you, but I know something has happened to James. Please," she reiterated, pressing the card firmly into his calloused hand, "call me when you find out anything."

Detective Simmons slipped the card into his shirt pocket and handed her one of his own. "Likewise, Mrs. Chambers, if you think of anything else, please give us a call."

"I will, Detective, thank you."

"Mrs. Chambers?"

Ariana turned back.

"One more question. Does your husband have a life insurance policy?"

Ariana knew he was just doing his job, but couldn't keep her gaze from turning to ice. "Yes, he has one through his job, but I think you'll find out when you start *investigating*," she leaned hard on the word, "that I'm not in any sort of financial difficulty. Of the two of us, I have the far bigger paycheck."

"Thank you, Mrs. Chambers." The detective rose from his chair and extended his hand.

Ariana shook it grudgingly, knowing she couldn't afford to offend him.

Back out on the street, irritation at Detective Simmons and at her own inability to do more fueled her pace as she headed back toward her apartment. The sun had set while she was inside, but the streets of midtown Manhattan still glowed. Not even the sky was truly dark; tonight it was more of a deep mauve, some low clouds having rolled in to reflect the light of the city back to its nocturnal denizens.

With the hours she put in at the office, Ariana had given up seeing the sun, but sometimes she really missed the stars.

She'd grown up on a farm, where the sky stretched as far as the eye could see in any direction, and the stars were visible almost every night. You could even see the Milky Way from there. But not here.

This was a city that felt no need for further adornment. Its boxy silhouette of concrete and glass and steel reflected back the sun during the day and allowed the city's own radiance to block out the sky at night, as if thumbing its proud nose at the only things that might rival it.

Ariana supposed it was just as well. The yawning emptiness of the night sky seemed designed to make humanity feel small, and New York was a monument to human achievement. Tonight though, she longed to look up into the stars and believe in something bigger than just herself.

CHAPTER 4

J ames thought he must be dead, but his mind cleared and he realized that if he were dead, it probably wouldn't hurt so much.

He slowly opened his eyes. Everything was still dark. *Great,* he thought, *I'm blind in addition to being almost dead.* Slowly, however, his eyes began to adjust to the low light, and he realized he wasn't blind after all, just lying in a bed in a dark room. He struggled to get up, but a voice from the darkness told him to lie still.

James froze as fear rippled through him. In the far corner of the room he could just make out the seated figure of a very large man. As he stared, the visual sharpened, bringing his captor into focus. It was hard to tell his age. His hair was black, springy, without even a hint of gray, but the carved expression on his face belonged to someone much older. A well-tailored suit did little to hide the defined musculature underneath.

James' mind raced as a cold sweat broke out on his forehead. *Kidnapped,* he thought, *I've been kidnapped, and this guy is here to guard the prize.*

"Not exactly," his captor snorted in retort.

Even as he thought it, James knew he was wrong. The power that clung to this man was more than just physical power. It was also money, probably very old money, and something else James couldn't quite put a finger on.

"Well, what then?" James said, trying to remember if he'd made his first comment out loud. "What the hell happened to me?" he asked. "Who are you? Where am I?" His voice began to rise in panic.

The man started to get up, but appeared to think better of it and returned his large body to the chair.

"My name is Ash Samson," he said, answering James as calmly as if they had just met at a friend's dinner party. "You're in my home. You were attacked in the park. Out for a late run, I believe."

James thought back. He remembered calling Ariana to ask her to sign the divorce papers. He remembered going for the run. And then something else. Something dark descending from above as he rounded a lonely curve. Something grabbing him by the neck and hoisting him into the air. Something sucking the life out of him. He began shaking his head from side to side in almost unconscious denial.

"No," Ash insisted, "your mind is not playing tricks on you. What you remember is exactly what happened. The woman who attacked you—" Ash stopped at James' confused look. "Alright, the *thing* that attacked you," he said, "was a vampire named Toria. She, unfortunately for you, has a taste for joggers."

"What kind of goddamned sick joke is this?" James demanded, swinging his feet to the floor. "Look, I don't know what happened to me or what part you played in it, but I'm going to leave now, and..." he broke off for a moment as Ash rose from the chair to his full height, but he swallowed hard and continued on, "...and if you just stand aside, I won't call the police."

"I'm afraid that's not possible," Ash said, his voice dark and level.

"Are you saying I'm not free to leave?"

"I'm not holding you prisoner, if that's what you mean." Ash returned to his former seated pose. "But you were basically dead just a few days ago."

"Days!" James knew he was yelling, but didn't care. "Days? Why didn't you take me to a hospital?" He raced on, not waiting for an answer. "My God, does my wife know I'm okay?"

"You're not okay," Ash replied. "And there was no time to get you to a hospital, James. The only thing I could do was to give you my blood."

James looked confused. "Are you a doctor?"

"No," Ash said patiently. "I'm a vampire."

"Oh, shit," James muttered, convinced now that he'd been kidnapped by a well-dressed lunatic.

"James, please. This will be much easier for you to understand if you just let me explain."

"How do you know my name?" James demanded, bracing himself for the next sinister twist.

Ash pointed to a pair of well-worn running shoes on the floor at the end of the large wooden bed frame. "There's a little pouch on your shoe with an ID card in it," Ash explained.

"Oh," James said.

"I am 3,000 years old," Ash began. "In my mortal life, I was known as Samson, and most of what has been written about me was true. I was a rash, barbaric young man, who, despite that, believed myself a servant of God. No, don't scoff," he said, when James couldn't keep the look of skepticism off his face. "Others believed it too."

"Right up until you sold your soul to Delilah?" James asked, wondering how this tale could get any more fantastic.

"That woman betrayed me," Ash said. When James made no comment, he continued on. "Since you seem to know the story, you'll remember I supposedly died in the rubble of a Philistine temple that I brought down in one final act of God-given strength." Ash shifted his gaze from James to stare at a spot on the wine-colored curtains. "Obviously, that wasn't quite what happened. Something happened to me that day, something that turned me into this." Ash gestured at the length of his seated body. "I don't know if there are other vampires older than me. All the ones I have ever known are ones I created or their progeny. As are you."

"Listen, that's a great story," James said, "really it is, but I have to go."

"Why does no one ever just believe me?" Ash asked to no one in particular. "In 3,000 years, you'd think someone would give me the benefit of the doubt." He let out an exaggerated sigh and pressed a button on a small remote control that sat on the arm of his chair.

The heavy curtains over the window beside the bed made a whirring sound as they drew open. Bright sunlight streamed into the room, lighting the space between the two men.

James lifted an arm to shield his eyes. "What am I supposed to do," he asked, irritated, "climb out the window?"

Ash smiled. "No, you are supposed to reach out your hand."

James was suddenly hesitant.

THE FIRST VAMPIRE — 15

"Come on," Ash prodded, "put that skinny arm of yours into the sunlight. I've told you I made you a vampire. Now I will prove it to you."

James stood and took one long stride, putting his whole body into the square of light coming in from the window. "I don't know what you expected to happen, but obviously I'm…" James' voice trailed off, as pain and confusion warred for the expressive territory of the newest vampire's face.

Moments went by, and still James stood there, burning, but not believing.

When he started to smoke, Ash got up, went over to him and gave him a push that sent him tumbling backwards onto the bed.

"Don't be a fool, James," Ash said. "It's exactly as I've told you. You will be extremely photosensitive for a few years."

"I'm smoking," James said, finally coming out of his stupor. His voice rose again in panic as he looked at the white wisps coming from his hands. "I'm actually smoking." His eyes flew to Ash's face. "I don't call that just being photosensitive." Now he started to yell. "I call that being a fucking, goddamned VAMPIRE! What have you done to me?"

"Saved your life?" Ash suggested.

James' skin began returning to its former color. "I have to go," he said, struggling to a sitting position. "I have to get out of here."

"James you aren't ready. How will you live? How will you feed?"

"Feed?" James cried. "Dear God, what have you done to me?" He gave Ash a look filled with all the horror his brain could muster. "I don't know why you've done this," he said after a moment spent struggling to fit this new reality into the world he thought he knew, "or even exactly what 'this' is, but I want to leave here and never set eyes on you again. So tell me what I need to know," James demanded. "Tell me what I need to know to be able to leave here and never come back."

Ash stiffened. "Very well," he said, grabbing the remote and returning the drapes to their closed position. "Follow me."

CHAPTER 5

A sh led him downstairs into an office where panels roughly one foot square, made of a rich, red wood James didn't recognize, covered all four walls. Thick beige carpet muffled their footfalls as they entered.

"Am I dead?" James asked.

Ash turned around. "No, James, you are most definitely not dead. You can still breathe and eat and do most other things you used to."

James' eyes widened.

"You will find, however," Ash continued, "that you have little desire to do any of those things. Your body needs more oxygen now than it did before. You can get some of your requirements of oxygen by breathing if you must, but your body has been changed into a very efficient mechanism for removing oxygen from human blood. It also uses some of the proteins in the blood for cell regeneration, but oxygen is the main requirement."

Ash crossed the room to his desk. James remained standing, uncertain how far he wanted to follow.

Ash pushed a button on the underside of his desk top, and two of the panels directly behind him slid open to reveal a small metal door. Ash pulled the door open, and only then did James realize he was looking at a mini-refrigerator. From it, Ash removed a vacuum-sealed silver bag. He handed it to James, along with a straw.

"Juice box?" James queried, both eyebrows raised.

Ash laughed. "I guess you could call it that, yes, but it's not juice. It's synthetic blood."

"Synthetic blood?" James repeated. "I didn't think there was such a thing. If you really have it, you shouldn't keep it to yourself," he said. "Lots of people could benefit from a synthetic blood supply."

Ash studied him for a moment, and James was briefly glad to have surprised him.

"One of my investments is in a small bio-tech company called Hemogen," Ash explained, "whose goal is to make synthetic blood for human use. They haven't perfected it yet, but they succeeded several years ago in making a highly oxygenated synthetic blood that met my requirements. Now, I keep funding them, and I have the formula and a constant supply." Ash nodded toward the bag. "Now drink."

"Uh… I'm not thirsty?" James suggested.

"No, but you soon will be," Ash said, "and I'll be honest with you, synthetic is not quite as good as the real thing. It helps stave off the worst cravings, though, and that's what I'd like to try with you for a while. I'd like to see if you can develop some control before you start feeding on humans."

"Dear God." James walked to the back of the room and sank down into the dark, supple leather of the sofa. The cold sweat had returned to his forehead, and he mopped at it with the back of his hand.

"The sweating only lasts a few days," Ash replied, as if it should be a comfort. "It's just a leftover reflex."

"Am I really going to want to eat people?" James asked.

"No, not eat. We're not cannibals." Ash pulled a short leather chair from in front of his desk, spun it around and took a seat facing James. "But human blood is what we crave. We can live on other things— synthetic blood, animal blood—but nothing is quite as satisfying as drinking from a live human." Ash went on, ignoring James' grimace. "You can drink without killing as soon as you develop a little control. It is in their infancy that vampires—at least those who don't choose to be killers—are the most dangerous, both to humans and themselves." Ash gestured again toward the bag in James' hand. "That's why I want you to start slow."

James couldn't believe he was listening to this. Nevertheless, he put his lips to the tiny plastic straw and took a sip.

A cool, metallic liquid coursed over his tongue, and blinding pain shot from his jaw. James dropped the bag and slapped both hands over his mouth. He gave a muffled yell and looked wide-eyed at Ash.

"It always hurts a bit the first time your fangs come in."

James resisted the urge to say "Fangs?" He was starting to feel like an echo. Instead, he ran his tongue along the back of his teeth. Shock forced his eyes wide as he felt first one new tooth and then another.

They jutted down from his palate behind his real teeth, very thin, but wickedly sharp. As he ran his tongue over them, he found himself wanting to bite down on the warm flesh.

He clenched his jaw shut instead and looked down at the silver bag in his lap. Almost against his will, he raised the bag once more. For a moment he simply stared at its shimmering surface, contemplating the liquid inside. He opened his mouth and bit down hard, sending his fangs right through the plastic.

He wanted it to be warm, but even the cool rush was like a red-hot poker to his brain. He closed his eyes, pressed the malleable plastic tighter against his mouth and sucked greedily. A tiny sliver of his brain recoiled in horror, but its cry was almost inaudible compared to the sweet sound of rushing blood. James ignored the voice of caution and drank on.

When the bag was empty and some sanity had returned, James slid back on the couch and put his head in his hands. It wasn't dignified, he knew, but at least it stopped them from shaking.

"There's no need to be ashamed, James," Ash said. "Just as before, you are what you choose to be. You can choose to be a wild beast or to manage your cravings. Both roads are open to you."

"Choose?" James asked. "Manage?" He raised a tear-streaked face, but his tone was strident. "Those are nice words, Ash. But I can never go back, can I?"

Ash's face softened for a moment, but then his mask of nonchalance returned. "No," he said dryly, "you can never go back to your old life. It will be many years before you can be in prolonged close contact with humans with any certainty of your control over your hunger."

"How long?" James persisted. "Can you do it?"

Ash nodded. "Yes, but I'm not sure how long it took. It was probably a hundred years before I even tried. Now though," he said, sounding to James as if he was trying to look on the bright side, "I work with humans every day, and I interact with them just as I am with you now."

James had stopped listening. "A hundred years?" The echo was back. "Ariana won't even be alive. No one will." James looked down at his hands and, without thinking, licked off an errant drop of blood.

His body shuddered at the taste, and James wasn't sure if it was from horror or pleasure. "Not that she'd want me like this," he whispered.

"Tell me about your wife," Ash said, his voice sounding odd and far away.

"Ariana?" James asked, looking up at his strange captor. "She's brilliant. She…" his voice trailed off as some instinct told him to be cautious. He didn't want to say anything that would intrigue this creature. If he couldn't protect Ariana from himself, he certainly couldn't protect her from Ash Samson. "We were getting divorced," he said flatly.

Ash looked surprised. "But you love her."

It was James' turn to look surprised.

"You called out for her in the park," Ash explained, "just before—"

James wondered at that for a moment, but then nodded. He did love her, it was true. Things had just gotten off track for them. She wasn't supposed to work 70-hour weeks. She wasn't supposed to miscarry their first child and not be able to have any others. The gulf between them, having grown slowly ever since they moved to New York, had become insurmountable after that.

"You will get used to your new life," Ash said, misinterpreting his expression, "but no, it will not be your old life. It will, at times, be difficult and lonely. Very lonely."

Ash rose and walked over to his expansive desk, leaning his tall frame on its fine finish as he turned back to James. "If it's too terrible for you, you can walk out the front door into the sunlight, and it will all be over. Or you can stay here and let me teach you to be a proper vampire."

So much for an ordinary life, James thought, dropping his head back into his hands and trying not to feel everything he'd ever known slipping through his fingers.

CHAPTER 6

Ash couldn't believe he had let James talk him into going to his apartment. It was risky and went against his better judgment, but he should have realized before now that James wouldn't be able to wear any of his clothes. They were simply too different in size. The things he had ordered from downtown would be delivered in a day or two, but he had ultimately agreed to this because he thought it would be better if James had a few of his own things.

Plus Ash felt sorry for the guy. First a divorce, and then getting turned into a vampire. It wasn't exactly James' week.

The squat brick building where James had lived was in a good location, but it sat sandwiched between two newer hi-rises, making it appear an ugly duckling by comparison. There was no doorman, so Ash went straight up to James' apartment.

He turned the brass key in a lock that was far sturdier than the door itself and let the plywood barrier swing inward. The tiny living room was pitch dark.

Two steps forward and a slight veer to the left, and Ash was standing in James' old bedroom. Light from the street filtered into this room because its plastic blinds were too short for the windows.

Ash opened the closet and raised a brow at the eight identical pairs of khaki pants hanging there. Neatly pressed, they made for easy pickings. Even as Ash stuffed a pair into the laptop bag he carried over his right shoulder, he began to wonder what had made him turn this particular man into a vampire.

He sighed as he selected a blue oxford shirt and stuffed it into the bag beside the khakis. It didn't really matter why. Like so many things, it was done and could not now be undone.

He turned from the closet and moved over to the dresser. James' wallet was there, as James had said it would be. Ash didn't take the wallet, but he did take the license from inside its front fold. Even vampires occasionally needed ID.

A pair of jeans grabbed from a drawer filled the remaining space in the bag, and Ash turned to go. When he did, he noticed a picture on the nightstand, illuminated slightly by the beam of light peeking in from the street.

A beautiful, smiling woman stared back at him from in front of some snowy backdrop. She was waving to the person taking the picture, her mane of dark-blonde hair shimmering in the sun, her sweater and jeans clinging to a stunning figure. Ash knew she must be James' wife, but he felt the vice grip of the past tighten around his chest as her dark eyes bored into him.

It can't be her. Not after all this time.

Instantly he was back with her again, her hair reflecting golden lamp light as her luscious body arched atop his own; warm night air caressing their bodies as they lay entwined in her bed. Every muscle of his body worshipping her perfumed skin, loving her fierce intellect, losing his soul in the bottomless depths of her eyes before he knew just how low those depths could go.

Delilah.

He snatched the photo off the small table and inspected it more closely. She didn't look exactly the same, but the soft, fierce glow radiating from her eyes was unmistakable. He'd know that black soul anywhere. He'd searched for it for 3,000 years—first at her home in Sorek, then, once he'd learned that he could see human souls, in the face of every woman he'd met down through the ages. And now he had found her here, by accident, married to another man. He slipped the photo into his bag and took the ragged breath habit told him he needed.

Blood and memories raced inside him, but he calmly retraced his steps back outside. After two blocks, he turned down a deserted side street and, making sure no one was about, broke into a full run and leapt into the sky, shooting straight up past windows and rooftops, until the air turned noticeably cooler and he could see the first rays of dawn glowing on the horizon. He took a deep breath, allowing the thin air to cool his exhilarated insides.

Feeling somewhat calmed, he turned and fell headlong, racing back toward the earth at full speed, stopping his nose only an inch from the pavement and righting himself with a slow flip. A satisfied smile lit his face. He normally didn't show off, not anymore, but his elation at finding Delilah made him burn with the desire to do many things he hadn't done in a long time. Which would he do to her first, he wondered?

With some surprise, he reminded himself that it didn't matter. Now that he'd found her, he had all the time in the world to see that the last chapter of their sordid saga was finally written.

CHAPTER 7

Ash suddenly wasn't in the mood to go home, so he walked down to the East Village where music boomed from the open door of the chic club he sometimes frequented when he was in the city.

Despite the early hour, the club was already packed with young, rich people of every variety. From hidden speakers in the rafters, loud Middle Eastern music, interspersed with odd bits of rap and pop, rained down on the crowd. The familiar, wailing notes made Ash feel at home.

He thought again of Delilah and felt rage and wonderment start to warm his cold insides. Scanning the crowd, he began threading his large frame through the crush of young bodies. He kept his eyes on the painted Moroccan tiles running the circumference of the room near the ceiling.

Each time a body in the crowd rubbed against him a pang traveled from his brain down to his jaw and then dispersed in tiny electric waves through the rest of his body. He was relieved to feel it. Time had dulled his hunger, but tonight he was starving.

Out of the corner of his eye, Ash saw a young woman moving toward the bar. She had warm olive skin and auburn hair that floated around her face in a flattering modern cut. She met his gaze for a moment, and Ash reached out to her mind, grateful to finally have found a suitable distraction.

As expected, the woman quickly looked away. Ash could tell she was flushed. Women were often ashamed of their reaction to him.

This young woman reached the bar and was waiting for her drink when Ash walked up behind her and put his hand on the small of her back. She turned to him, eyes alight and smiling slightly.

Ash returned her smile and bent as if to whisper something to her over the din of the crowd. He put his lips lightly against her ear and mouthed the words, but spoke the invitation with his mind.

Forgetting about her drink, the woman answered him by taking his hand and leading him through the crowd. Tobacco smoke and svelte, gyrating bodies obscured his view, but after a few moments, they got close enough to the far wall for Ash to see that cushioned platforms were set up in each of the rear corners of the room. He moved ahead of the young woman toward a spot just vacated by a couple heading for the dance floor.

Ash reclined his long body along the outer edge of the platform and drew the young woman down beside him, keeping her between him and the other occupants of their pillowed dais. The woman turned, half beside, half on top of him, and put one hand inside his coat. Her small fingers ran lightly over the hard muscles of his chest.

The sensual rhythms snaking from the speakers cast a spell on the crowd. The couple next to them had succumbed. Ash could see their entwined arms through the dim.

The young woman seemed to feel it, too. She moved closer to him, and Ash waited for the predictable heat of anticipation to course through his body. It had been many months since his last feeding.

He cupped the girl's cheek in his hand and drew her ruby red lips to his. They were hot and moist and moved willingly under the pressure of his own. He remembered this. He remembered the way it had made him feel.

At his silent prompting, the girl withdrew her mouth from his and pushed herself up higher on the cushions to give him access to her exposed neckline. He stared for a moment at her soft red dress, her smooth skin, and her pounding pulse, savoring the beauty of such a singular combination. He tightened his grip on her mind and wound his hand into her hair. Its silkiness reminded him of Delilah. He gritted his teeth in frustration, but then brightened, remembering that he had just been given the opportunity to finally exorcise her from his memories.

He hesitated for a moment when he realized that the burning hatred he still felt for Delilah might be one of the few emotions he had left. Growling under his breath, he put it out of his mind. He had found her, and he would have his revenge. That was all that mattered.

He angled the woman's head slightly to make her neck less visible to others and sank his teeth into her flesh. As he'd hoped, the first gush of blood past his lips quieted his ghosts.

A second later, she whimpered in his arms, and Ash realized he had been too rough. His hold on her mind was strong though, and he quickly gentled his approach to ensure she felt no pain.

He drank from her until he knew she could stand no more, but he didn't intend to kill her. He ran his tongue over the wounds in her neck, covering them with his saliva. The wounds would heal before she even recovered from her swoon.

Checking his watch, Ash reluctantly repositioned the auburn haired beauty so her body no longer lay across his own. Then he rose and extricated himself from the crowded bar. He needed to get back to James.

Outside, a sudden tingling sensation broke through his musings, telling him he wasn't alone. Resisting the urge to look over his shoulder, he shook the tail of his overcoat back into place and started walking in the general direction of his townhouse. He crossed block after block, but the sensation of being watched remained.

When he came to the corner of Central Park, he decided to take a detour. Inside its stone walls, gravel crunched beneath his feet, and he could now make out another set of footsteps behind him. Damn, he thought, the Council must have someone trailing him again.

Ash rounded a curve and ducked behind a large tree. The trunk of the massive oak shielded him completely. Moments later, a very blond man walked by, wearing denim and cowboy boots. Ash waited for someone else to appear, then turned his attention back to the blond cowboy and did a double-take. He could normally pick out a vampire from a hundred yards, but he'd almost missed this one. *How strange for the Council to send someone so very young,* he thought.

The young vampire passed out of Ash's field of view, and he left the shelter of the old tree. Instead of continuing toward his townhouse, he turned in the direction the blond one had gone, curious about his young follower.

After a few steps the young one paused, causing Ash to wonder if he'd gotten too close. One so young shouldn't have been able to sense him at all. Ash kept walking until he stood just behind the other vampire's shoulder.

"Why are you following me?" they both asked in unison.

The boy spun around. "You!"

Ash looked down and gave a little smile. "Surprise," he said, grabbing the vampire by the collar and pulling him up to his own eye level. Unexpected warmth washed over him—much like the warmth from a human body. Ash dropped his head and sniffed up the side of the boy's face. "Who are you?" he asked, genuine puzzlement creeping across his harsh features.

"Lucas Benson," the boy said, coupling the pronouncement with a careless shrug. "Most people just call me Luc."

Ash studied the young vampire. "Been in the city long, Luc?"

Luc shook his head. "No. This was my first gig for the Council, and here you up and spot me on the first day."

Ash almost smiled, but he was annoyed at the Council's intrusion into his privacy, not to mention their incompetence. He set Luc back on his feet. "Where are you from?" he asked.

"Georgia," Luc answered, backing up several paces to put some space between them. He looked up toward at the towers of the Time-Warner building, still visible over the tree line. "Just figured after a hundred years I should see someplace new, I guess."

Ash's jaw dropped, and he covered the distance between them in an instant, his hand clamping around Luc's throat. "That's not possible," he declared through gritted teeth. "I don't know what game the Council is playing, but there's no point lying to me. You can't possibly be a century old. You still give off enough heat you could almost pass for human."

Luc struggled to speak, and Ash dropped him abruptly.

"Get yourself another assignment," Ash said, as Luc sputtered and rubbed his throat. "If I ever find you following me again, I'll kill you."

He stepped around Luc, making it clear he was dismissed, but then turned back. "And tell the Council the same goes for anyone else they send. I'm tired of humoring them."

And now that he had found Delilah, he didn't want them getting in the way. She was his alone.

Chapter 8

Full of disapproval, Nancy's voice crackled out of the intercom speaker on Ash's desk. "Miss Toria to see you, sir."

He forced himself to put down the dossier he'd been reading. Everything about Delilah, or as she was called in this life, Ariana, was in that folder. Ash routinely used a private detective to investigate executives of companies in which he was planning to invest. When he'd called to ask Tom to gather background on a prominent New York fund manager, Tom hadn't considered it strange at all. He'd prepared the dossier over the past two weeks. Ash had memorized it in minutes.

Nor had her boss, Roger, considered it strange when Ash called to inquire about subscribing to their newest fund. The man had been quite ecstatic, actually, even inviting Ash to dinner to bring him up to speed.

Ash checked his watch and made his way to the second floor living room to find Toria's petite body lounging on his couch. Stunning as ever, she wore dark jeans that barely covered her pubic bone and a black crocheted sweater that, from a distance, appeared quite modest, but upon closer inspection left little of her smooth torso or black lace bra to the imagination. Her hair was sculpted into sleek dark ringlets. Ash frowned when he noticed her stilettos propped up on his coffee table.

Toria laughed and dropped her feet to the floor. She let her eyes roam over his physique, taking in his crisp cotton shirt and dark slacks. Ash saw warmth in her expression, but all she said was, "How very Brooks Brothers, Ash." Business casual was not to her taste.

"You're late, Toria," he pointed out. "I called you two hours ago."

Toria raised her eyebrows and put her feet back up on the table.

Ash sighed. He knew it was the wrong approach. "I'm surprised I had to call you at all," he said. "I thought when we spoke in the park that you needed my help." He looked at her with genuine confusion. "What happened, Toria? It's been weeks."

Her heels again dropped to the floor. Behind him, Ash heard the hall door open and cursed himself for not telling Nancy to keep James busy. Toria stood as the newest vampire came around the corner.

She turned to Ash. "Aren't you going to introduce me?"

Ash gave an inward groan. "I believe you've already met."

James came toward them, and Toria's dark eyes widened. "Him?" She pointed at James. "You turned *him*? Why?"

Ash saw James grow paler. "James," he said with a long-suffering sigh, "this is Toria. She's an old friend of mine, one of the Council Elders, and," he hesitated, knowing this wasn't going to go well, "the one who attacked you in the park."

James lunged at her, but Ash stuck out his arm and caught James across the chest.

"Damn it, Ash!" James cried, realizing he was pinned.

Toria didn't even flinch.

"James, calm down," Ash ordered. He looked from James to Toria and back again. "Look at her, James. Look closely. You should know you can't harm her. You should know she's much older than you."

"I don't care," James exclaimed. Nevertheless, he did as he was instructed and stopped fighting. Ash released his grip.

"Answer me, Ash," Toria demanded. "Why did you turn him? It's been centuries since you made another."

Ash ran a hand through his dark hair and cast a baleful eye at James. "I don't really know," he admitted. "I guess I just thought it might finally be safe, if he was properly instructed."

Toria rolled her eyes, and looked James up and down, taking in his khaki pants and button-down blue shirt. "He was better off dead," she said finally.

"How dare you?" James yelled, taking a long step in her direction. This time Ash didn't stop him, and James grabbed Toria's arm and spun her around. "You left me for dead!" he shouted. He pointed at Ash with a shaking hand. "He saved me."

Toria shook her arm free of James' grasp and laughed. "No, young one, he didn't. And don't make the mistake of thinking there's real human feeling still lingering in the dead heart of your newfound friend here." She looked at Ash. "Whatever he did, he did for his own reasons."

"Toria," Ash began.

"Don't take that tone with me, Ash," she shot back. "You're the one who's always preaching restraint. We're killers. Why would you go and make another one?"

"I won't be a killer," James insisted.

Toria turned again to James, her gaze filled with scorn. "You already are," she said. "The sooner you accept that, the better it will be for everyone."

Ash sighed. "It doesn't have to be that way, Toria. And though I don't judge you for the choices you've made, I don't want to force that choice on James."

"And did you tell your new pet that when you made me, we went on a killing spree?"

Ash gave her a pointed look, but remained silent.

Toria sank down onto the couch once more, her expression cold and haughty. "I didn't think so," she said. "Tell me Ash, when are you going to let your new pet out for his first walk?"

James gritted his teeth. "I would like to see Ariana."

"What?" Ash's head snapped around to look at his charge.

"I've been thinking," James said, "and, while I agree with you that I can't go back to my old life, surely I can check in on her? From a distance?"

Ash shook his head. "You know that's not possible."

"No, I don't," James said. "I don't know anything because I haven't left this house since I first woke up here."

"James," Ash began.

"No more juice boxes, Ash." James got up and started back toward the stairs. "I'm going out… tonight."

He left, and Toria turned to look at Ash. She batted her eyelashes and smiled sweetly at him. "That went well."

Ash longed to smack her. "Surely you didn't come here just to smirk?" he asked through clenched teeth.

"Actually, no, but I might start dropping in for that in the future. I came to talk to you about the vampire abductions."

"Abductions?" Ash queried. "You make it sound like the culprits are little green men."

Toria said nothing, but pulled a file folder from black bag at her side. She stood and poked one end of it into Ash's broad chest.

Ash took it from her and began paging through its contents. Seven. Eight. At least nine missing. They were mostly young, but not newly made, so suicide wasn't a likely answer. Sometimes the minds of the new ones couldn't adjust to what they had become. They often killed themselves within the first year of their turning.

"I don't understand," he said, still looking at the last page. "These are not fledglings. A couple of them are quite old. Are you telling me they are all missing?"

Toria nodded silently.

"Who could pull this off?" he asked.

"You mean besides you?" Toria raised a dark, sculpted brow.

Ash was taken aback. "Me?"

"There was some talk after we figured out what was happening that you were the only one capable of kidnapping or killing these particular vampires. Or of hiring humans to do it for you."

Toria poked a manicured nail into his chest, anger flaring in her eyes. "I had almost quelled the suspicion against you until you sent Luc back with the message that you were going to kill anyone they sent to follow you from now on. It made some of the Council question what you have to hide."

Ash closed the folder. "You know I don't have anything to do with this," he said.

"I know," Toria replied, replacing the folder in her bag. "You don't care enough about vampires to go to all this trouble."

Ash sighed and sat down on the arm of the sofa. "Perhaps, but I do care enough to offer my help."

Toria moved to stand in front of him. "I'm not even sure what to ask you to do," she said. "I first thought it must be humans. Now, I'm not so sure. The Council is officially investigating all the individual cases, but I've been unofficially investigating for weeks; now they seem to have tapered off. There has only been one in the last month, and I'm running out of leads."

She folded her arms across her chest and looked down at the floor. "I've even stooped to asking Keller for help," she muttered.

"Keller?" Ash's brow shot up. "The monk? Since when is he in New York? And I thought he'd vowed never to be in the same hemisphere as you." It almost made Ash smile. It was a rare male who could resist Toria. When she'd set her sights on the handsome Irishman, Ash had assumed he was a goner. Not so. The man was a true believer and had resisted Toria to the very end with a fierceness Ash had seldom seen. It had only made her want him more, of course. Inevitably, she turned him, thinking to rip him from the arms of God and into her own, but Keller just hated her more.

"He finally got tired of hiding out, apparently," Toria said. "He's a scholar, and the best place for him to be a scholar is here."

Ash heard the note of sadness creep into her voice. They all had so many regrets.

"And is there anything in the history books about disappearing vampires?" he asked.

Toria pursed her lips. "Not unless this is the beginning of the apocalypse."

"What?" That got his attention.

Toria shook her head. "It's nothing. Keller is still a monk. He reads signs as well as books. The Verses speak of the end of the children of Lilith as one of the signs of the end of days."

Ash shook his head. "Don't waste your time on fairy tales, Toria," he said. "Whatever is happening, there's a logical answer, and we'll find it."

"I know," Toria said with a frown, "but my gut tells me something is wrong. I just can't figure out what it is."

Ash didn't state the obvious. If the abductions had stopped, they might never know the answer. "How about a hunt to improve your spirits?" he asked, wanting to change the subject.

"With you?" Toria's disbelief was unmistakable.

Ash shook his head. "No, not with me. With James."

Toria's dubious look remained for a moment. "All right," she agreed finally. "I'll take your pet out, but I won't pull any punches."

"I wouldn't expect you to," Ash said, rising to stand beside her. "Tell me, do you think you can get him set up at Council House too?"

"My, my, aren't we full of requests tonight?" Toria asked, giving him a speculative glare.

"Do you want my help or not?" Ash asked pointedly.

Toria's skewering gaze relented, so Ash continued. "James is some kind of computer whiz. He needs to stay busy, and I figured the Council could use him. If you don't agree…" He let his voice trail off, not wanting to owe Toria too many favors. Or make her think he had any other reason for wanting James out of his house.

Toria thought for a moment. "No, you're probably right. I'll get a room set up at Council House and be back for him in a couple of hours." She gathered up her bag, stepped closer, and put her hand on Ash's chest. "Just promise me you'll see what you can find out about the missing vampires, Ash. This is serious. I can feel it."

Ash nodded, surprised by the earnestness in her gaze.

CHAPTER 9

After seeing Toria to the door, Ash went in search of James. As expected, he found him in the downstairs den playing a video game. "If I'd known how many hours a day you could spend with that thing I'd have bought it weeks ago," Ash commented.

James didn't look up. "I have to leave here, you know," he said, leaning sideways as something exploded on the huge screen.

Ash sighed, unsure why he was so worried about this particular vampire. He'd made others and never doubted their ability to fend for themselves—-even the very first one, who had been a complete accident.

Almost 400 years after he'd crawled out of the rubble of the Philistine temple, Ash remained ignorant of his true nature. He had clung to humans, trying to blend in, to pretend to be what he was no longer.

He'd still been a soldier then, one of the famed Jewish mercenaries in the army of Alexander of Macedon, whom time would christen Alexander the Great. The man had been a genius at exploiting the weaknesses of his enemies. On that particular night, however, one of Alexander's most impossible victories had also turned out to be one of the simplest.

Alexander had advanced far into Central Asia but left insufficient troops and legitimacy behind to preserve his hold in other parts of his newly conquered empire. A rebellion had sprung up in one of the provinces, and Alexander took part of his force back into the interior to quell it.

They made short work of the rebels, with the exception of their leader and one small band who took refuge in a nearly impregnable location. The Sogdian Rock was a natural phenomenon that rose over two miles into the air. At that time of year, it was covered in ice and snow from base to summit.

When they arrived, Alexander had demanded the rebels surrender, but they had laughed at him, asking where he planned to get winged soldiers. So Alexander sent a call through his ranks for men brave enough and strong enough to attempt to scale the ice in a night assault. Alexander promised a king's ransom to the first 12 to make it to the top, and 300 men, including Samson, volunteered. Each of them was given a strip of red cloth to wave as a way to signal their successful ascent.

Samson had conducted night raids with many of the men who volunteered for this mission. They knew his strength, and he and 11 others were chosen to go first. The others would follow in their steps, up their lines.

It was not an easy ascent, even for him. At that time, he wasn't yet able to fly, so he was left to pull himself up the sheer wall of ice with the rest. He was luckier than most, though, because the cold affected him less. He could leave his hands ungloved, and his strength was not sorely tested. Still, a careless handhold could have sent him plummeting to the valley floor, as it did at least 30 of the others. He hadn't known at that point whether such an injury would kill him.

He was first to reach the top, where he unfurled his red banner. Down below, Alexander waited for night to fully fall and then moved the rest of his force into hiding.

In the morning, Alexander rode out and summoned the stronghold's messengers. He told them he'd found soldiers with wings, and the several hundred men at the top unfurled their banners, to the dismay of the rebels. Not knowing how many of Alexander's men had managed to do the impossible, the rebel leader surrendered immediately.

Ash and his men were allowed some amount of pillage and plunder, but not as much as usual because Alexander intended to take a bride here and secure these lands through political alliance instead of fear. The men fed, raped, and stole with varying degrees of success and enthusiasm. Many of them merely demanded a fire and a meal.

Ash found a ramshackle lean-to that served as a sentry tower at the outer rim of the rampart. He knocked its lone occupant unconscious and dragged him inside, so he could feed and shelter his body from the few hours of sun that were approaching.

He was finishing off the unconscious rebel when Memnon happened across his hiding place. Memnon was one of the Shield Bearers, an elite fighting force built by Alexander's father, Phillip. He was a valiant warrior, and Ash had admired his skill and his loyalty to Alexander.

Nevertheless, when he saw the horror of what he'd become reflected in Memnon's shocked eyes, Ash lunged at him full force, fangs bared. Memnon managed to draw his sword, but it only hit a glancing blow across Ash's chest and shoulder. Ash knocked the sword away, grabbed Memnon, held him, and drained him almost dry.

When he felt Memnon's pulse beat tire, saw his many valiant, even heroic deeds, Ash was overcome with horror at himself. He'd never allowed himself to develop close ties, even before he became a blood-drinker. Now he'd killed the one person he might have called friend in several hundred years. He'd killed someone who deserved to live.

Ash bent to lay the man's body on the floor, and a drop of blood from the wound in his shoulder fell onto Memnon's lips. They twitched. It was almost imperceptible, but Ash was certain he'd seen it.

Not sure what he was doing or why, he slid his dagger out of its sheath and cut his own wrist. More blood flowed over the fallen hero, who eventually began to drink. Ash had saved him—and become aware of another terrible power that he possessed.

Memnon never forgave him, of course. Ash had robbed him of his hero's death and cursed him with a weakness that rivaled even his new strength.

From then on, the two of them had existed in an uneasy disharmony, like reverse-polarity magnets at either end of a short tether. They were each nomads, but being the only two of their kind, they tended to wander in close orbit to each other, not companions, but co-habitants of their dark world.

A final, unfortunate choice of resting place had buried Memnon under the hot ash of Vesuvius. Ash had been training gladiators in Pompeii, but Memnon hated the debauchery of that city and had chosen to spend his days in one of the white-washed crypts outside Herculaneum, a city just to the north of Pompeii and on the less-fortunate side of the volcano.

When the eruption came, debris from the spewing mountain had blocked out the sun. Ash escaped Pompeii by swimming, underwater, across the Bay of Naples. Only later did he learn that Herculaneum had been completely destroyed, buried under so much ash and rock that no attempt would be made to resurrect it.

He'd not heard from Memnon since that day.

Ash sighed and returned his attention to his newest addition to the vampire race. "You're right, James. It's time for you to leave here. Tonight you will go out to feed, and what you do afterwards is up to you."

James rose from the couch. "When do we leave?"

"Not for a few hours yet," Ash explained. "Toria will be back for you later, after she's gotten your room set up at Council House."

"Toria?" James asked, his distaste obvious. "I thought the whole point of this imprisonment was to keep me from turning out like her."

"Not exactly," Ash said, hesitating. "Well, yes, but she'll be a fine chaperone for one night. She knows perfectly well how to feed without killing, and she respects my views on that point. The fact that she chooses not to follow them…" Ash shrugged. "Well, that is a choice you, too, will have to make. I just want it to be your choice and not something your cravings or lack of instruction force you into."

"That's noble of you," James commented. "And just where will you be during this trial run of your new pupil?"

Ash frowned, not liking that he actually felt a little guilty. "I have dinner plans," he replied.

"Hot date?" James queried.

Ash felt the knife turn. He'd grown to like James in their few weeks together.

"No," he said brusquely. "Business dinner."

CHAPTER 10

Ariana sat alone at a small outdoor table at an Italian restaurant on Manhattan's Upper West Side. Red-checked tablecloths and the rich aromas of bread and wine should have made her feel at home, but she laid her fork across her full plate of pasta and wondered why she was here.

She and James had come here together. Not in many months, it was true, but since his disappearance, she'd felt his absence more strongly than before. Tonight it weighed on her, and she didn't understand why.

She and James had been growing apart for a long time before the separation, even before her miscarriage. That was the moment she had known it was over, though—when the doctor had told them she could never have any more children. She'd seen the light go out of James' eyes then, and knew she would never be able to bring that light back.

Now, instead of accepting the fact that her husband was leaving her, which she'd only sort of gotten used to, she was supposed to accept that he was dead. Her mind told her it was true. It had to be. Grown men, especially predictable, reliable men like James, did not go missing for weeks on end and suddenly reappear.

Something terrible had happened to him, something so terrible that he would not be coming back. She shuddered at the thought and felt tears well again beneath her eyelids. She tried very hard not to dwell on what the "something" might have been. It was hard not to know, but it was worse to speculate.

Like a dripping faucet in a nearby room, the low sound of conversation from the table behind her began to intrude on her melancholy. At first she tried not to listen; then she just tried to hide the fact that she was listening. She still couldn't make out any actual words, but the voice that spoke them held her attention because it was the richest, deepest voice she had ever heard. Each time the man spoke, it rolled over her like warm thunder, as if his voice vibrated on the same frequency as her skin.

Finally, her curiosity got the better of her, and Ariana left her table and made her way toward the ladies room. After checking her makeup and waiting an appropriate interval, she returned the same way she had come.

From this direction, she had a full view of the Voice and he of her. She met his gaze and the rest of the room seemed to shift out of focus. For a long moment, there was nothing but black eyes meeting eyes that were blacker still. Ariana had never met anyone with eyes as dark as hers, but the Voice's eyes were blazingly dark.

Hello, lovely one. The Voice again. Only this time it was in her head. His lips never moved. And what lips they were, Ariana noted. Sculpted was the right word, but she had never longed to touch sculpture the way she longed to know the feel of those lips.

Then she was standing at his table, though she didn't remember walking over. Something told her she should be alarmed, but alarm was not the emotion she felt.

She looked down at the stranger as he sipped his wine. Easily more than six feet, he should have looked ill at ease in the restaurant's delicate wicker chair, but his almost unnatural grace made it seem protected rather than burdened by his muscular frame.

Ariana watched his strong, smooth hand uncurl from the stem of the wine glass and arc into his hair. No, it wasn't fear that was making her breath come faster. She started when another voice said her name.

"Ariana," the other man said, "we were just talking about you. Funny that you should be here."

Ariana turned to see who the Voice's companion was. "Roger," she said, more than a little surprised to find her boss sitting there. "What are you doing here?"

She realized how dumb that question sounded just half a second too late to stop it. "I mean, it's great to see you outside the office for a change."

Roger smiled. "Ariana, meet Ash Samson."

Ash Samson. She should know that name.

Suddenly the Voice was standing at her side, and there was a shock of recognition, both of the name and of the man. The name she now recognized as belonging to one of Tailwind's newest and largest investors. As for the man himself, she couldn't say how she recognized him, but she had the unmistakable sensation of having seen him before. More than that, of knowing him somehow.

"Mr. Samson, what a pleasant surprise." Ariana said, extending her hand. "I'm Ariana Chambers."

"Ariana." His voice was low and hard, his face enigmatic. "That suits you." He bent and took her hand in his, kissing it lightly, but his eyes never left her face. Ariana sucked in a ragged breath and jerked her hand away.

Luckily, her back was toward her boss, she thought. He would undoubtedly have put her reaction down to pure rudeness. She looked at Ash Samson. His mysterious smile had turned into a smirk, and the look in his eyes was even more predatory than before. He hadn't mistaken it for rudeness.

"Won't you join us?" Roger asked. "Our discussion actually concerns you."

"Ah, no, I'm afraid I can't. I'm here with a friend." The lie came without effort because she was suddenly desperate to get away. Her senses and defenses weren't ready for the likes of Ash Samson.

"Your friend can join us as well," Ash said. "We'll all have dessert."

"No, no," Roger chimed in, inadvertently saving her. "That won't be necessary. Tomorrow is soon enough to talk business, Ariana. You enjoy the rest of your evening, but let's plan to meet in my office first thing."

Thank you, Roger, she thought.

Ash frowned for a moment. "I won't be able to join you then, I'm afraid. I have a prior commitment." The frown cleared. "Roger, you can fill Ariana in first thing tomorrow, and I will send a car for you both at 7:00 so we can clear up any last details over dinner."

"That sounds fine to me. Ariana?" Roger's question was polite, but Ariana knew she wasn't expected to have plans more important than coddling a big client.

"I look forward to it," she said, giving Mr. Samson her most award-winning smile. "It was nice meeting you Mr. Samson, but now, if you'll excuse me…" She let her voice trail off to avoid repeating the lie that she wasn't alone.

"Of course. And please call me Ash."

"Ash, then. It's been a pleasure." Ariana turned. "Roger, I'll see you in the morning."

"Good night, Ariana."

Ariana made her way around Ash Samson and some large potted plants to get back to her table. She quickly paid her check and left, thanking providence she didn't have to pass them to leave the restaurant.

⚜

He hadn't been prepared to see her in person yet, Ash thought. That was supposed to come later. Tomorrow, perhaps, after he'd persuaded Roger to go along with his plans.

No matter. Even if she'd noticed his reaction to her, she would not have understood it. He wasn't sure he understood it himself. It was almost as if nothing had changed.

The first time he'd seen her had been in Sorek. She had been in charge of laying the banquet for his entourage, while he discussed trade with her stepfather. He couldn't remember if he'd ever had that discussion. All he remembered was her.

She'd worn a dress the color of sapphires, with gold bands at her waist, her temple, and around her upper arms. Then as now, though, her dark eyes were what drew him. That night there had been an invitation in them. He'd never suspected it could be a trap.

Making his way to her room once the house was asleep, he'd opened the door to find her brushing her long dark hair by candlelight.

"Come in," she said, never turning to look at him.

He did as she asked, closing the door behind him. She turned, and for a moment they just stared at each other, rooted to their spots on either side of the room. With one accord they moved closer, coming to stand within arm's reach, but not touching.

Delilah was tall for a woman, but her gaze came only to the level of his throat. He put a finger under her chin to raise her eyes to meet his, but he was the first to look away. Her gaze unnerved him—but that was why he had come. "I can tell you see me for what I am," he said, surprised that it was true. So many people could not. They saw only the judge or only the warrior, seldom the man.

Without a word, she stepped forward and put a hand on his chest, causing him to draw in his breath. He remembered he'd wanted to talk with her, but then she'd parted her lips, and the time for soul-searching was over. He'd brought his lips down onto hers, and Delilah had returned his kiss, pressing her body against his, sending him the message that she saw everything he was and still welcomed him to her bed. His mouth went from tentative to ravaging, taking hers in an act of possession almost as fierce as lovemaking.

And what lovemaking it had been. On that night and all the nights that followed, they had thrilled to each other's touch, reaching heights he'd not seen before or since.

How she must have laughed at him, he thought. He'd been such a fool to be taken in by her, never guessing the truth, even when it was staring him in the face months later in the form of a Philistine soldier.

Ash shook his head to try to clear it. All that mattered now was that he'd finally been given the opportunity to make things right.

As the night wore on, he plied Roger with food and drink at several of the finest—and some not so fine—establishments in the city. By the time he put Roger into a cab, he had the man eating out of his hand. Money talked in this town, and he had more than enough to convince Roger to part with Ariana for a while.

Chapter 11

Outside his posh prison, James felt newly powerful. Just walking down the sidewalk gave him a sense of his strength that he'd never felt while locked up in Ash's townhouse. Indeed, he felt stronger now than he ever had. He lengthened his stride, and Toria fell effortlessly in step.

"Where are we going?" James asked, turning to face her and marveling at how quickly he'd gotten used to the idea of what they were about to do.

Toria laughed. "As you know, I like to hunt Central Park."

James' taste of freedom turned sour. "Not there," he said.

Toria ignored his baleful glare. "I figured you'd say that. Don't worry. There's another spot I think will do."

She turned right onto 51st Street, and James followed. As usual, Toria was all in black. This time it was a short, body-hugging leather dress paired with knee-high, black patent leather boots with silver eyes and black satin laces. Her dark hair hung in long, loose curls down her back. James watched her hips sway as she walked and couldn't decide whether she looked more beautiful or more deadly.

He, on the other hand, still looked like a regular guy. He didn't particularly like Toria's sense of style, but his khaki pants and button-up oxford didn't seem appropriate either. He looked more like a stock boy at Best Buy than one of the undead.

Putting his wardrobe concerns aside, James tried to take in all the sights, sounds and smells of his beloved city. This was his home, but, seeing it for the first time through non-human eyes, it was completely new. Each tiny detail assaulted him.

He might have been bothered by that, except that he knew he had an eternity to explore each one if he chose. Exhilaration blossomed in his mind. He'd already been giving some thought as to what he'd do with his new lease on life.

Toria turned into a small park lodged between two tall glass buildings. Actually, "park" was an overstatement. It was mostly concrete, with a few trees planted among the chairs and tables. Most of the lights were out.

Toria went only a few short steps past the gate and took James' hand. She leaned against the concrete wall and pulled him close. He stiffened, but didn't pull away. "Toria," he jibed, "I didn't know you cared."

"Don't be a wise guy," she whispered. "I'm just trying to be inconspicuous."

"Why?" he asked.

"There are two boys at the other end of the park."

James turned to search out their shapes in the darkness.

Toria leaned against the wall and closed her eyes. *Search for them with your mind, James, not your eyes.*

James turned to be certain she hadn't spoken out loud. He still wasn't used to vampire telepathy.

He closed his eyes and tried to concentrate the way Ash had taught him. Toria's hands rested on his waist to steady him, and her voice sounded again in his brain, like whispering fingers that beckoned him forward.

Without leaving where they stood, they crossed the concrete courtyard. Sure enough, two young men sat on a bench some distance apart, trying not to sit too close to each other but also trying to hide the fact that they were passing a joint back and forth. They were probably in their late teens, James thought. One was tall and lean with a hard build and dark skin. The other was shorter, younger, and the color of milky coffee.

"Closer," Toria prompted.

James moved closer to the young one, so close he could see the short whiskers just below the boy's ear and the slow drumming of his pulse beneath his skin. He was captivated for a moment. Back in his body, he felt his mouth go dry and his fangs began to unsheathe.

He studied the boy's eyes, and the shape of his face began to fade away. In its place his whole life was revealed. James saw the boy's drunken mother, his work-a-day father, and the boy's ambition to have a better life. He saw his reason for taking this night job at a swanky midtown restaurant even though it made him tired during school and was far from his home. He saw his guilt for smoking dope on a school night, paired with his desire to escape for a while from what waited for him at home.

"James," Toria whispered, using her actual voice this time. She seemed far away, but he lost his view of the boy and felt for a moment as if he were falling from a great height. At the last moment, instead of falling to earth, he was sucked back into his own flesh.

"God, that's weird!" James exclaimed breathlessly.

"Enough practice. Let's move. Grab hold of his mind as we approach and don't let go. Take hold of his flesh and drink until he starts to fade. And then stop." Toria looked at him with a question in her eyes.

"I've got it," James assured her. "Jedi mind trick, social drink, and then stop."

He started walking toward the pair, found the younger one again and whispered an introduction into his brain. As stoned as the kid was, he probably could have walked right up to him, James thought. He briefly wondered if that was the reason Toria chose these two—easy pickings for the newest vampire. Poor bastards, he thought. Oh well, he didn't intend for them to even remember what happened. He didn't intend to kill them. He didn't intend to disappoint Ash.

He registered a moment of surprise at that thought, but was quickly distracted by the now detectable scent of the two boys. The smell of them, of their sweat, their flesh, and their blood mingled with the sweet aroma of marijuana. James felt a little high himself.

Suddenly he tasted blood, and it was like a lightning bolt to his brain. He realized he was gritting his teeth, and his fangs had cut his own lip. It didn't matter. He sat down on the bench and held the boy immobilized, using his body as well as his mind. Both were so new, he didn't trust one or the other not to fail him.

Quickly he sank his teeth into the boy's salty flesh, trying not to think about what he was doing. Soon he didn't have to try. Blood poured down his throat, burning as it went. It seared like fire, yet it seemed to heal and strengthen instead of scalding. The boy gave willingly, pouring forth his blood and more of his life, more of himself than before. In a flash of insight, James knew the boy welcomed this, welcomed it as the only extraordinary thing to ever happen in his young life. Too bad he wouldn't remember.

As the flow of blood and memories slowed, James lifted his head. He gently rested the boy's head against the wall behind where they sat. He even remembered to lick the young man's wounds.

Fairly pleased with himself, he turned to see what had become of Toria. She stood behind him, holding the now limp body of the other boy. She took a step closer and dropped the kid on the bench next to his friend.

"My God!" James yelled. "What have you done? We weren't supposed to kill anyone!"

Toria raised an eyebrow and gave a half-hearted shrug. "No," she said, "*you* weren't supposed to kill anyone. And you didn't. Ash will be pleased, but that's not the way the world works, James, and you might as well learn that too."

James was stopped from continuing his tirade by the shocking realization that something was happening to the dead boy. He was beginning to glow. It was faint at first, but it kept getting brighter, as if someone was slowly turning a dimmer switch all the way to high.

James looked around, afraid the light would draw attention, but no one was coming. As a matter of fact, the park was no lighter than before. Not even the end of the bench where he sat was illuminated. And yet the boy shone with a light that almost hurt his eyes. When it seemed impossible for it to get any brighter, the light moved. It expanded beyond the bounds of the boy's body and separated from it, rising from the bench to a standing position with the same basic shape and features as the boy's body.

The figure in the light looked at James for some time, and briefly at Toria. Finally it moved over to the younger boy and kissed him fondly on the forehead. Then it rose into the air and disappeared.

James was speechless for a long moment. "Did you see that?" he finally managed.

"Yeah, they all do that," Toria said. She studied James' shocked countenance. "You mean Ash didn't even tell you we can see souls?"

James gave her a confused look, so she continued. "We can see the souls of humans when they leave the body. Some vampires can see human souls even before they die. Ash can see traces of souls in people. I keep telling him he should set up a psychic hotline. He'd make a killing." Toria looked down at the dead, soulless body of the young man. "No pun intended."

James was stunned into silence once again. He shook his head in disbelief. "You mean we really have souls?"

Toria gave him a puzzled, pitying look. "Not *we*, James. They. They have souls. Humans. Not vampires."

The implication of what she said hit him hard. He had been an atheist for most of his adult life, and now he'd lost the soul he'd never believed existed.

The irony was that he was in exactly the same place as before—on the road to hell. Only now the road was longer, he knew his final destination, and there was no way to make it right.

James rose slowly from the bench. Without warning, he flew at Toria, pushing her across the dark courtyard and into the brick wall opposite their little bench. His hands closed tight around her throat.

"You killed me, you bitch," he spat. "It doesn't matter that I'm still here walking around. I'm as good as dead."

Toria laughed, and the sound of it enraged James even more. "Everything is a goddamned joke to you, isn't it?" he yelled. "Ash, me, human beings, you think we're all here for your amusement."

Toria's smile disappeared, and her eyes grew hard. In a flash she brought her arms up between James' and broke his hold on her neck. Her foot followed, aiming a powerful kick into the middle of his chest that sent him flying back over to the bench he'd just vacated.

Toria strode over to him and belted him another blow with her closed fist. "You want to see a joke, James? Look in the mirror. You have fangs and the only sustenance your body needs is the lifeblood of these..." she gestured to the two prostrate youths with undisguised distaste, "...creatures."

She grabbed him with one hand by the collar of his shirt and lifted him off his feet. "And yet here you sit, trying desperately not to be what you are—a predator."

She threw him back against the wall. "Ash hasn't even taught you to fight properly. What good is all his strength if you can't use it?" She aimed another blow, but he was able to duck in time to avoid getting his face smashed. Her fist left a dent in the wall beside his head.

"You have decent instincts," Toria said, pulling her hand back. "If you decide you want to learn to be a real vampire, come find me." She wiped the dust off her hand onto the hem of her short dress. "Otherwise, I'm done with you." She turned away.

"Wait!" James pleaded, reality setting in. "What about them? We can't just leave a body lying around—can we?"

Toria removed a knife from the top of her boot and walked over to the dead boy. Pulling his head back, she neatly slit his throat, dragged him over to the base of the nearest tree and dumped him onto the hard earth.

"There," she said, replacing the knife in her boot. "Case closed." She turned to James. "That's another reason I like parks. When cops find a body and no blood, they just assume it drained into the ground or that the person was killed elsewhere and dumped. Either way—no mystery, no investigation."

"What about him?" James motioned to the still unconscious boy next to him.

"With any luck, he'll wake up and run away," she said, already heading back toward the gate. For reasons he chose not to explore, James followed.

Chapter 12

Council House looked almost exactly the way James had imagined it: a dark doll-house with weeping statues and massive stone pillars.

Those pillars were connected by a low brick wall topped by iron railings with jagged metal teeth. End to end, the outer wall encircled half a mid-town block in its imposing embrace. At the main entrance were two larger pillars, each crowned with a marble orb, and from the face of each pillar hung a huge iron lantern, each one almost as tall as a man. The lanterns signaled the entrance to the building's protected courtyard. Beyond the courtyard loomed the six above-ground stories of the mansion.

James fought back his fear. He couldn't stay holed up in Ash's house forever, but it would have helped if Toria had said a single word to him on the walk over.

When they reached the front doors, Toria pushed through them and strode in without looking to see if James followed. He did and shut the doors behind him.

Inside the entryway, Toria was in quiet conversation with another vampire. After a brief exchange, she departed across the main hall, her heels clicking on its marble floor, and up a tremendous set of winding stairs.

The other vampire, who appeared an innocent, sandy-haired youth, looked at James and held out his hand. "I'm Evan," he said.

James shook the proffered hand, wondering why the gesture seemed so out of place.

Evan gave a nod to his left. "Come with me, and I'll show you to your room."

James followed Evan's slender figure around the corner and down a hall to an elevator. Noting his puzzled look, Evan smiled. "When the house was expanded, it was easier to put in an elevator than another staircase," he explained. "Plus, there's no flying allowed in the house. Do you fly, James?"

"No." James shook his head. "At least, I don't think I do."

Evan pursed his lips as they got into the elevator. "It's been many centuries since Ash made another vampire. There will be many here who are curious as to your abilities." He punched the button for the third floor.

Again James shook his head. "I don't know much more than they do, I'm afraid."

"It might be wise to keep that to yourself for a while, until you get a better sense of where you stand," Evan offered.

"Don't vampires get stronger with age?" James asked. "Why would anyone think I could do anything?"

Evan stepped out onto a rich burgundy carpet as the doors opened on the third floor. "Our strength does increase with age, that's true, but where you start depends in large part on how far removed you are from the original vampire—Samson."

"And how far removed are you?" James asked his new host.

Evan smiled. "Pretty far. My real name is Ivan. I was born in Russia during the reign of Peter the Great, and was made a vampire by some of Toria's line, several times removed from her."

He stopped at the end of the long hallway at the next to last door, pushing it open to reveal a small but functional room complete with a bed, a mini fridge, a desk, and a laptop computer. A neutral, patterned rug covered most of the wood floor. There were no windows.

James crossed the threshold ahead of Evan and made for the laptop. "What's this for?" he asked.

"We have a network here. You should find log-in information in the desk drawer. You'll have to put in some information, and then you'll have access to our website, calendar, and all sorts of useful information. You'll also have a house e-mail account."

James was already pulling out the desk chair and powering up the machine. "Great. Who does your web development?"

Evan shot him a puzzled look.

"I am—was—in software development," James explained. "I was chief engineer at a little start-up company downtown."

"Oh, well, in that case, I'll see if I can't find the answer for you. Right now I have no idea."

As James' attention drifted, Evan headed for the door. "I'm sure Toria will be up sooner or later. I'd offer you the rest of the tour, but there's a map on the website, so I'm guessing you'll get to it in your own time."

He crossed the threshold and was pulling the door closed when he suddenly stopped and popped his head back in. "Oh, the room next to yours toward the elevators is vacant, and the room on the other side is occupied by a monk, so it should be quiet up here."

James turned and smiled. "Thanks, Evan." Evan closed the door behind him, and James began filling out the login page for the Council House network.

He lost all track of time until the smell of burning flesh hit his nostrils. He left the computer and opened the door to the hall, inhaling left and right. After a moment, it was clear that the noxious smell was coming from the room at the end of the hall. What had Evan said? That it was occupied by a monk?

James knocked loudly on the door. How unfriendly could a monk be? he wondered. And who ever heard of a vampire monk?

There was no answer, and no sound came from inside. James pounded again and called out, "Hey, are you okay in there?"

Finally, the door opened and a lean, green-eyed vampire stared down at James. He wore no shirt, just plain brown pants. James caught a glimpse of the room behind him and decided that brown must be his favorite color. A plain khaki-colored blanket lay across the bed, and what looked like a brown robe fell across the back of the desk chair. It took a moment for James to register that the room had a window and that sunlight was streaming across the desk and onto the floor. *Why would a vampire take a room with a window?*

"Are... are you okay?" James asked again, a little unnerved by the strange light emanating from those green eyes.

"I'm fine," the monk said haltingly. He studied James for a moment, finally asking, "Do I know you?"

"No," James answered, "I just arrived today." He looked again at the unexpected sunlight. "Well, make that yesterday. I'm in the room next door and… well, I thought you might be in trouble. I smelled something burning."

The monk smiled slightly. "It's kind of you to ask, but as you can see, I'm perfectly fine." Suddenly his smile fell, and he turned around. "Tell me, do you see any burns?" he asked, indicating his own back. "Do you see any scars even?"

James perused the perfect, pale flesh and shook his head. "No, nothing. You look fine."

"Then you see my problem," the monk said.

James didn't. "I'm James," he said, trying a different tack. "What's your name?"

"Keller," the monk answered, turning around. At last James felt like he was making progress.

"And you're really a monk? With what order?"

Keller stiffened. "I studied in Ireland, at Clonfert, when I was still a monk."

James' brow furrowed as he again took in the brown robe. "You're not a monk now?" he asked.

Keller stuck his arm out into the beam of sunlight that cut across the narrow room. James flinched as he held it there, remembering too well the pain it caused.

"Who ever heard of a vampire monk?" Keller said bitterly, echoing James' earlier thought even as his arm began to smoke. "I was lucky to escape my order with my life when Toria turned me into this."

Keller removed his arm from the beam of light, and James watched as the skin bubbled and began to heal itself.

Keller watched it too and laughed. "Even if they had accepted me, how can I be a proper servant in this body—this body which cannot suffer?"

James knew the question was rhetorical, but couldn't stop himself. "This body that has no soul?"

Keller's eyes widened and he grabbed James by the shoulder. "Dinna say that!" he demanded. "Do not ever say that. You don't know."

"No, you're right, I don't." James acknowledged, "Just like you don't know that God no longer hears your prayers. Perhaps he still does, even if your order no longer considers you fit to serve."

Keller stepped back and smiled. "I have been told as much recently by another of our kind. Perhaps the both of you are right. Perhaps the children of Lilith can be redeemed."

James shook his head. "Who's Lilith?" he asked.

Keller stared back at him. "Has no one told you of your origins?"

"Ash told me he was the first and he didn't know exactly who or what was responsible," James said.

"Ash told you?"

"That's right. He's the one who made me," James admitted, remembering Evan's advice a little too late.

Keller looked at him with decidedly more interest. "Is that right? Well, that's most disappointing."

James eyebrows shot up. "I'm sorry?"

"I had hoped that Ash's long forbearance meant he had seen the error of his ways. It appears not. Is he killing again as well?"

"What? No. Absolutely not. He didn't even bite me, Toria did. He saved my life."

"Saved your life?" Keller scoffed and walked over to a stack of books. The small room was quite littered with books. There were stacks on the desk and stacks on the floor. James could make out the Council laptop unplugged at the bottom of one such pile. Out of another, Keller finally pulled the book he wanted.

"The Verses," he said, "were written in the first or second century by a Christian prophet who was visited by a young vampire, a vampire who claimed to have been born of a human mother."

"Aren't we all?" James retorted.

Keller gave him an annoyed glare and reverently caressed the small leather-bound volume. "This particular vampire had not been turned, but was rather gradually turning into one of us. He claimed to have been told by his mother that his father was one of the children of Lilith, and he asked Sirach, the prophet, to tell his future. The result," Keller passed him the volume, "is a retelling of the early Jewish legends of Lilith, combined with a foretelling of the role of the children of Lilith in the last days of Earth."

James paged through the text. It looked like a book of the Bible, except for the repeated references to Lilith. "So you never told me—who is Lilith exactly?"

"Lilith was the first wife of Adam. She proved too willful to serve Adam as a proper helpmate and so was banished from the Garden of Eden. She was cursed, relegated to darkness and demons, but since, unlike Eve, she never ate from the tree of knowledge, she remained immortal."

James handed the book back. "What does that have to do with us?" he asked.

"Nothing," a voice answered from the doorway.

James turned to see Toria leaning casually against the door frame.

"It's a fairy tale and a complete waste of time." She motioned for James to join her in the hallway. "I have a job for you if you are interested in doing something productive."

James turned back to Keller. "We'll talk later, okay? I would like to learn more."

Keller smiled at him, noticeably ignoring Toria's presence. "Any time."

James closed the door behind him and looked up at Toria. "I guess this means you're speaking to me again?"

Toria shrugged. "I think being out from under Ash's wing will be good for you, so I wanted to give you a project."

"Something you need?" James asked.

Toria shook her head. "No..." she broke off as the smell of burning flesh once again greeted them both. James winced and saw Toria do the same. For a moment he thought she might storm into Keller's room, but she quickly composed herself and motioned for him to follow her into his room.

"As I was saying," she continued as James shut the door, "the Council recently expelled one of its members, a fairly new arrival to the city who goes by the name of Lucas Benson."

"Expelled? Why?" James queried, a worried look on his face. "Does this have anything to do with the vampire disappearances?"

Toria glanced at him sharply. James shrugged in response. He didn't like having to admit to listening at keyholes, but he wanted to know what he was up against.

"No," she replied dryly, "he just made a big mistake on his first assignment."

James snorted. "Oh, great. No pressure."

"No, not really," Toria replied. "The Council doesn't yet know that I'm having him trailed. I just want to know if there is anything to report." She handed him a small piece of paper. "I have his address from the Council network. Maybe tonight you could go downtown and see what he's up to now that he's no longer working for us."

"I see," James said, taking the paper from her hand. "What should I expect?"

Toria shook her head. "I don't know. I don't think he's likely to try to kill you, but I can't be certain, so just do the best you can without being seen and don't take any chances. It's not that important."

James hesitated, but decided that the time for hesitation was long past. "Okay," he replied.

Toria turned and headed for the door. "Thank you, James. Now you should get some rest, and if you want my advice, stay away from Keller. He's not been totally sane since I turned him, and he's not to be trusted."

She pulled the door shut behind her and left James wondering just who here *was* to be trusted.

CHAPTER 13

Delilah sensed that this man in her arms needed absolution. How blindingly ironic that fate had led him to seek it here. She felt Samson draw in a deep breath and slide his hands down to meet hers. He guided them both across the room, only dragging his lips from hers when he lowered himself onto the edge of her bed.

He pulled her forward, and she willingly followed his lead, coming to sit astride him. His strong hands slid slowly back up her arms and then down to capture her breasts, seeming to test their weight through the sheer fabric of her dress.

She could feel that he was already hard for her, but he didn't seem in a hurry. He hooked his finger into her v-shaped neckline and slowly slid the blue fabric over, exposing her left breast. He teased her nipple for a moment with his thumb as it grazed past, then bent his head and took it in his mouth. She rose slightly to meet him, and he wrapped his hands around her taut bottom.

She sucked in her breath as his mouth closed around her flesh and he began to suckle her with unashamed delight. His mouth was hot, his devotion slavish, and her hands went unbidden into his glorious hair as a bolt of desire rammed through her, forcing her to arch harder against him.

⚜

Ariana didn't want to wake. She wanted the dream.

She almost laughed out loud. James would have said that was her whole problem, she thought. She always wanted the dream, always shot for the moon.

She roused herself, put her feet on the hard wood floor of her apartment, and stared out its floor-to-ceiling windows onto the city below. How many people out there were doing exactly what she was doing—getting up, getting ready for another day of trying to grab the dream? Probably all of them.

She padded to the bathroom, plucking her Blackberry organizer off the dresser on the way so she could read e-mail while she brushed her teeth.

Nothing from Roger.

She wasn't sure what that meant. Why had they been discussing her last night? She was the number two person at the fund. It was only natural her name would come up.

But there was nothing natural about the way Ash Samson had looked at her. Or about the way she had reacted to him. Or her bizarre dream. Just thinking about it made her blush.

Really, nothing like a pornographic dream to make a client meeting even more awkward, she thought as she rode the elevator up to the 32nd floor of the mid-town high rise that housed her office.

Ursula, their receptionist, occupied her usual place behind the sleek glass desk that greeted visitors to Tailwind Investments. "Hi, Ariana," she said. "Roger has been unofficially looking for you."

Ariana looked at her watch. It was only ten minutes past 8:00. She glanced back at Ursula with a raised eyebrow.

"I know," Ursula replied, a hint of sympathy showing from behind her thick glasses. "He's been in for at least an hour."

Ariana gave a wan smile. "Thanks for the warning, Urs."

Roger and Ariana brought different strengths to the management of the fund. Ariana was brilliant and insightful, but deliberate in her work. Roger was given to flashes of genius, interspersed by periods of what Ariana considered excessive hyperactivity and vacillation.

Ariana opened her office door, hung up her coat, and checked her messages. There was nothing urgent, so she decided to bite the bullet and call Roger.

He picked up on the first ring. "Ariana, I'm glad you're in. Do you have time to come up and talk now about the Samson matter? He's in more of a hurry than I thought."

"Sure, Roger. I'll be right up."

She took the stairs and then blamed the exertion for the fact that her heart was beating faster when she got to Roger's door. She was surprised that she felt a little nervous to knock, but knock she did and, hearing some sort of noise, she entered.

The noise was actually Roger's razor, but he motioned for her to come in as he finished his shave. He stood in front of the 14-foot windows of his corner office, and Ariana couldn't see him clearly until she got closer. He looked like hell.

"Late night?" she queried, coming further in and taking a seat in one of the two red leather chairs that faced Roger's tremendous desk. She had teased him mercilessly when he first ordered them several years ago, about making their office look like a bordello. Roger was a great guy, but he had no taste.

When the last of yesterday's shadow was gone, Roger wrapped the cord around the razor and threw it into a desk drawer. He sank down into his chair, put his elbows on the desktop and stared at Ariana through bleary eyes. "Remind me to only see Ash Samson at business functions from now on," he said. "No more social get-togethers."

"Ash did this to you?" she asked. Further inspection revealed that Roger was still wearing the same clothes he'd been wearing at the restaurant last night. "My god, Roger, were you out all night with him?" Her voice finished on an unnaturally high note.

"You don't have to sound so surprised," Roger remarked dryly. He put his head in his hands and groaned. "I don't even know where the time went. After dinner we went to his club and had a few drinks." He looked up at her. "Not that many, I didn't think. Then we were in some other room and there were dancers, and..."

"Just stop right there," Ariana interrupted, putting her hand out to emphasize the point. "I get the picture." *And it's not a pretty one at that—at least not as far as Roger's part of it.* Roger might be a multi-millionaire, but he was still basically a middle-aged finance geek. Definitely not the party animal type.

"I wish *I* did." Roger groaned again. "Get the picture, that is. Then again, maybe it's better I don't remember." Roger lifted his head. "At any rate, I'm not going to dinner with him tonight. You're on your own."

"Roger!" Ariana's voice was too loud, and Roger's grimace told her that loud alarm was not going to be a successful strategy today. She started again. "Why don't you tell me what this is all about before we make any plans."

"I think the plans are already laid," Roger said, sounding oddly resigned, "but I can fill in some of the details for you. You know Ash has become one of our biggest investors recently."

Ariana nodded.

Roger looked at her intently. "Right," he said, "but Ash has several billion dollars in total investable assets. He's only invested a small portion of that with us to date." Roger leaned back in his chair and rubbed his forehead. "What I do remember from last night is that he is pleased with what we're doing here and wants to explore a larger investment. A sizably larger investment." He rubbed his forehead a little harder.

"So we wine and dine him while he's in town and he leaves us a big check?" Ariana fervently hoped it was that simple.

Roger dropped his hand and began to absently finger the worn spot on the elbow of his plaid shirt. "I'm afraid it won't be that easy," he said. "He's talking about numbers large enough that just managing his new money would require an expansion of our staff here. We would also need someone to manage the process of extracting him from his current investments and getting him into whatever new investments we came up with."

"Wow."

Suddenly Roger wouldn't let Ariana get any questions out.

"He asked me who my best person was," he said, continuing on in a rush, "and of course I said you. He wants you to come to his London offices. I'm not sure for how long, but if he we have to, we can do the whole transition with you there. You can develop and execute the exit strategy with his people, you and I can develop the new strategy, and we'll staff the research and execution out of this office."

Ariana's mouth hung open. *How could so much have happened in one night?* "You're shipping me out to London to be some guy's personal investment adviser?" she asked. She wasn't about to get demoted because some big shot snapped his fingers; she'd worked far too hard for that. "What about my work *here?*" Ariana couldn't believe Roger would sell her out so quickly.

"We're talking about another billion dollars, Ariana," Roger said. "There will be plenty of work, no matter where you are. We'll probably start another fund just for this and bring in a few other investors later on."

Outrage turned to shock. "A billion dollars? Why, that will more than double the size of the current fund." Ariana's brow furrowed, and she looked hard at her boss. "Roger, are you sure you've thought this through?" she asked.

"No," he said, his voice muffled because he'd put his head back down in his hands. "Ash just sprang this on me, too, which is all the more reason you have to go to London. With you there, it will be easier to stall him if we hit snags or need more time."

Ariana stared out the window for a moment wondering why everything suddenly seemed to be out of her control. "I guess I agree with you," she said finally. "It seems I have to go to London."

Roger looked a little surprised. "It's not for good, Ariana. You should look at it as a promotion. It's certainly more than we've bitten off so far. If this goes well, you'll have plenty of chops to start your own fund if that's what you want."

He was right on all counts, of course, but it didn't erase her sense of unease.

CHAPTER 14

Once she left Roger's office, the day went by in the usual flurry of activity. Before she knew it, it was half past 6:00, and Ariana had no choice but to prepare for dinner.

She went into her office bathroom and gazed at her reflection with a critical eye. She was not unattractive. She had great long, shimmery hair, full lips and dark eyes, but she suspected her eyes and strong bearing scared men away. She had a real talent for sizing people up in an instant—seeing into what made them tick. Most men didn't like that, especially in a woman who made more money than they did. She smiled wanly. At least she wouldn't have to worry about that with Ash.

That was a dangerous line of thought, she immediately told herself. Ash was a client. It wouldn't do to start thinking of him as a potential romance.

Even as she lectured herself, she remembered the way she had felt last night during the brief moments when they had made eye contact.

There was no forgetting that, but self-control was her specialty. James, though in the end he didn't like the result, was the one who had taught her that she had the power to control her own destiny.

An interlude with Ash, whatever form she allowed it to take, had one goal—a successful business transaction that she could build on to start her own fund. Her goal of working for herself and being a screaming success was within her reach even sooner than she'd imagined.

And that was pretty cool, Ariana thought with a self-satisfied smile. No man was going to get in the way of that, no matter how scrumptious he was.

She winced as she thought of James. Wherever he was, she hoped he knew that he had never been in the way.

Had she simply spent too much time at work? No, there was no single, simple explanation. *And don't forget,* chimed the little voice that sometimes argued in her defense, *James was the one who left you*. Ariana sighed, knowing this argument with herself had no end.

Ash's car arrived promptly at 7:00, and she was downstairs waiting for it. It was the usual black sedan. She climbed in as the driver held the door. Somehow she'd expected something slightly more dramatic.

Before she even had time to relax into the drive, the car came to a halt in front of a posh Park Avenue townhouse. The driver came around to get her door, and Ariana stepped onto the sidewalk.

Ash had pretty good taste, she thought, admiring the upward view. She loved these old townhouses, with their unique, elegant architecture. Faded, dark red stucco rose three stories above the sidewalk, adorned with elaborate carved overhangs at the roof and above the windows. A large brick pillar flanked the stairs that led up from the sidewalk to the front door. Or rather, front gate.

The stairs stopped at an archway protected by a locked wrought iron gate. Similar black bars adorned the windows on the lower floor, protecting them from overly inquisitive passers-by.

Ariana ascended the stairs, followed by the driver, who brushed past her and opened the locked gate. They both stepped into the entryway and, after locking the gate behind them, the driver turned and gave a brisk rap of the brass gargoyle knocker that adorned the mahogany front door. It had an empty echo, but Ariana thought the gargoyle was a nice touch.

The driver retreated back down the stairs, and someone opened the door. For a moment, all Ariana could see was a small, dark silhouette as the light from inside spilled out onto the stoop along with a rush of warm, fragrant air.

"Good evening, Miss," the elderly woman said in a clipped British accent. She motioned for her to come inside, and Ariana's eyes adjusted enough that she could tell the woman wore a black dress with a pristine white apron.

"I'll let Mr. Samson know you've arrived, Miss. Please," the woman pointed to a small sitting area, "have a seat."

The maid's wiry figure disappeared down a hall to the left, and Ariana crossed from the foyer into the beautiful sitting room she had indicated.

No, beautiful was the wrong word, Ariana thought. More like exquisite, in a masculine sort of way. The floors were a deeply varnished wood, so dark they were almost red. Antique Persian rugs covered much of them, and Ariana speculated that just the few she could see must have cost a fortune. Especially the one in the center. It depicted scenes of what looked like a stormy romance. Ariana stepped in to get a closer look.

A footstep clicked on the floor behind her, and she turned to discover herself staring into a rock-solid chest.

"Do you like it?"

Ariana looked up and drew in a breath. Ash. "Oh, yes," she breathed, hoping the double entendre wasn't too obvious.

Ash smiled down at her and graciously touched her elbow, turning her around. He was still very close. Leaning forward, he pointed toward the interplay of colors on the rug. "King Herod ordered the women of his court to create this rug to tell the story of Samson and Delilah. Herod and Samson came from the same region, and Herod fancied himself a similar romantic warrior."

Clearly it was even older than Ariana had imagined. She turned to face him again. "And how did you come by it?" she asked.

Ash smiled. "Oh, let's just say I took it off the hands of someone who didn't fully appreciate it."

She couldn't help smiling back, though her thoughts were otherwise. For heaven's sake, the rug was priceless, and he just kept it lying around on the living room floor. Suddenly she realized the obvious. "I suppose it caught your eye because he's your namesake?"

Ash looked confused for a moment. "What? Oh, that's right. The family name." He smiled rakishly at her once more. "Actually, I bought it because of her."

"Her?" she asked, not quite catching his meaning.

Ash nodded toward the rug, and Ariana turned again to look at it. The scene at their feet showed a woman alone in a courtyard.

Ariana studied her. She was a dark beauty, indeed. The legendary Delilah. Ariana smiled and looked back over her shoulder at Ash. "So she's your secret love?"

His broad smile faded. "Something like that."

Ariana moved farther around the rug. It truly was a work of art. Elaborate scenes of love, betrayal, murder, and retribution flowed masterfully from one into the next. Only... Ariana moved around the rug to examine the final scene more closely.

Every other scene seemed to match the Biblical version of the story, at least as well as Ariana could recall it. Samson saw Delilah, wanted her, and she allowed him into her bed. Delilah eventually coaxed him into telling her that his hair was the secret of his great strength, and then she betrayed him.

Samson was taken prisoner, and in the final hour, asked God for the strength for one last act of retribution. God restored his strength, and Samson pulled down the pillars that supported the temple, burying himself and his captors.

But the story on the rug went one scene further. It showed Samson climbing from the rubble.

"I thought Samson died at the end of this story?"

Ash shrugged. "Maybe the women of the court just wanted a happy ending," he suggested. "Isn't that what women are supposed to want?"

Ariana raised an eyebrow at him over the expanse of rug. "I would have thought you had a pretty good read on what women want." That wasn't what she had intended to say at all.

Now it was Ash's turn to raise a brow. "Careful, I might take that as a compliment."

"Well," she pointed out, "Roger didn't seem able to keep up with you. Not even for one night."

Ash laughed and smiled in a way he clearly intended to be sheepish, but humility, Ariana noticed, didn't sit comfortably on him. "I must confess that I don't go out like that every night, but last night, there was much to celebrate." His eyes focused on her more intently.

"You mean the deal with Roger?"

"Of course. Roger is a genius, and he tells me you aren't far behind. It will be a great pleasure to watch you work."

A bell tinkled somewhere in the distance, and Ash stepped back from the rug.

"Dinner is apparently served," he said, motioning for her to precede him through a door on the far side of the sitting room. "It's this way."

A series of quick turns brought them into a formal dining room. This was a rarity in New York, and Ariana was delighted to see that it was set formally and just for two. She couldn't say why, but having to share Ash with strangers making small talk would have been too much for her to bear. She wanted to get to know him.

The realization made her stop short, so that Ash almost ran into her. "Is everything all right, love?"

The casual endearment uttered in that voice of his made her skin tingle. What was it about this man that he had such sway over her after one meeting?

She suddenly realized she hadn't once thought of James since she'd arrived. A sick feeling crept into the pit of her stomach and lodged itself there like underdone hamburger. She walked farther into the room without turning back to explain.

Ash followed and pulled out a chair at one of the places for her. He took the place set to her right.

The same little maid who'd let Ariana in earlier now appeared to pour them both wine. Ariana took advantage of the interruption to get her thoughts in order and give herself another lecture on keeping business separate from pleasure. She was determined to get the discussion back into safer territory. "So tell me more about your plans," she invited. "Roger gave me the bare bones, but that was about it."

"Well," Ash took a sip of his wine, "over the years, my financial house has been allowed to get a little too diversified. I have investments in projects of all sizes, all over the world. I want to consolidate the management of at least a portion of my assets, and I want to do it with Tailwind Investments, with you and Roger."

"And you think I need to come to London to assist in executing the transition?"

"Not assist, Ariana." Ash's tone was newly serious and careful. "You, assuming you come, will have complete control of the process. My London advisers will take direction from you."

He seemed to want her pretty badly. "Who are they?" she asked.

Ash shrugged. "A couple of suits I hired away from Goldman Sachs to work full-time for me and a couple of others."

"Won't they be reluctant to work with me since I'm essentially going to be taking away part of their job?"

Ash shook his head as he spoke. "I don't think so. They are already overworked. Plus, they know they don't have the expertise you and Roger bring to the table."

Ash paused while the maid placed salads in front of them. "Thank you, Nancy," he said, quickly turning his attention back to Ariana. "My lead adviser, Justin, and I have discussed this at some length, actually, and he's one hundred percent on board."

Ariana opened her mouth and started to speak, but thought better of it. Even if she could come up with a hundred good objections, they didn't really matter. Roger was counting on her to make this work, and make it work was exactly what she would do.

"This will be good for your career, Ariana," Ash said, surprising her. "You've achieved much in a very short time. I would never ask you to do anything to jeopardize your professional future."

"Thank you." Ariana turned her attention to her salad, not knowing what else to say. Sensitivity to her career aspirations was an unexpected development.

Soon salad was replaced by grilled wild salmon on a bed of vegetable couscous.

"You know, Ariana," Ash said, setting aside his perfectly weighted silver fork, "other than your resume and your successful management of my money to date, I don't know much about you."

Though she found his impersonal tone comforting, a smidgen of dread crept into the pit of her stomach, marring her enjoyment of the perfectly cooked fish. *It's a completely legitimate question*, she told herself. No need to read anything too personal into it.

Ariana smiled brightly. "What more do you need to know?"

Ash half returned her smile, but his gaze was piercing. "Everything."

Spending time with this man was definitely going to be bad for her digestion, she thought. "Everything isn't really that much, I'm afraid."

Ash looked skeptical, forcing her to continue. "I went to under-grad and law school at Duke, then to Stanford for an MBA. I worked in the San Francisco office of a private equity fund for a few years, and then came to New York to work at a hedge fund, which is where I met Roger. When he left to start his own fund, I went with him."

"Did you meet your husband in California?"

Ariana wasn't prepared for that question, and her bewilderment must have showed on her face.

"I'm sorry," Ash said, compassion warming his dark eyes. "Roger told me. I didn't mean to pry."

"No, no." Ariana recovered her composure. "It's all right. James and I did meet in California, while I was still in grad school. He was working for a software company in Silicon Valley." She didn't like where this conversation had strayed. "How about you?" she asked. "Is there a Mrs. Samson?"

"No. There was once, but... it didn't work out." He looked away from her, taking a long gulp of his wine

Soon Nancy served dessert, and they ate in awkward silence. After the plates were cleared, Ash rose and came behind Ariana to pull out her chair. "Let's go into my study. I need to give you something." She rose, and he pushed her chair back under the table. "And I need a drink."

Ariana followed him from the dining room into a wood-paneled office. "So you'll be back in London next week?" she asked.

"That's right. I'm going back the day after tomorrow on the over-night flight." Ash strode around to the other side of his desk, picked up a manila folder and handed it to her. "I had Justin pull together some initial information for you."

Ariana resisted the temptation to open it and dig in. When it came down to it, she really did love her work.

"When would you like me to fly in?" she asked instead.

"I'd like to get things rolling as soon as possible, but I know this is short notice. When do you think you can get your plate clear here in New York?"

"Well, today is Friday." Ariana started to think out loud and turned to stare at a spot on the wall as she often did when trying to concentrate. "It will take me at least a few days to work out with Roger how my responsibilities here are going to be divided and how we want to function going forward with me in London. Plus, I'll probably need a day to tie up a few personal things since it looks like I might be away for an extended period." She turned back to Ash. "So, maybe Thursday of next week?"

Ash came around the desk and walked over to one of the panels on the side of the room and pressed a button Ariana couldn't see. The panel slid silently to the side revealing a previously hidden, but well stocked, bar. Ariana heard the clinking of glassware before Ash handed her a glass half-full of caramel-colored liquid.

"Shall we?" He made a motion as if to toast, and so Ariana raised her glass.

"To the fulfillment of wishes," Ash said.

Okay, that was weird, she thought, as she touched her glass to his and took a small sip of the amber liquid. Cognac, she guessed, but she wasn't an expert on after dinner drinks. A nice chocolaty Bailey's was more her style, but this was smooth and warm; its comforting heat helped quell some of her nagging doubts.

"You'll stay at my house, of course."

So much for the quelling of doubts, Ariana thought, turning and setting her glass on the desk to cover her unease.

"I have a large manor house outside the city," Ash continued. "I'll have Justin copy all the necessary documentation and bring it over. Then the three of us can work from there." He paused and must have seen her hesitation. "Of course, I also have a flat in the city proper that I will put at your disposal," he said, "but I think you'll be more comfortable at the house. I'll have an office set up for you there, and we'll all have plenty of room to work without getting in each other's hair—so to speak." He smiled slightly at what seemed a private joke.

There now, Ariana thought. *That all sounded perfectly reasonable.* In fact, Ash had been perfectly reasonable all night. No hint of the predatory sex god she had glimpsed at the restaurant the night before. Maybe he had been a one-sided creation of her sex-starved imagination. That would be good. She wasn't ready for real temptation.

"Sounds perfect," Ariana said, finally showing a hint of a smile. "I've never been to a manor before. If it's even half as cool as your James Bond bar service over there, I'm sure it will do just fine."

Ash laughed and moved closer to her. "It has a few surprises." His voice took on the seductive rumble she remembered. Ariana was a little surprised, but she liked the idea that he might have a wicked streak after all. She liked it so much she did something totally inappropriate. She took a step and closed the distance between them.

Then she promptly lost her nerve.

God, she was a mess, she thought as she stood there frozen, staring at the smooth skin at the collar of Ash's shirt.

His hand came up and one finger lightly lifted her chin until she allowed her eyes to meet his. And that was the real mistake, she thought. Suddenly it was as if the mask of the polite Ash she'd had dinner with fell away to reveal the man—no, what had she called him? Right, the predatory sex god—inside.

Ash smiled down at her and the spell was cast. *Don't stop there, angel.*

She couldn't tell if he'd actually said it or if it was in her imagination like the other night, but it didn't matter. The Voice was back. She reached up and put a hand lightly on his chest.

His smile disappeared and was replaced by a look of such intense desire that Ariana almost turned away from the force of it. Almost, but not quite.

In an instant, his arms were around her, his lips came down to find hers, and Ariana was awash in the heat and motion of his lips and his fingers. She was being crushed between the two, but she didn't care. The urgency of his touch warmed her insides where they had been cold for so long. She returned his kiss with a fervor that terrified her.

Ash groaned and moved his hands lower down her back. Ariana was both relieved and alarmed to know that she wasn't the only one so affected.

One of his hands pushed its way up into her hair. He bent her head back slightly and deepened the kiss. Ariana felt suspended beneath the sensual onslaught of his mouth.

Then, suddenly, Ash pulled himself away. He still looked at her with hunger, but now there was distance between them.

Ariana was confused. Confused and more than a little ashamed of herself.

"Ariana." Ash's voice sounded as strained as she felt. "I think you should go."

Ariana turned silently to get her bag and prayed her shame wasn't visible on her face. She'd come on to a client, for God's sake! And now they might lose that client. Roger would kill her. And James… she no longer owed him her loyalty, but this still felt like betrayal.

"Ash," she turned around, prepared to make a very long and unbecoming apology.

"Don't," he whispered. "Don't apologize. I want you. I want to get this deal done. If you come to London all these things and more are possible." He handed her the folder she had laid on the desk and would have forgotten in her distraction. "I just didn't want to scare you away tonight."

His words rang true, Ariana thought, but still, she hesitated. She met Ash's gaze and was glad to see that he looked worried.

"Come to London, Ariana," he said. "I promise you won't be disappointed."

He turned and pushed a button on a console on the desk. "I'm going to have Nancy see you out."

Ariana nodded, not wanting any front-door goodnight awkwardness to pile on top of the I-just-came-on-to-a-client-whom-I-just-met awkwardness.

"Where did you find her anyway?" *Great, merciful change of subject.*

"Nancy?" Ash queried. "Oh, she's been with me for ages."

CHAPTER 15

On his way to the warehouse, Luc picked up a homeless man and sat him on the back of his motorcycle. He wouldn't stay upright, so Luc climbed on in front of him and wrapped the man's arms around his shoulders, holding him in place like a stinking, slobbering sweater. The man nestled his head between Luc's shoulder blades. Luc grimaced and gunned the engine.

In under a minute, they were pulling around the side of the large concrete structure he'd selected to house his business venture. At one point, when this part of town had still been industrial, it had stored goods for shipment out of the nearby docks and rail yard. Now, with its small office and subterranean warehouse space, it suited Luc's needs.

He carried the man through the empty space on the ground floor, his cowboy boots kicking up dust around his feet. At the back of the cavernous space, Luc took a set of flimsy metal stairs down to the cage level, turning on lights as he went.

The warehouse space on the lower levels was two stories deep and, except for a row of makeshift cages, almost completely empty. Everything about his operation was shoestring, but he'd made sure the cages were sturdy enough to do the trick. One wall of the warehouse was divided into eight concrete cubby-holes, four on top and four on the bottom. Luc assumed they'd been used to store smaller, loose freight at one time. But now the four on the bottom were each outfitted with a fourth wall of steel bars, each two inches thick and three inches apart. He was fairly proud of his handiwork, as no vampire had yet been able to escape.

Luc walked further into the darkened space. Inside the cages sat three young vampires—two males and a female. They had been there quite a while, long enough that they had stopped screaming and trying to talk to him every time he came in. Quite a change from when he'd captured them over a month ago. Vicious killers, each of them. Or so they fancied themselves. Luc didn't feel one bit of sympathy for them. Even if he did, what was one month out of their wretched eternal lives?

There was a fourth cage, but it remained empty. He'd gotten distracted by his brief stint as a member of Council House and never captured a fourth. Not to worry. Since Ash Samson had gotten him kicked out, it was back to Plan A without distraction.

Luc forced his mind back to the task at hand and crossed to his workspace on the wall flanking the cages, where a stainless steel prep table gleamed in the low light. It had a sink in the middle with a drain that was connected into the cages by a series of plastic hoses.

Luc laid the man on the prep table, quickly snapped his neck and waited for the inevitable. As the soul departed, Luc said an earnest prayer that it come back to a better life.

Then he went to work, pulling a hook down from the ceiling and removing the man's right shoe and sock. One short incision with a small knife freed the Achilles tendon, and Luc slipped the metal hook through it. He removed the head with one stroke of a large cleaver.

The cleaver went into the sink and the head up on the high end of the slightly slanted table. Luc closed the eyes as blood began to drip into the narrow channels in the table and flow toward the drain.

A bright yellow control box dangled from a nearby chain. When Luc grabbed it and pressed the black button, a pulley system cranked on overhead and raised the man's body so that it hung, neck down, over the sink. Blood slopped into the drain and began to run through the feeder system. Luc added the contents of a small bottle to the flow and made one last incision down the length of the man's torso.

Sticking his hand in near the pelvis, he raked the man's innards into a large bucket. Those he'd save to add to the next batch of synthetic blood to make it go farther. He put the bucket into the big freezer that sat against the opposite wall.

As Luc washed his knives and his hands, precious pints flowed out of the homeless man and into the three succubi in the cages. Luc let the water run, glad to stay off to one side where he couldn't see them sucking blood from metal spouts. It wasn't natural.

Once they'd drunk enough to sustain them, and the sedative began to take effect, he came around and pressed a button on the cages' control panel. The three chains fastened to three vampire wrists began to slowly withdraw into the back wall of each cell. Once in place, three small blades came out and made three incisions, and vampire blood began to flow through the channels he had carved in the concrete walls, ultimately collecting in a five-gallon plastic bucket that sat on the floor to the right of Luc's prep table. It would be filled in one drawing.

Once the draining process was underway, Luc set the timer for the cell doors. It was time to let this bunch go.

He took the elevator back up to the street level. He'd had enough of vampires for one night.

Or not, he thought as the elevator doors opened into his upstairs office to reveal a khaki-clad vampire rummaging through his files.

CHAPTER 16

When he awoke, James found himself behind the bars of one of the cages he had observed earlier, when he'd followed the sound of running water down a rickety metal staircase onto a narrow catwalk above Luc's operating theater. He'd only watched the gruesome sight long enough to assure himself that Luc wouldn't be coming back up for a while. Apparently, he'd misjudged.

A polite cough had interrupted his search of Luc's files. He'd turned, and was caught totally off guard by the fist that whipped out and caught him underneath the chin. He got a glimpse of blond hair, a denim jacket, and fangs just before he lost consciousness.

Now he cursed his carelessness. He might have just solved the mystery of the missing vampires, but he couldn't tell anyone. And there was no sign of his blond captor.

As the hours ticked by, James went over all the things he'd done wrong. If he ever got out of this, Toria was going to be furious at him. But that was not the most immediate of his problems; he was starting to get hungry.

He wondered if Luc would let him starve. That didn't seem to be the purpose of this little enterprise, but then, he was a prowler, not a specially chosen victim. Maybe Luc was some sort of demented vampire serial killer.

That thought motivated James to get up and try the bars. Whatever they were made of was more substantial even than it looked because the bars didn't budge. The clanking rattle of the elevator door startled him.

"Rise and shine, Jimbo," Luc called out as he crossed the concrete floor. He paused in front of James' cage and stood looking down at his newest captive.

"It's James, and how do you know my name?" James asked.

Luc exhaled loudly and grabbed one of the bars. "I got a visit earlier today from Toria. She explained about your little secret mis-

sion." Luc smiled suddenly. "I, of course, assured her you were doin'
just fine."

James' eyes narrowed. "Does that mean you're going to let me
out?"

"No," Luc replied, "I can use you for my purposes and still keep
my word to Toria. You won't be harmed in any way."

"What purposes? And what happened to the three vampires who
were here earlier?" James demanded.

Luc leaned against the bars, looking offended. "I let them go,"
he said. "What else? I'm trying to run a business here; I'm not some
murdering psychopath." He glanced up at the dark ceiling a full story
above the top of the cage. "But it's kind of hard when you can't be out
before dusk. Maybe I should get a receptionist."

James laughed out loud. He couldn't help it.

Luc glared at him. "What's so funny from in there?"

James wasn't entirely sure himself, but he tried to explain. "I was
just imagining that help wanted ad," he said. "Vampire seeks agreeable
human to answer phones, provide snacks."

Luc flashed a mega-watt grin. "That would work," he said
amiably.

James shook his head, wondering how Luc could seem so harmless, yet clearly be so deadly. "Maybe you should just get a website
instead," he suggested.

"A what?"

James blinked, feeling Luc's confusion mirrored on his own features. "You know, the internet, web pages, e-mail..."

When no recognition sparked on Luc's face, James gave a sigh. "I
think you'd better let me out."

As soon as he said it, James recalled the horrible sight of the homeless man being fed to the other vampires, but he put it out of his mind.
His first priority had to be getting out of his cage. "Look," he said, "I
can help you get set up so you don't need to deal with your customers
in person so much. Who are your customers, by the way?"

Luc hesitated and finally gave in. "Vampire blood will heal pretty
much anything," he said, "including wrinkles. I mix it into a little

face lotion, and the ladies can't get enough of the stuff." He stuck his hand through the bars, "I've been thinking of expanding, and I can definitely use the help, but I want your word that you'll actually do it if I let you out."

James looked at the outstretched hand, considered his options for another fraction of a second, and shook it. "Deal," he affirmed. His role seemed harmless enough.

Luc hit a button on the side of the row of cages and the door to James' slid open. He stepped gingerly out.

"So, where do we start?" James asked. "I don't suppose you have a computer?"

Again Luc just stared at him.

"Okay, I'll have to get you a computer, maybe two. Then I can start getting you set up." James checked his watch. There was still time to swing by to check on Ariana before the sun came up. He could spec and buy the computers tomorrow.

"Who's Ariana?" Luc asked.

James raised a surprised gaze back to Luc. "I guess all vampires can do that?"

"More or less," Luc answered, moving a step closer. "Who is she?" he repeated.

"No one, really," James muttered, unsure why he was suddenly nervous. "Just a girl I knew before. She lives near here."

Again, Luc's fist caught him by surprise. He staggered back from the force of the blow, tripping over the bottom of the cage door. Before he could rise, Luc shoved him farther in and slammed the door.

"What are you doing?" James demanded.

Luc gave him a pitying look. "Teaching you a lesson your precious Ash should have taught you already."

With that, he turned and left.

⚜

Four days later, Luc returned to check on his prisoner.

"Hello, James," he said, when he'd made his way down to the cage level. James' bloodshot eyes stared back at him, not really seeing him or the young girl at his side. "Did you think I'd forgotten about you?" Luc asked.

James wiped the saliva from his mouth, and Luc thought for a moment he might respond, but he just grunted. Luc knew he was starving. He pressed the button to open the cage door.

With the door open, James finally saw the young runaway Luc had brought. He backed up, but his nostrils flared, and Luc knew they were what would lead him to her.

"I've got a little something for you," Luc said. He gave the girl a gentle shove in James' direction. It was hard to say which of the two of them was more addled, she from whatever drugs she was on or James from starvation.

James tried to turn away from her and face the wall, but the stupid girl thought she was there to service him. She wasn't totally wrong, Luc thought.

"Hey," she said meekly, moving closer and tucking a loose strand of hair behind her ear. Luc couldn't put a name to its current color, but he suspected it would be blond if it were clean. She was just a tiny thing—a tiny, broken thing he'd crooked his finger at inside another abandoned building. She'd come so willingly, he'd barely even had to speak to her.

When James didn't respond, the girl reached out and touched his arm, the ragged sleeve of her sweatshirt falling back to reveal a dainty, bruised, and blue-veined wrist.

Luc knew the instant James' fangs unsheathed, the instant the last bit of reason fled his burning brain. James grabbed her wrist, spun around and pounced on the girl like a wild animal. Liquid slurping sounds followed, but the girl had spoken her last. Luc heard her neck snap as they went down.

When James could drain no more, he raised his head from the limp form cradled in his arms.

Luc saw that he now recognized him, but the fever had far from passed.

"More," James pleaded, spraying drops of blood as he talked.

Luc tossed him a few bags of synthetic blood and went upstairs, leaving the cage door open.

Eventually, Luc heard the rumble of the elevator as it rose from below. The doors opened, and James stood there looking at him, his clothes covered with blood, his face wrought with regret.

"Why did you do that?" James asked, stepping gingerly into the room as if unsure he deserved to be there.

"I didn't do anything," Luc answered, being deliberately callous. "You killed that girl." He picked up a pencil off his desk and twirled it between his fingers. "I just wanted you to know what you were capable of—and incapable of—before you went to pay a visit to your human girlfriend." Luc pointed the pencil at James. "Tell me, James, what does your girlfriend look like? Is she older than the girl you just killed? Taller? Shorter?"

James started to answer and then stopped. "I don't know," he said.

Luc could see realization dawning. "Because you don't have any idea what that girl downstairs looked like, do you? You never saw her as a person—only as food."

James sank onto the couch, head in his hands.

"It will be a long time, James, before you can trust yourself to be near humans in that way again. By then, you won't be doing people any favors by showing up when they've thought you were dead. Trust me." Luc came to stand in front of James. "You are dead to her, James, and she needs to be dead to you. Unless you're prepared to turn her into one of us."

Luc got the horrified look he'd hoped for. James swallowed hard. "No, never that."

CHAPTER 17

Ariana scanned the mob of people at the gate area as she exited the jet bridge at Heathrow. *Travelers always look one of two ways,* she thought, *excited or exhausted.* Today she was one of the excited ones. In fact, she'd been excited all week.

From the moment she'd left Ash's townhouse, the bustle of change had taken hold of her life, leaving her mercifully little time to reflect on James' disappearance or her attraction to Ash until she was buckled into her seat on the runway at JFK. By then, it was too late to chicken out.

Ariana made her way through the gray terminal to the baggage claim area and grabbed her suitcase. After wrestling it onto its wheels, she looked around for the promised car service. Some part of her hoped Ash had come himself, but a sign with her name printed on it told her otherwise. A uniformed driver took her bag, and she followed him to a long black car that sat waiting outside the terminal. They headed northwest out of the city, and its concrete scenery soon gave way to more bucolic surroundings. Golden fields rolled past, inter-rupted by an occasional stone wall or square hedge.

The hypnotic effect of the passing landscape renewed Ariana's reflective state, and again she struggled to understand all she was feel-ing. She wanted to chalk her excitement up to her love of a new chal-lenge and unexpected travel, but she knew she wasn't being honest. In spite of all her misgivings, a large part of her excitement centered on Ash Samson.

Which was odd, given that she barely knew the man, but perhaps that was the lure. He was a mystery.

He was also a client, she reminded herself. With everything she'd lost—her child, her marriage, her husband—she couldn't lose her career, too, at least not over something as stupid as a romantic misstep with a client. She wouldn't let that happen.

The car slowed and turned into a pebbled drive, and all Ariana's practical thoughts evaporated as around a winding curve appeared the most astounding house she could have imagined. It was made of bricks the color of pale clay and had more windows, towers, and chimneys than Ariana had ever seen at one time. Framed against the crisp blue sky, the manor seemed not so much a house as a massive stone feature of the otherwise open landscape.

Flanking each side of the main part of the house were two separate wings, each turned perpendicular to the manor's front facade. Ariana couldn't tell how far back they went or if she was even seeing all of the impressive structure.

As the car slowed to a stop in front of the entrance, Ariana tried unsuccessfully to tame the expression of wonder she knew had settled on her face. When the driver came around and opened her door, she couldn't resist getting a better look.

As she was craning her neck in an effort to judge the size of the place, a gray-haired woman in a dress and apron opened the front door. She smiled broadly as Ariana dragged her gaze from the house to its occupants.

"Come inside dear, we've got several rooms all made up for you." *An English maid,* Ariana thought as she ascended the few stone steps to the door. *She looks and sounds just like what you'd expect.* Sort of like a younger Miss Marple, though, in truth, the woman's age was hard to guess. She was almost completely gray, but her eyes shone with the brightness normally reserved for the young.

"It's nice to see you again, dear. I'm Nancy." The woman took Ariana's coat. "And this," she said, indicating the man who closed the door behind them, "is Ben."

Ariana murmured a surprised "Hello again" to Nancy, a little ashamed not to have recognized her at first. She turned to Ben and introduced herself, shaking hands with both of them, though they each seemed ill at ease with the gesture.

"How was your flight, miss?" Nancy asked. "Not too tiring, I hope. Airports these days..." She gave an exasperated sigh. "Makes one almost rather walk to one's destination. Or take a nice slow boat."

Ariana warmed to Nancy immediately. The woman was clearly in her element here at the manor. "No," she answered, "it was rather restful, actually. The week before, with all the preparations for this trip, was the tiring part."

"Oh, I'm sure," Nancy said. "Well, we have a very nice room for you. I know you'll settle in comfortably in no time. Why don't I show you up, and Ben will follow shortly with your bags."

Ariana hesitated as a thought struck her. She wasn't here on vacation, after all. "Perhaps I should check in with Mr. Samson first and let him know I'm here?"

Nancy started up the stairs. "Oh, don't worry, Miss Chambers, we'll tell him you've arrived, but he'll not expect to see you before dinner, which will be served at 8:00. I'll come fetch you myself, since this house can be a bit difficult to find your way around in at first."

Ariana followed the maid up to the landing and then right down a long corridor toward the south wing of the house. She didn't dare fall behind, but found herself wanting to stop and peer into the endless rooms that revealed themselves as she passed by. Finally, Nancy stopped in front of a door and opened it with a small flourish.

Ariana stepped inside and was immediately glad she had agreed to stay here. No flat in the city could possibly be as sumptuous as this.

The room had mostly white furnishings, but the walls were a deep blue, making a beautiful frame for the garden she could see out the two large windows. She walked over to get a better look and noticed her feet actually sinking into the plush, beige carpet. A peek into the bathroom revealed similar opulence, with peach-toned marble and gold fixtures.

Nancy opened the door on the other side of the room, and Ariana followed her over. "This connects to your private study in the south wing," Nancy explained.

Ariana stuck her head in and saw that the study was small, but complete with all the modern technology she could ask for—but no files. "I believe Ash said Justin would be bringing over some files?" she inquired.

"Oh, one of the salons on the first floor has been designated as the main work area," Nancy said. Her prim demeanor shifted as she giggled. "The other maids have taken to calling it the 'War Room.'"

Ariana smiled. It sounded perfect already.

Nancy, quickly recomposed, made her way out with a polite bow and an admonition for Ariana to let her know if she needed anything before 8:00.

The door closed, and Ariana gave in to the temptation to throw herself onto the giant bed. She lay there for a few moments marveling at the rapid pace of change in her life, and checked her watch often. It was a quarter past 6:00. Just enough time for a long hot shower and then to answer a few e-mails before dinner.

She quickly stripped and made her way into the bathroom. There was plenty of hot, stinging water, and Ariana stood under it for almost half an hour. Long hot showers were one of her guilty pleasures. Since she had no other clothes, she slipped into the plush white robe that hung on the door.

She left the sanctuary of the bathroom reluctantly, but was happy to discover that her bags had been deposited in the bedroom while she showered. She started to unpack and wondered what was appropriate to wear to dinner at a billionaire's English manor house, finally settling on off-white slacks and a lavender cashmere sweater.

She dressed quickly, grabbed her hair dryer, and went back into the bathroom. She loved her long hair, but she hated having to dry it. Maybe she would go short, she thought, but James had always liked it long.

Tears sprang unexpectedly to her eyes as she realized she no longer had to worry about what James liked. She put the hair dryer down and held on to the vanity with both hands.

Oh God, she thought, as tears started to fall. What was the matter with her? He had been about to divorce her anyway.

But he was still her husband. When she couldn't reach James, she'd put off sending back the papers, so their divorce had never been finalized.

In a terrible way, at least her title was more fitting. She certainly felt more like a widow than a divorcee, and it was her own fault. She'd refused to acknowledge the fact of her divorce, holding on to memories of her marriage until the very end, as if the divorce were a bad dream. Now the dream had become a nightmare, and because she'd refused to let any of the acreage of her heart go fallow, all of it had burned to cinders.

Ariana wiped her eyes on a towel and re-started the hair dryer. In time, she would change her hair. In time, she would move on. But not yet.

Chapter 18

Samson woke slowly, noticing that no light yet strayed in from behind the curtains of Delilah's single window. He seldom woke before first light unless something was wrong. His pulse quickened as he turned and realized that Delilah wasn't beside him.

He sat up and felt his heart sink as he missed the weight of his long, sacred locks. Filled with dread, he looked back and saw them shorn and still lying on the pillow.

His mouth dropped open, but no sound came. He wanted to scream and rage, but sat dumbfounded. *Delilah.* The inescapable conclusion tumbled about in his brain, but he could make no sense of it.

He looked around the room, confirming that she was truly gone. She was, but she hadn't left him alone. At the bedroom door stood a Philistine soldier. The man pulled the door open, and a dozen of his heavily armed companions burst into the room. One of them ordered Samson to his knees.

He obeyed, but not from fear. He had never known fear. He had known hurt and betrayal, or so he'd thought, but Delilah's betrayal made him feel physically wounded, unable to fight or even stand.

One of the men threw a robe over him, and they led him into the street and trussed him over the back of a horse like the household goods of some desert nomad. He knew where they were taking him and what would be his fate. The Philistines would kill him.

Delilah had condemned him to death.

He couldn't see anything but the ground and the dusty underside of his unfortunate mount from where he hung, and he wondered if Delilah watched her handiwork from some upper window. The thought of her there, hiding, laughing at him, finally roused him from his stupor.

Samson pulled himself down from the horse and used his tied wrists like a giant hammer. Even without his divine strength, he was a frightening physical specimen. His fists connected with bone and three guards went down in rapid succession before one of them succeeded in hitting him with a short spear.

It pierced his side and pain lanced up into his brain. He staggered and fell forward onto his knees. With his feet bound, he was unable to rise, but he continued to swing his arms, even as the rest of the guards assailed him. Blows rained down on his head and upper body. A well-placed kick cracked one of his ribs and sent him over on his side into the dirt. More kicks followed. Still Samson would not stay down.

He propped his weight on his bound arms, trying to stand. Another kick sent his elbow popping in the wrong direction. He felt the tendons tear and bones snap. A dagger followed his broken forearm into the dirt, pinning it there in a bloody pool. Staked to the ground, there was little he could do, but he flailed on, taking blow after blow, until he lost so much blood that consciousness finally, mercifully, left him to his fate.

⚜

Ash woke before the sun had set. There were no windows in his room, of course, but he always knew the position of the sun. And he always rose early when he dreamed of her.

He dressed quickly and grabbed his PDA from the nightstand. The orange light was flashing, and Ash's brow furrowed as he listened to the message.

Quickly he returned the call.

"Justin Markham here," a voice answered on the third ring.

Justin was human, but he was a trusted friend and had worked for Ash for over a decade. His official title was financial advisor, but since he knew what Ash was, he occasionally pitched in and filled more secretive roles.

"Justin, it's Ash. I just got your message. What's going on at Hemogen?"

"Hi, Ash," Justin said brightly. "Are you back in-country?"

"Yes, I'm at the manor. I flew in last night. I hope I didn't need to stay in New York?"

"No, no," Justin said. "I'm not even sure there is anything going on at Hemogen. I just figured I should let you know the chief technician out there thinks some notes and samples may have been taken from the lab."

"He thinks?" Ash asked. "What does that mean? Either we had a break-in or we didn't."

"That's just it," Justin explained. "There wasn't any obvious evidence of a break-in; they haven't even called the police, but Faulkner is positive the samples were not just misplaced. The notebook he's not as sure about, but I think it can't be coincidence."

"Do you suspect corporate espionage or something else?" Ash asked.

"I don't know," Justin responded. "Both the notes and the samples relate to the synthetic blood research, which could be lucrative if they ever succeed, but that's quite a remote possibility at present. I would have expected any thief worth his salt to target the more advanced disease cures Hemogen has been working on."

Ash was silent while he turned the matter over in his head.

"It's probably nothing to worry about," Justin pointed out. "I'm told the notes and samples are unlikely to be of any real help to anyone in making marketable synthetic blood."

"That may be," Ash said, making up his mind, "but if anyone went to the trouble to steal them, I'd like to know why. Call Tom Pinkney."

"Are you sure he's up to it?" Justin asked. "We've never used him for anything more than background checks in the past. He's been off the force for quite a while now."

"He's up to it," Ash said. "Plus, I want to keep this quiet. Get him contact information, surveillance tapes, whatever he needs to figure out if it was an inside or an outside job. Then we'll go from there."

Ash heard a pencil scratching against paper in the background.

"Okay, then," Justin said, "I'll give him a call first thing in the morning."

"Fine," Ash said, already eager to be done with this conversation.

"Oh, how was New York?" Justin asked. "Did you decide on any new projects?"

Ash waited the space of a heartbeat, wondering if he should tell his friend the truth.

"I did," he said guardedly, "but not any of the ones we had discussed."

"Oh?" Justin's voice registered mild surprise. "Why's that? Something better come along?"

Ash grinned. He couldn't help it. "You could say that, I suppose."

"What's going on, Ash?" Justin said, clearly unused to the playful side of Ash's personality.

"You won't believe this," Ash said, "but I found her. I finally found her—working at a hedge fund."

Nothing clicked for Justin. "Found who?" he asked. "I'm afraid you've lost me."

"Delilah."

The word hung heavy between them for longer than Ash would have liked.

"Are you sure?" Justin said finally. "I mean, you couldn't possibly be mistaken?"

He sounded hopeful, and Ash suddenly regretted telling him.

"It's her," he answered, trying not to grip the small phone so tightly as to break it.

"Well," Justin said after another long pause, "if she's as bad as you say," Ash could hear when he started grinning on the other end of the line, "I can't wait to meet her."

Ash frowned. "You'll get your chance, actually. She's here."

There was another stunned silence. "Here, as in London?" Justin queried.

"Here, as in already at the manor."

"Wow," Justin said, exhaling loudly. "For a man with all the time in the world, you certainly didn't waste any. How'd you manage that?"

Ash chuckled. "I hired her," he said. "I'm going to put some money under the management of her company, Tailwind Investments. She's going to be managing the transition of funds from here, so I need you to come out tomorrow and bring everything she'll need to start the process."

"Tomorrow?" Justin exclaimed.

"Yes," Ash confirmed. "I told her we'd been discussing this move for some time, so you have to seem prepared."

Justin snorted. "Lucky for you we had been planning something along these lines. I've even heard good things about Tailwind, not that I suspect you care."

"Not really," Ash said. No price was too high for the reward he had in mind.

Justin was quiet for a moment, and Ash sensed a change in his friend.

"Tell me," Justin said, "how does this little scene end?"

"The way I always planned," Ash replied. "Like for like."

"So once you've won her affections, given her back her memories, and had your long overdue lovers' quarrel—what then?"

"Then I rip her heart out."

Justin's flip tone disappeared. "Ash, I hope you mean that figuratively."

Ash wasn't sure.

"Just don't do anything until I get there, Ash. Okay?"

No reply.

"Ash?"

"She will be here when you get here."

Ash knew Justin wanted to comment on the weakness of that promise, but he wisely changed the subject.

"Did you ever find out anything about Toria's missing vampires?" he asked.

Ash frowned into the phone. "No, nothing, but the disappearances seem to have tapered off at least."

"Good," Justin said. "With everything else that's going on, we need to tackle one problem at a time."

CHAPTER 19

Ariana hit "send" on a final message to Roger just as the expected knock sounded at her bedroom door.

"Hi Nan—" Ariana stopped before getting the last syllable out. "I mean, hi, Ash. I was expecting Nancy."

"I'm sorry to disappoint," he said, his voice as low and primeval as Ariana remembered. As he spoke, his eyes raked her from head to toe, and Ariana felt heat trail down her body.

"I trust you had a good trip?" he said, meeting her gaze once more.

Ariana nodded, feeling oddly tongue-tied. "The trip was fine."

Ash laid his palm flat against the door and pushed it farther open. Careful not to brush against him, Ariana squeezed by to join him in the hallway. They walked the length of the hall in silence as Ariana tried to take in the details of the house and the man.

Ash was dressed casually in black pants and a dark blue linen shirt. An expensive watch glittered on his left wrist as he reached up to run a hand through his hair. Dark strands parted, then sprang back into place.

"I love your house," Ariana said.

Ash looked down at her, his carved face lit by an unexpected smile. "Would you like a tour?"

"I'd love it," she answered, catching some of his enthusiasm.

Ash showed her through the main part of the house, opening doors to salons, guest rooms, reading rooms, and libraries.

"How long have you had this place?" Ariana finally asked, noting that, for all the interesting contents of each room, there were no tales of guests or former owners.

Ash frowned slightly. "It's belonged to my family for over 400 years."

"Wow," Ariana exclaimed, "that's kind of amazing. I'd love to hear about them, your family."

"This," Ash said, opening a door on the second floor, "will be your work space while you're here."

Ariana let the change of subject pass and poked her head into the room Ash indicated. Her eyes traveled over the collection of computers, white boards, boxes, and small desks that surrounded the one large table in the center of the room. "War room, indeed," she said, laughing.

"What?" Ash asked.

"Oh, nothing." Ariana shook her head. "I'd love to see more, but I'm sure Nancy is already wringing her hands that we are late for dinner."

Ash gave her a peculiar look. "Right on the money, as always," he said. He reached out as if to grab her hand but stopped short. "Come on, then. Down we go." They went back toward the center of the house and down the main staircase.

On the first floor, not far from the kitchen, a table was laid in what Ariana now knew was only one of at least three dining rooms. This one was very informal, and the table was roughly the same size as the one they'd shared at their previous dinner in Ash's townhouse.

Once again, the food was impeccable and they passed the meal in companionable conversation, mostly about her work.

It's torture, Ariana thought. She didn't want to be companionable. She didn't know what she wanted, and apparently neither did Ash. One minute he was looking at her with naked hunger, and the next minute he went back to seeming like a casual acquaintance. It was strange to think this was only their third meeting.

"Would you like to finish our drinks out on the terrace?" Ash asked. They had waved off desert, opting for cordials instead.

"Oh, yes," Ariana exclaimed. "I'd love to see what the stars look like out here."

"It's a little chilly out," Ash commented. "Do you have a jacket?"

Ariana shook her head. "I think it's still buried in a bag somewhere in my room. No, wait," she called, deciding she must be a little jet-lagged. "Nancy took the jacket I was wearing when I came in. I don't know where she put it."

Ash pushed his chair back. "Wait right here. I'll go and get it for you."

A moment later he reappeared holding her short wool coat. Ariana rose and slipped into it, pulling it tight around her. Ash's hands lingered on her shoulders, but he did not turn her around. Instead, he ran his hands around the collar, pulling her hair free.

"I like you as a blond."

What an odd thing to say, Ariana thought. She'd been a brunette for a while in college, but she was basically a dark blond and always had been.

She turned and walked past him into the hall, but Ash didn't follow.

"Aren't you coming?" she asked.

"I think drinks may not the best idea after all."

"Lost your nerve?" she asked, smiling at his suddenly serious expression.

"Yes." His response was blunt, his face oddly pained.

Ariana looked quickly away, suddenly desperate to get back to the sanctuary of her room.

"I guess I'll say goodnight then," she said brightly, taking two steps in what she fervently hoped was the right direction. She did not want to have to ask him to escort her.

When Ash said nothing after a few steps, Ariana breathed a sigh of relief that she'd started in the right direction. Of course, one wrong turn and she might still be wandering the halls in the morning.

"Oh," she said suddenly, "will your other advisors be joining us tomorrow?"

Her rapid shift into work-mode seemed to throw him for a moment, but he recovered quickly. "Yes," he responded. "Justin is coming up tomorrow afternoon."

"Great. I'll come down early and start trying to get a handle on the contents of the work room first thing."

She left him standing there nodding as she made what she hoped was a beeline for her room.

❧

Ash went over to the sideboard and poured himself a full glass of brandy. The sweet burn of the liquor did nothing to dull the ache that had settled somewhere underneath his breastbone.

She'd betrayed him, he told himself. She was the same calculating woman who'd bargained away his life for a few coins. He couldn't forget that. He'd waited 3,000 years for his revenge. He would make her love him and then take her life. Like for like. He just couldn't lose what was left of his soul in the process. Then again, he thought, maybe Toria was right; maybe there was nothing left to lose.

CHAPTER 20

Memnon hated the lights of the city. Even more, he hated its infernal noises. After 2,000 years encased in rock, the constant cacophony was unbearable, forcing him to intersperse his above-ground activities with periods of solitude. It had taken some time, but he'd finally found a place both dark and quiet enough to meet his needs.

Taking the grimy steps down into the subway station two at a time, he hopped the turnstile and meandered down to the end of the platform. The station's only other occupant was a woman of indeterminate age asleep on a bench under an equally indeterminate number of coats. Her eyes didn't open as Memnon passed, so he walked straight toward the tracks and stepped off the edge.

No train approached, so he walked down the middle of the track bed deep into the tunnel. Dirt and garbage crunched beneath his feet. About 60 feet in from the station, the tunnel passed underneath a grate that was open to the street, and bars of eerie blue light shone down onto the tracks. Memnon kept walking, watching the blue light pass over his white skin and then fade into the distance behind him. Finally, he came to a point where only blackness greeted him, and he allowed his muscles to relax.

A few more feet brought him to an unused tunnel that branched off from the main line. Down that tunnel was a small maintenance closet, with just enough room for him to squeeze in. Crumpling his large, lean frame into the small space took a few moments, but he didn't mind. The dark confines of his new home comforted him, reminding him of Herculaneum, of all the years he'd lain buried there, frozen in ash and rock.

He hadn't planned on that, of course. He'd expected to see something extraordinary, or he'd expected to die.

He had first gone to Pompeii, but corruption and debauchery had already drained all the humanity from its inhabitants. He couldn't stand to be around them, so he'd journeyed farther north to the smaller village of Herculaneum.

It was a fateful choice. The eruption happened in daylight, but the cloud that spewed forth out of the mountain had blocked out the sun. He might have escaped from Pompeii, as it was only covered over by about ten feet of debris, but Herculaneum was on the other side of Vesuvius, where the eruption buried the town under 75 feet of scalding ash. It had felt like the entire inside of the mountain had come down on his head.

Then came the silence. For so long, nothing moved or spoke, just the occasional vibration of the offended earth. It was so quiet it took some time for him to realize he wasn't dead. It took even longer for him to realize he wasn't going to die.

At first the hunger tormented him, reducing him to the point where he begged the gods to take his life—but they refused. Lack of blood brought insane ravings and threatened his mind, but his body did not die.

Finally, to take his mind off the hunger, he reached out with it into the earth, trying to see. He saw only death initially, the corpses of all those who had perished. Slowly, life returned, beginning with the minutest creatures—the grubs, the worms. Finally, creatures returned that he could sense with his other faculties—a nesting mouse, a scavenging bird; all these were company to him.

For years, they were his only company. The human race abandoned Pompeii and Herculaneum. He could actually feel the collective attention of the world as it faded. When he realized this, he tried to seek it out. What was the world looking at now that it had forgotten the tragedy into which he had been baked like a berry in a pie?

Eventually, he could see what the world saw. Or at least part of it. He could see other vampires. There was only Ash and the one other in the beginning. The other one he didn't know and could not explain. Ash, on the other hand, was familiar. Ash being alone, being a soldier, being miserable. Same old Ash.

He saw him make first one, then another vampire, and that horrid woman, Toria. Then came still others. From his hole in the rock Memnon watched their entire vampire family bloom like nightshade across the globe.

And for what purpose? To hide in darkness? To assuage the loneliness of creatures who should never have existed in the first place?

What a waste, Memnon thought as he closed the flimsy metal door of his new resting place. No matter, things would soon be made right. This new age demanded a new leader, one who would do more than hide in the dark pretending to be human.

He smiled, delighted to finally be a soldier again.

CHAPTER 21

A riana woke from a troubled sleep as the sun's first rays lit the room. For a moment, she didn't know where she was. Then she remembered Ash's magnificent home and the pained look on his face last night when he brought their evening to an early end. That look had haunted her dreams.

Nevertheless, she planted her feet in the soft carpet and vowed to put Ash out of her mind. She was here to work, and since work was the only thing she had left, she couldn't afford to screw it up.

An hour later she opened the door to the war room to make good on her vow. Three laptops were set up on the large white table that occupied the center of the room. She walked around the table, following the tiny aisle that had been left clear between the center table and the stacks of boxes that took up most of the far wall.

Reaching her destination, she removed one of the laptops and replaced it with her own, then watched the screen flare predictably to life. With that small success under her belt, Ariana got to her feet and looked around the room to try to figure out where to start. At least a dozen document boxes sat on the floor along the wall to her right. It looked like as good a place as any.

She pulled the first box out from the wall and took off the lid. A single sheet of white paper indicated that the box contained the offering memoranda and subscription agreements of some of the funds in which Ash's money was currently invested.

She pulled the lid off the second box. It contained proxy statements and annual reports for various public companies. The third box held similar documents for private companies of which Ash owned all or a portion of the equity.

She looked at the front of each of those boxes. The fund box was labeled one of twelve. The public company box was one of six. The private company box was one of fourteen.

Ariana let out a breath she didn't realize she'd been holding. She hoped Justin had already done a summary of all these. If not, this was going to take forever.

She walked down and pulled the lids off the other three boxes—real estate, bonds, and "other," respectively. The "other" box was only one of four, so Ariana decided to start there.

Halfway through a catalogue of art, antiques, boats, and cars, Ariana heard the door open. She looked up over her computer screen to see Nancy gingerly poking her head into the room.

"Morning, Nancy," Ariana said with a smile.

"Good morning, Miss Chambers. What can I bring you for your breakfast?"

Ariana thought a moment. She was hungry. "Do you have eggs?" she asked. "I could go for some scrambled eggs and a glass of juice if it's not too much trouble."

"Not at all," Nancy replied. "I'll be back shortly."

Ariana wondered at the new formality as Nancy disappeared from the doorway. She took her glasses off and got up to stretch.

The sun had fully risen and Ariana went to look out the window. The war room faced the back of the house and looked down on an elaborate garden. Manicured hedges topped by budding flowers created a cloverleaf shape around a fountain at its center. Gargoyles spit arcs of water out to the four winds. Classical urns filled with more flowers guarded the entryways to various paths that led off in different directions from the center cloverleaf design.

In moments Nancy was back bearing a tray laden with food. Ariana ran to hold the door for her.

"Oh, thank you, dear." Nancy carried the tray around to where Ariana's computer was set up. She removed the cloth napkin that had covered half the tray, and Ariana looked down at a veritable feast of eggs, ham, cereal, yogurt, juice, milk, and coffee. "Wow. Nancy, you didn't need to go to all this trouble," she said. "I don't even usually eat breakfast."

Nancy smoothed her gray dress and cast a baleful eye at Ariana. "Well, a few good breakfasts won't do you any harm, especially if you're going to be getting up with the chickens."

Ariana laughed. "You needn't worry about that. I'm not usually a morning person either. Once I get over the jet lag, you won't see me until long after the sun is up."

"You and the master will get along well then," Nancy said pertly.

Master? Ariana repeated silently, just managing to hold her tongue. "Is he a night owl, too?"

"Quite, I'm afraid," Nancy said. "He gets up late and works in his study for several hours before we are even allowed to check on him. You probably won't see him until this afternoon when Mr. Justin gets here. He's due in at 4:00, I believe."

"Oh." Ariana was disappointed.

"If you'll excuse me, Miss Chambers." Nancy gave a little bow and moved toward the door.

Ariana frowned. "Nancy," she called out.

The older woman looked back at her.

"Please call me Ariana. Even though I'm working here and not just a house guest, I'd much prefer it if we were informal."

Nancy smiled. "We're British, Miss Ariana. We can only be so informal, but I will try." Nancy took two more steps and then turned back once more. "I'm sorry if I was a little terse earlier. I didn't realize yesterday who you were, and I was worried I had been too casual in my attitude toward you."

Ariana stared blankly at the woman. "Who am I?"

Nancy laughed. "Not what I expected when Ben told me you were a multi-millionaire, a successful businesswoman, and that you've come here to take over managing the master's fortune."

Now it was Ariana's turn to laugh. "It sounds infinitely better when you say it like that. In reality it's a lot of number crunching and drinking too much coffee, getting too little sleep and having to increase my eyeglass prescription twice a year."

Nancy harrumphed and headed for the door. "All the more reason to eat a hearty breakfast," she called out over her shoulder. "Or," her voice dropped to a conspiratorial whisper, "to snag a rich husband."

Ariana couldn't hide her surprise. Was Nancy matchmaking? She decided to nip this in the bud and smiled gently at the older woman. "As you mentioned, Nancy, I don't really need a rich husband."

Nancy's smile never faltered. "Well then, I guess that leaves you free to appreciate the master's other... qualities." Her gray brows wiggled naughtily on the last word. "Just ring the kitchen when you're done with the tray, dear." She exited through the swinging door, before a puzzled and slightly shocked Ariana could finish setting her straight.

Chapter 22

Around 1:00, Ariana decided she needed a break, so she picked up the empty breakfast tray and set out to find the kitchen. A few minutes stroll in what she thought was the right direction and a turn down a short stair brought her to her destination. She swung open a well-varnished wooden door and poked her head inside.

"Hello?" she called.

Nancy and Ben both hopped off the stools on which they'd been sitting and stood as if they were in the infantry.

"Miss Chambers," Nancy said with an air of shock, "you should have rung for one of us." She scurried to take the tray from Ariana's hand.

"Oh, it's all right, Nancy. I needed the exercise. In fact, I thought I'd take a walk in the garden out back, but I wanted to ask if there was good route for an hour's walk or if there was anything to be aware of out there."

Ben's wizened forehead creased as he thought for a moment. "If you leave the house from the center doorway and go down the stairs into the garden, take the path on the left, at nine o'clock, and follow it until you come to a fork. At the first fork, go left. You'll come to two more forks. Go right at both of those, and you'll be back at the center fountain in about an hour."

"Left, right, right," Ariana repeated. "Got it. Thanks, Ben."

Ariana retraced her steps back through the manor's empty halls to the main entryway and out the back door. Much-welcomed sunlight warmed her face, and Ariana stood for a moment to let it sink in. She felt a strange sense of relief, but put it down as a natural reaction to the first rays of spring sunshine. No house, no matter how sumptuous, could compete with that.

Passing between two urns filled with lavender flowers, Ariana started down the left-most path. The shaped hedge rose gradually as she meandered, starting out about hip high at the path's entrance and growing so that it towered over her head.

Occasionally there was a break in the hedge to showcase some kind of flowering plant or bush. Ariana had no idea what any of them were. She'd never had much of a green thumb. She was really only good at one thing—making money. She smiled to herself. You might say she had a green thumb after all.

After about ten minutes, Ariana came to a junction. In the center was another fountain, smaller than the one up by the house, but Ariana liked it better. In this one, sculpted mer-children played with dolphins that sporadically shot streams of water out of their blow holes. The children were extraordinarily lifelike, except for their tails, with each posed as if he had just managed to avoid getting squirted by one of the playful fish.

Paths led off from this juncture in three directions. Not exactly a fork, she thought, but she took the path to her left as Ben had instructed. She wondered for an instant how long it would take someone to find her if she took a wrong turn and got lost. She had no idea how big this garden-cum-maze really was.

Banishing that thought, she quickened her pace and soon the path opened into what seemed like a room. The hedge on her left fell away in a large semicircle while the hedge on her right continued straight ahead. In the green, open space between them was a reflecting pool. Two benches of white marble veined with gray sat along its edge.

A clinging vine covered much of the hedge in the "room" that was formed around the pool, and Ariana went to get a closer look. The vines had large, heart-shaped leaves and were covered in closed blossoms. They must not yet be in season. Ariana reached out her hand.

"You shouldn't touch those."

Ariana drew back as if she'd been burned and turned around to see who had spoken.

A pale young boy with brown hair stood about three feet behind her, wearing a sheepish look on his face.

He smiled shyly at her. "I'm sorry. I didn't mean to scare you. It's just that moonflowers are temperamental, and they are Mr. Samson's favorites."

"Moonflowers?" Ariana queried, still waiting for her stomach to dislodge from her throat.

The boy moved to stand beside her; he couldn't be a day over 15. *What was he doing out here?*

"That's right. They're closed during the day, but open every night when the light of the moon hits them." He swung his hand in a wide arc. "This is the moon garden. Almost all the flowers in this space are night blooming."

Rapidly losing his shyness, the boy stuck out his hand. "I'm Eric. My father's company does the landscaping for the manor and I help out. I plan to be a botanist. Mr. Samson says I can go to any college I want if I can keep the moon garden blooming year round."

Ariana shook her head slightly as she shook the boy's hand. "That's great, Eric. And it's nice to meet you. I'm Ariana. I also work for Mr. Samson. I'm staying at the manor for a while."

"You're American?"

"That's right. I'm from New York." Ariana still couldn't get used to saying that. She'd been in New York for years, but she didn't feel like a New Yorker. She was and would always be a Southerner at heart.

She looked back at the flower-laden vines. "Do they bloom every night? I think I'd like to come down and see that."

"Oh yes. The moon will come over the hedge tonight just after 11:00. All the flowers will open within about two minutes, though, so you have to be on time."

Ariana smiled. "Thanks for the tip." She took a step back toward the path. "I guess I'll continue my walk. I didn't realize this was a maze when I started out. If I go right at the next two junctures, that will bring me back to the manor?"

The boy nodded. "That's right. And remember, if all else fails, you can always find your way out of a maze by putting your hand on one wall and keeping it there as you walk. It won't be the shortest way out, but it will always get you to the exit eventually."

Ariana couldn't hide her surprise, but it made sense. The entrance of the maze did have to connect to the exit somehow. If you followed one wall continuously you would eventually come to the other end. "Hmm. I hope I never need it, but that's pretty cool. Thanks, Eric."

The boy smiled and waved. "You're welcome."

Ariana enjoyed the rest of her walk immensely. Eric's friendly demeanor had somehow made the whole maze less threatening and much more of an adventure. Each turn revealed some new spectacle—a fountain, an unexpected flower or sculpture. It really was an interesting walk.

She hadn't expected that. The maze had seemed so man-made, and Ariana preferred nature wild. That's why she never went to Central Park. It always felt like a giant soccer field to her. Not real. This maze was designed to revel in being not real—to the point of being surreal. It was a unique approach.

Back at the house, Ariana put aside the box of "other" that she'd gone through in the morning and pulled the box of fund documents closer to her chair. No more putting off the inevitable. She began a list of the funds, their liquidity dates, and early withdrawal penalties. Presumably Justin would be able to tell her the amounts Ash had invested in each fund and at what time.

Her list grew as she made her way through the box. When she began to squint, she noticed the fading light outside and checked her watch; it was 4:30. She was momentarily proud of herself for keeping her mind off Ash for virtually the whole day. Just then Nancy again poked her head in and announced that Mr. Justin had arrived, and she would be serving tea for the three of them in the room across the hall in 15 minutes.

Ariana moved to tidy up the stacks of paper that now cluttered the table. After getting some of them back in order, she hefted the first box she'd looked through back into its place along the wall. Taking a step back, she ran into something.

She couldn't stifle a little scream as she whirled around. "Jesus!" she exclaimed, when she realized the something was Ash. "Is everybody around here trying to give me a heart attack?"

"I'm sorry to startle you," Ash said, grinning and not looking at all sorry. "I came to see how you were doing and to let you know Justin has arrived. I believe Nancy is setting out some refreshments."

Ariana studied him as she tried to catch her breath. He was stunning in dark jeans and a white cotton shirt. His dark hair and eyes contrasted against the fine white fabric. His eyes, as always, seemed to bore holes into her.

She turned away, stepping over a box to get back to her computer. "I know. I'm just tidying up here." She looked up at him again. "I'll be there in a minute."

Ash stood for a moment, and Ariana got the distinct impression he wasn't used to being dismissed. But he took the hint without comment and went across the hall, leaving Ariana with a moment in which to reign in her unkempt workspace and even more unruly thoughts.

CHAPTER 23

Ariana slid back the door to the sitting room and looked at the two men. Ash stood in front of an unlit stone fireplace with his back to the door. He didn't turn when she entered, and Ariana wondered at the tension visibly tightening his broad shoulders.

In a chair facing her sat a tall, lean man with dark hair that was graying noticeably at the temples. He rose and came toward her, the creases in his gray suit springing back into perfect position.

"You must be Ariana," he said with a broad smile that revealed impeccably perfect teeth. He surprised her by kissing her hand instead of shaking it.

"I can do that," he said impishly as he raised his head. "I'm English."

Ariana laughed. "And you must be Justin?"

His gray eyes watched her closely, and his smile faltered for a brief moment. It was quickly restored, and Ariana dismissed the twinge of foreboding it created in her gut.

"That's right," he said. "Justin Markham at your service." He gave a small bow and released her hand. "I hear we'll be spending no small amount of time together over the next couple of weeks. I'm delighted you seem a pleasant enough person and not some black-clad, pencil-thin, stiletto-wearing urbanite."

Ariana looked down at her jeans and sweater set and marveled that her favorite outfit had finally come in handy. Justin handed her a cup of tea and motioned for her to sit in the chair next to his.

Ariana sank down into the soft leather and took sip of tea. Ash still stood at the fireplace, one elbow resting on the mantle, but he had turned to face the two of them.

"So, Ariana, tell me a little about yourself," Justin said. "I guess you know I was at Goldman Sachs in London for more years than I care to count before I came to work for Ash. What's your story?"

Ariana turned to Justin. His warm gray eyes invited her to talk, but she was ever-conscious of Ash's eyes on her as well. "There's not much to tell, really," she said. "I grew up on a farm, went to college, went to law school, went to business school, and then worked in private equity and at a hedge fund before joining Roger Plumber at Tailwind."

Justin's keen gray eyes studied her again. "You are too modest, Ariana. You were at the top of your class at prestigious schools, a star performer at every place you ever worked, and you've been almost as big a part of Tailwind's success as has Roger."

Ariana put her teacup down in its delicate saucer. "All of which makes me decidedly uninteresting at parties, I'm afraid."

Again, Justin's eyes lingered on her face, seeing too much. He opened his mouth as if to say more, but was interrupted by Ash's sudden burst of laughter.

Ariana wondered what he found so amusing. She was about to ask him, but Justin continued on as if nothing had happened. "Perhaps," he said, "but I'm sure it makes you very interesting at work, and, speaking of work, we should probably get started." Justin rose from his chair and made his way over to the cart of refreshments Nancy had presumably wheeled in earlier and started stacking finger food on a delicate china plate. "I'll just bring a few of these sandwiches with us so we don't go hungry," he said, smiling in her direction.

Ariana rose to follow Justin as he headed for the door, but Ash didn't move. "Aren't you coming?" she asked him.

He didn't even turn to look at her. "No, you two go ahead. You don't need me, and if you do, just ring Nancy to send for me. I'll be in my study."

The weight of her disappointment took Ariana by surprise. Why did he affect her so? She looked at him, still standing against the mantle like some ancient warrior who'd been dropped into the wrong century. *Oh, brother,* she thought, almost embarrassed at the direction of her thoughts. When she turned to the door, it was to find Justin again watching her a little too closely.

"Shall we?" she said brightly, indicating the door. Justin turned and preceded her into the hallway.

Thankfully, the awkwardness passed once they were elbow deep in documents. Justin was frightfully bright and organized, and his rakish but good-natured sense of humor made the time pass quickly.

When Nancy rang for dinner, Ariana was caught off guard. She looked down at her jeans, then up at Justin, who had continued to work. "I need to run and change," she said. "Can you finish up here without me?"

"Of course. Run along," he replied, gesturing toward the door with a mock stern look. "You don't want to keep the fearsome Nancy waiting."

Ariana closed her laptop. "Thanks," she said as she bolted out the door. She didn't want to keep Nancy waiting, but she also didn't want to show up at dinner in jeans when Justin was in a suit. And she wanted to look nice for Ash.

But not too nice, she cautioned herself as she perused her closet. Deciding simple was best, she traded her jeans for a little black skirt and some black strappy sandals. Matched with her off-white sweater set, it was elegant, without being too dressy or too sexy. Perfect.

Ash was standing in the main foyer talking to Ben when Ariana came down the stairs. He, too, had changed and was now wearing an impeccable dark suit with a soft blue shirt and tie. Silver cuff links adorned his sleeves. *Master, indeed,* Ariana thought. If she didn't stop finding things to admire about this man, she was in danger of becoming as besotted as Nancy.

Ash turned as she approached, rewarding her with a slight smile.

"Good," Ariana said lightly, trying not to notice how his eyes raked her from head to toe. "If you're out here it means I'm not late for dinner."

Ash's smile widened. "You look stunning," he said, his voice barely above a whisper.

Ben disappeared down the hallway in the other direction, and Ash steered Ariana toward the main dining room with her arm through his.

Trying to ignore the feel of his body next to hers as they walked, Ariana searched for a neutral topic of conversation. "Justin says he's worked for you for twelve years," she said, rather proud of herself for sounding so casual. "You must have a lot of faith in him."

"I do." Ash nodded.

"So, I'm still curious as to why you're throwing him over for me and Roger."

Ash turned to look at her. "You know, you won't have many clients if you keep advising them all against using your services. What would Roger say if he could hear you?"

He was right about that, but Ariana couldn't shake the feeling that she didn't have the whole truth. Did it matter? Roger would say definitely not.

Ash escorted her into the dining room, and Ariana reluctantly slid her hand from his arm and took a seat opposite Justin. Ash sat at the head of the table, and an improbable feast flowed forth from the kitchen, served on the most beautiful, delicate china Ariana had ever seen.

"I see Bill is back in residence," Justin commented two dips into his soup.

"Yes, I had him come up for the weekend to keep you two sustained while you sort out where all my money is."

Justin harrumphed. "I know quite well where it all is. I've just never been able to persuade you to do anything sensible with about half of it until now."

Ariana tucked that little tidbit away.

"Who is Bill?" she asked. "Whoever he is, he's amazing."

"Bill O'Neill is an up-and-coming London chef. I helped him start his first restaurant, and he occasionally does me the honor of a private showing."

Soup bowls were whisked away by two young maids and replaced by a succulent Cornish game hen with spring root vegetables.

"Ariana, I have to admit I'm intrigued by how a farm girl gets to be a New York City power broker." Justin looked at her with a warm gaze and one eyebrow slightly raised.

"I don't know if power broker is the right term," Ariana demurred. She looked again at Justin and knew he wouldn't be satisfied with a polite brush off. Ash was rather pointedly studying his plate, though he didn't appear to be eating.

Ariana took a deep breath and shook her head. "I don't know the answer myself. I was just never satisfied. I always felt like there was more to learn, more to do. And somehow in the process of trying everything, I found something I excelled at."

Justin smiled and cut an odd glance at Ash, who was now scowling. Ariana began to wonder why, but his deep frown soon lifted and the rest of the meal passed in pleasant conversation, though Ariana felt like an outsider for much of it.

Ash and Justin had worked together for a long time and were obviously good friends. She envied Justin that. Ash seemed at ease when they talked.

With her, he wasn't at ease.

Because I want you. The Voice was suddenly back in her head, and Ariana felt a blush spread to her cheeks. She looked at Ash. He and Justin were discussing a particular biotech company that Justin thought Ash should sell his interest in. Shit. She'd rather it turn out that he was a telepathic pervert than that she was a crazy pervert.

A slight smile crossed Ash's face. Ariana looked down before he could catch her studying him.

"Oh," she exclaimed, looking at her watch. "It's almost 11:00."

Ash looked at her, still wearing that mysterious little smile. "Past your bedtime?"

"No. I wanted to go see the moon garden."

Ash's gaze stayed locked with hers. "I'll take you." He slid his chair back.

"I didn't know you had a moon garden here," Justin said. "In fact, I don't even think I knew there was such a thing. I'll come along if you don't mind. I'd quite like to see it."

Ash gave Justin a pointed look, which Justin just as pointedly ignored.

This wasn't good at all, Ariana thought.

"You know, on second thought," Ariana said, "I'm suddenly feeling tired. I must still be a little jet lagged. If you two don't mind, I'm going to turn in." She rose to go.

Ash and Justin both stood. "Not at all," Ash said. "Pleasant dreams."

"Good night, Ariana. I'll see you in the morning."

"Good night." Ariana pushed her chair back under the table and for the second night in a row beat a hasty retreat to her room.

⚜

"Exactly what are you up to?" Ash said to Justin when he was sure Ariana was out of earshot.

"I'm just trying to get to know her," Justin replied. "She's going to be in charge of your money for some period of time, so I need to be sure she knows what she's doing."

Ash shot him a skeptical glare.

"Okay, fine," Justin admitted. "If you are really plotting some terrible end to this little play you've set in motion, I want to find out if she's as bad as you say. So far, I have to tell you, I don't see it."

Ash frowned. "Maybe not, but it's there. It's her and it's there. When she was Delilah, I didn't see it until it was too late, and I won't make that mistake again." He pushed his chair farther back from the table and stared down at his friend. "It's noble of you to try to protect her, but don't get in my way on this, Justin."

Justin slid his own chair back and went over to the sideboard to pour himself a drink. "Fine," he said when he turned back to Ash, "but you should try to keep a little more of an open mind before you do something that may only add to your long list of regrets."

Ash gave a low growl and stalked from the room.

CHAPTER 24

Ariana smiled and rolled toward him, never opening her eyes, pressing her naked body against the length of his.

"Ariana," he whispered.

Ash groaned and ran his hand along the smooth curve from her waist to her thigh. His thumb rubbed the hollow just inside her hip bone, finding it as soft as he remembered.

Ariana opened her eyes. There was a moment of surprise and confusion until Ash looked deeply into them and whispered to her mind, *It's only a dream.*

"I know," she replied, smiling sleepily at him before pulling his head toward hers.

Their lips met, and Ash tightened his grip on her hip. He kissed her deeply. He wanted her to dream about this even after he was gone and to think about it all day tomorrow. Justin be damned.

Her body cleaved to his like a magnet, seeming to remember its place nestled into the hollows of his larger frame. Her mouth welcomed the forceful invasion of his tongue.

Ash wanted to punish her. He wanted to stay and lose himself in her.

He didn't know what he wanted.

He dragged his mouth away from her full lips and moved it slowly down to her left breast where he took her nipple in his mouth and suckled hard. Ariana threw her head back and gave a breathless moan.

It's her, all right. His Delilah. He'd made love to her in his dreams a thousand times. He knew everything about her. He knew where she liked to be kissed, how soft or hard she liked everything he did to her. It gave him an advantage, but he told himself it was only fair. His 3,000 years of suffering should count for something.

The hand on her hip slid inward, over her pubic bone to the warm, moist folds between her legs. She was so wet for him, the knowledge almost did him in. He had enough power to make her think this was a dream, but he couldn't create desire from nothing. She wanted him, and it was heady knowledge.

Ash hesitated, resting his head between her breasts. Ariana reached for him and pulled him back to her.

"Don't stop," she whispered.

Ash claimed her mouth once more, pillaging it with his tongue as his hand pillaged her warm center. Her hips writhed against him in a rhythm he still remembered. When she broke off their kiss and threw her head back, Ash wanted so badly to be inside her. He wanted to feel her body close around his in that one passionate embrace that was like no other. But this wasn't how it was supposed to be.

Not giving himself time to think, he slid farther down her naked form and turned his face first one way and then the other against the soft insides of both her thighs, feeling her flesh quiver against his cheek. When his tongue finally descended on her needy flesh, she gave a shuddering moan that reverberated through both their bodies.

Joined to her once more, Ash forced himself to go slow, to let his tongue be warm and heavy. Then he pressed and sucked at her in ways her writhing hips told him her body remembered. When her breath started to come faster, Ash raised his head and looked at her.

She was magnificent in desire, her body a curved temple where he had wanted to worship until his last breath left him. Little had he known that she had been conspiring to bring him to that very end, all those years ago!

He looked down at his erection straining against the front of his jeans and refused to speculate on how long it had been since that had happened. Instead, he turned his attention to the silky feel of her skin as he slid his hand slowly along the outside of her thigh.

He wanted nothing more than to feel that skin pressed against his own flesh, urging him on, but the sheer force of his desire gave him pause. *No*, he thought, that wasn't quite right. It scared the hell out of him.

He took a deep breath he didn't really need and then soothed her back to sleep. Rolling to the edge of the bed, he watched as her breathing slowed.

What was he doing? He had loved Delilah so much. When she betrayed him, he'd thought none of it was real, that she'd been out to get him all along.

Now, here she was again, with no memory, hardly even knowing him, and she responded to his touch with the same fever as before. And he to her, even though it should be impossible. For heaven's sake, she'd only been here two days, and already things weren't going according to plan.

Ash levered himself off her bed and forced his traitorous eyes to focus on the door. He got to the other sided of it without turning back and then made his way to his room at the other end of the house. Even at that distance, however, his mind refused to give him any peace. He grabbed two bags of blood from a small refrigerator he kept in the corner. He had a microwave, but skipped it, draining them both cold.

He had to put Ariana out of his mind. He had a plan for her. He just needed to stick to it. He meant what he'd told Justin. He'd been fooled by her before, and she still threatened to get the better of him, but this time he was forewarned.

Chapter 25

James strained to hear Keller's response, but missed it. He couldn't believe he was actually listening at a keyhole. The door to his own room stood open, ready for him to make a quick escape. He'd been spending most of his free time this week at Luc's, honoring his bargain, but his investigation had brought him back to Council House. He'd been about to knock on Keller's door when he heard the two voices from within.

"Is it ready?" Keller asked.

"It is," an unfamiliar voice answered. "All that remains is to deliver it."

"How soon?"

There was a brief pause. "Soon. We cannot afford to delay. Already the half-human one pushes the bounds. The blood of Lilith is seeping into the blood of Adam, corrupting it from within. It's not enough that she has created us. She seeks a portal back into our world."

"All strains of Lilith need to be wiped out, Keller. You know this. She is an abomination. We are only ever one human-vampire pairing away from creating a creature strong enough for Lilith to enter."

"I will be pardoned?" Keller asked.

"You will be celebrated, Keller. Maybe not at first, but, with time, even they will see that you did what was best."

"The order will restore my name?"

"They will," Keller's guest responded. "You will be restored and added to the annals at Clonfert. As if you never left."

The sudden shifting of furniture sent James scuttling back into his room. He closed the door gently, just as Keller's door opened.

One pair of footsteps faded down the hall toward the main staircase. James sagged onto his small bed in relief. He hadn't been discovered, and now he really had something to tell Toria.

A knock at his door startled him. *Stay calm*, he told himself as he pulled the door open. *Keller can't suspect.*

But it wasn't Keller. "You're right," the other man said, baring his fangs and forcing his way into the room.

Oh crap, James thought, immediately realizing he had no defenses. Power dripped off this one, whomever he was, much as it did Ash.

Wait, James thought, grasping at straws. Maybe he couldn't overpower him, but that didn't mean he was defenseless. He opened his mouth and screamed.

The intruder started, and it took him a second to recover; but when he did, he belted James a blow across the face that threw him across the room.

⚜

"Memnon, what are you doing?" Keller demanded, coming out of the room next door.

"Just taking care of a loose end," Memnon replied. "Nothing for you to worry about."

"No," Keller insisted. "Don't hurt him."

Memnon hesitated. "We can't let anything get in the way, Keller," he explained. "Our plan—God's plan—is almost ripe, but your nosy little friend here overheard everything. We can't let him tip off the others."

Keller frowned. "He won't say anything. Why don't we just tell him the truth?"

"We can't take any chances," Memnon argued.

"Alright," Keller acquiesced, "but we're so close. Can't you hold him wherever you've been keeping the others? Then, when everything is ready, he can be included."

Memnon frowned, but was forced to agree. He couldn't risk alienating Keller. He needed his help.

He swung the unconscious James over his shoulder and headed for the window at the end of the hall.

CHAPTER 26

Ariana groaned and turned away from a single beam of sunlight forcing its way between the heavy drapes. She blinked once, then twice, remembering the dreams in which she had succumbed to the skillful caresses of her newest client.

Great, she thought. *Just great. Today wouldn't be at all strained.*

Then she smiled. She didn't know what the real Ash would be like, but dream Ash was... dreamy.

Deciding she couldn't stay in bed all day fantasizing about Ash, or Samson, or anyone else her fevered brain might decide to cast him as, Ariana put two feet on the floor and told them to carry her to the shower.

She wasted no time, but Justin was already hard at work when Ariana stepped into the war room less than an hour later. He greeted her with a warm smile. "You're looking refreshed. I trust you had a good sleep?"

Ariana smiled, remaining noncommittal as she walked around the table to peer over his shoulder. "What are you up to so early?"

"I was feeling a wee bit guilty that I didn't have everything netted out for you," he answered. "I'm just putting the finishing touches on the overview. I'll have a more detailed summary by this afternoon."

"Great. I could stand to devote some time to my other projects anyway," Ariana said, crawling under the table once more to unplug her laptop. "My other files are in my room, so I'm going to work up there for a while. I'll be back by tea time."

Justin laughed. "It does amaze how quickly you Americans take to tea time."

"It's a great custom," Ariana said. "I wish we had it. New York is always so rushed; I don't think I could manage that much time out of the work day on a regular basis."

Another thought struck her as she turned to go. "Will Ash be joining us today?" she asked.

Justin shook his head. "He usually observes something between London and New York time when he's here because so much of his business is transacted out of New York. He gets up in the afternoon and works in his study. He might come down for tea. Seldom before then."

Ariana smiled and left the room, unsure if she was relieved or disappointed.

The first thing she did upon returning to her room and getting her laptop plugged back in was to send Roger a detailed report. He'd sent her some information on prospective investments, and more would be coming tomorrow by courier, which was good because, from what she'd seen so far, there were considerable sums that could be moved right away. The rest would have to be staged to minimize penalties and take advantage of the best investments Ash was already in, but there was lots of room for improvement. Roger would be happy.

Tea time rolled around before Ariana had even finished responding to yesterday's e-mails and going through the materials Roger had sent. She made her way downstairs, assuming tea would be served in the same place as yesterday. She met Nancy halfway there.

"Hi there, dear," Nancy greeted her. "I was just coming to tell you that tea is being served on the back terrace today. It's so warm out, the master thought it would be a nice treat."

"Thanks, Nancy." She still couldn't get over Nancy calling him "master."

Nancy continued past Ariana down the hall, and Ariana headed for the terrace.

Outside, it was a warm evening. The sun hung low, turning the clouds to cotton candy from one side of the horizon to the other. Ash faced westward, seeming to admire the pastel tableau, and Ariana stood for a moment admiring him.

He was dressed informally in dark slacks and a gray sweater. The muscles of his shoulders and back stretched the soft, light wool as he lifted and replaced his teacup.

Ariana longed to walk up behind him and let her hands roam over that rugged terrain. She wanted to do to him what he had done to her in her dream. She wanted to know if his hair was as soft as it looked.

Justin appeared before her thoughts could get too far away from her. "Go on, then. He won't bite," he said.

"What?" Ariana exclaimed. "Oh," she said, realizing he was telling her to help herself to the tea cart.

Ash turned, again wearing that enigmatic little smile. "Ariana, how are you?" he asked. "Are you finding everything you need here?"

"Oh yes," she said. "I'm glad I didn't insist on staying in the city. I would have regretted not coming here." *In more ways than one*, she added silently.

"Me too," Justin added, walking toward Ash and reaching for the tray. "Unparalleled luxury and all the cookies you can eat."

Ash laughed, and Ariana's insides reverberated with the sound. She turned to look at him; he stopped laughing when he met her gaze.

"I trust your room is satisfactory?" he asked. "Have you been able to get any sleep?"

His eyes bored into her, and Ariana shook off the impression that he knew just exactly how she'd been sleeping. "The room is lovely, thank you. And I've been surprised at how well I've been sleeping here. Maybe it's all the fresh air."

"The country doesn't agree with some people," he said. "Gives them nightmares."

Ariana's smile didn't quite reach her eyes. "I appear to have left all my nightmares in New York," she said. "Nothing but pleasant dreams to report so far."

A wicked grin lit Ash's face, turning up the handsome meter yet another notch. "Good," he said, seeming inordinately pleased with himself.

"That's right. We don't want you tuckered out when you're moving all Ash's money around," Justin chimed in. "Can't have you forgetting a zero someplace."

"On that note, Justin," Ariana said, "would you be so kind as to pour me a cup of tea? I have been running at a little bit of a caffeine deficit since I got here."

Justin moved immediately to fulfill her request, accompanied by the bell-like music of cup touching saucer. "My lady," Justin said, handing her the tea with a ginger cookie on the side.

Justin piled a stack of cookies onto a plate and turned to go back inside. "I'm almost done with the summary I promised you. Ariana. Can you pop in when you're done so we can go through it?"

Ariana nodded. "Will do."

She rested her cup and saucer on the glass top of a small table that occupied one corner of the terrace, and Ash moved to join her. Alone with him, she couldn't resist indulging her curiosity.

"Dropping a zero would hardly put a dent in what I've been reviewing, Ash. Would you mind if I asked how you amassed such a fortune?"

Ash frowned, and Ariana wondered if she'd overstepped.

"Much of it has been in the family for generations," he explained, still frowning. "The parts I've built in this life have come from well placed investments in small companies and well timed takeovers of big ones. Not very interesting really."

Ariana was surprised. "Oh, I don't think that's true," she said. "If you're able to see a good idea and help turn it into a reality, I think that's very interesting. It's part of why I do what I do, in fact. To create and build things, to be able to go home at the end of the day and say I made something better."

If she'd expected Ash's expression to lift, she was mistaken. If anything, his look darkened even further.

He searched her face for a long moment. "You should go back inside," he said, taking a deep breath. "I'm sure Justin's eager to show you what he's been up to all day."

Ariana couldn't hide her disappointment. He was so unpredictable, moody even. She knew he was drawn to her, but he pushed her away at every turn.

But it was probably for the best, she decided. She didn't really want to become entangled. Not now. Maybe not ever. Not after the fiasco she'd made of her life with James. Ariana sighed and, wondering if she needed her head examined, left one of the most intriguing men she'd ever met standing alone in his garden.

Back in the war room, she discovered Ash was right. Justin was eager to show her what he'd been working on all day. He'd somehow whipped up a 40-page "summary" of what he'd been doing for Ash for the last few years and where all Ash's assets were.

Tea notwithstanding, Ariana wasn't feeling quite up to the task, so she excused herself and took the stack of paper up to her room where she guiltily dropped it on the floor next to her desk. It was two hours before dinner. She just wanted a nap and a shower.

The shower helped her relax, and she wrapped her long hair in a towel before lying down on the bed. It would dry while she slept.

Chapter 27

When Ariana woke, her room was completely dark. She glanced over at the illuminated clock and realized she'd slept well through dinner, which was okay, since she wasn't hungry. Just wide awake.

Not wanting to work, she pulled on a pair of jeans and a tee shirt and opened the door of her bedroom. She'd seen a library when Ash had given her the tour, and thought it wasn't far. That seemed like the perfect thing for a bout of insomnia.

She peered cautiously out into the hall. At 3:00 in the morning, the hallways of the manor were as black as pitch, except for tiny shafts of blue moonlight that crept from under some of the doors of the east-facing rooms. Ariana felt old fashioned wishing for a candle, but the moonlight provided little illumination and did nothing to alleviate the overall feeling of creepiness. She was reminded of the Haunted Mansion ride at Disney World. If she passed a mirror, she'd probably scream.

After walking for what seemed like far too long, Ariana reached the panel doors she was searching for. The dark wood slid open at her touch and closed just as easily behind her.

Inside, she flipped the light switch and breathed in the scent of old paper, dust, and leather. She loved libraries. *Once a nerd, always a nerd,* she thought with a smile.

The room was large. Shelves lined three of its walls, all filled to the brim with glorious books. A few chairs were scattered about, along with a couch and a desk. There was even one of those rolling ladder contraptions to reach things on the highest shelves.

Where to start? She scanned the shelves from where she stood just inside the door and decided to proceed methodically, beginning on the left and working her way around the room.

The first shelf was devoted entirely to battles and warfare. It looked like there were books on every battle since man first picked up a club.

The next shelf held more general history. Ariana paused to run her hands over some of the spines. *This was more like it,* she thought. Her hand paused over what looked like an original manuscript by Plato. *How on earth?* She would not have guessed Ash was a book collector. *The war books maybe, but these? Wow.*

She resisted the temptation to linger, knowing she might also be tempted to take one down and run her hands over its pages. The desire to touch pages that had been touched by some of the greatest minds in history… She forced herself to keep walking. More of the same graced the wall opposite where she had come in. Ariana marveled at the pages and pages of knowledge, some of it quite ancient, that was assembled in this room.

She passed the two large windows without bothering to look out. She knew nothing out there, even if she could have seen it in daylight, could compare to the wonders in this library.

The shelves in the far corner appeared to be devoted to theology, even some occult books. Oddly, some of these were not dusty, as if someone had handled them quite recently. Ariana walked to the nearest one and pulled it from the shelf.

There was no title on the cover. She carefully opened the black leather-bound volume. There was no title page either. It merely began—"In the beginning, God created them. Male and female, he created them."

Was this an old Bible? she wondered. No, not quite. That wasn't the first verse of the Bible. Ariana had attended enough Sunday school to know that. She read on.

"The male was called Adam, and the female was called Lilith. And they were stewards of the Earth, but Adam came unto Lilith and tried to make her will as his own. Lilith turned from Adam and from God and fled the garden God had made for them and went into darkness. And God was not pleased."

Ariana's eye skipped down a few passages. "Lilith and her children were doomed to walk in darkness, never knowing human comfort. Adam was given a new mate, Eve, but he was destined to know no peace, either in his own house or in the houses of the generations after. And Lilith and Adam sired many lines. And so the curses stand, not to be lifted until the end of days."

Ariana read the passage again. She didn't know what this was, but it definitely wasn't the Bible. There was more, of course. Some of it was familiar. Eve and the apple, the tree of knowledge of good and evil, the new punishment of mortality and nakedness for Adam and Eve. All that was there. So where did this first wife Lilith come from?

Ariana shut the book. Some things were better left undiscovered, and she had an overpowering intuition this was one of them. She returned the book to its place and sat down behind the large, leather-covered desk at the far end of the library from where she'd entered. Its big matching leather chair was comforting, and Ariana found she needed it. That book had given her the willies.

She put her elbows on the desk and looked around wistfully. *What a pity to have a library full of books you don't dare to touch,* she thought.

She slid the chair back and was about to return to her room when something caught her eye in the slightly open desk drawer. It was a manila folder. A white label at the top had her name typed in bold, block letters. Ariana Katherine Chambers.

She had that feeling again—the feeling that she should put the folder back and forget she ever saw it. She opened the folder anyway.

Inside was her resume and what looked like an investigative report. Her entire life was spilled out over a half dozen white pages. Everything was there—where she grew up, her high school GPA, her first job, her wedding date, a criminal background check consisting of some youthful traffic violations, and even an entry on James' disappearance.

Why had Ash felt the need to have someone go to so much trouble to get information on her? Her resume and bio were on the fund's website for heaven's sake. Did he really need to know all this just to decide to invest with them?

She wasn't sure, but she thought she might be angry. Before she could figure it out, something else drew her attention. Removing the folder had uncovered a stack of white stationery paper. The top page had her name written on it.

Over and over and over.

Ariana hesitated a full minute, but then reached in and removed the stack of paper from the drawer. The entire page was more of the same—just her name, written over and over again in a handwriting she knew was Ash's. She'd seen his signature enough times over the past few days to recognize it.

Too bad she hadn't recognized he was a lunatic, she thought. No, instead she had decided she wanted to sleep with him.

Oh, shut up, she told herself. *This is serious.*

Maybe there was some more sensible explanation. She looked at the next page. It too contained her name and also another—Delilah. *What the hell?*

Ariana hurriedly replaced the stack of paper in the drawer. Most importantly, she couldn't let on that she knew he was a psycho.

Wait, how could he be a psycho? He was an established businessman. He bought and sold companies. He interacted with people all the time. He had amassed a fortune. He didn't exactly fit the serial killer profile. *Shit. Maybe I'm the lunatic,* she thought, shaking her head.

"You're really quite the potty mouth these days, Delilah." Ash's deep, alluring voice came out of nowhere, but Ariana wasn't surprised. It was almost as if she'd been expecting him.

CHAPTER 28

Ariana turned quickly. Ash stood at the other door. It was just out of her peripheral vision, and she hadn't seen it open.

He looked stunning, a god in blue jeans, just rolled out of bed. His soft gray button-down, not living up to its name, revealed far too much of his bare chest, and Ariana found herself longing to touch him. She remembered her fevered dream and felt her cheeks flush.

"It's nice to see you, too," he said.

"What?" It finally dawned on Ariana that he kept responding to things she hadn't said out loud. Who did that make the lunatic?

"Neither of us, I'm afraid," Ash said, sliding the wooden door closed and coming to stand in front of where she sat frozen, half-facing his big desk. "I'm just a man on a quest, and you, well, you just aren't fully awake yet, love."

He stopped in front of her and reached across the desk to grab the letter opener. Then he put his hands on the chair arms, trapping her where she sat.

He knelt down to bring his eyes level with hers. "I don't know how to tell you any of this," he said, "so I'm just going to show you."

Ariana's breath caught in her throat as he raised the letter opener; to her surprise, he didn't plunge it into her heart but rather into his own wrist. Not too far. Just about half an inch. He twisted it a little, like you'd twist a juicer to get the last few drops from an orange. Blood flowed down his hand.

"Drink," he ordered.

Ariana's eyes widened.

"Yes, I know how this must seem to you." Ash quickly took two fingers and wiped up the trail of blood forming on his arm. He pressed the bloody fingers to her mouth.

Ariana squeezed her lips shut and slammed her body back as far in the chair as it would go. She didn't know what was happening here, but it was definitely not good.

"That's where you're wrong, love," Ash said. "Everything about this is good. In fact, I haven't felt this good in a few thousand years."

Ariana put both feet on his chest and pushed as hard as she could. He was only holding the chair with one hand, so they both went rolling in opposite directions. Unfortunately, she wasn't getting any nearer to the door.

Ash leaned back against the desk drawer that had stopped his tumble and laughed. It wasn't even an insane laugh, she thought. He seemed genuinely amused.

"I am amused, love," he said. "I have the strength of ten men and yet, again, you managed to get the jump on me."

Ariana resisted the temptation to push the chair back farther into the corner. "Will you please stop doing that!" she said. She was mystified by what was happening and tapped into the temper she rarely showed.

Ash laughed again. "I'm sorry. It takes some getting used to, I know." He stopped laughing but didn't rise from where he sat on the floor. "I wasn't planning to tell you like this, you know."

"What—that you're some kind of whack job?" she asked.

"No," he said, eyes glittering, "that I've been alive for thousands of years, and I've spent most of them looking for you."

Ash slowly rose to his feet. The look in his eyes had turned menacing, and Ariana knew her first taste of real fear. He closed the distance between them without ever taking his eyes from hers. When he got to where she sat cringing in the chair, he planted his feet on either side of hers and grabbed her by the arms, lifting her so they were face to face.

"Ash..."

He cut her off with a bruising kiss. Ariana felt dizzy and wondered how her body could still respond to him.

He lifted his head and smiled at her, revealing the tips of his fangs. Ariana's eyes widened in panic. She struggled in his grip, to no avail.

"Trust me, you want this," he told her.

He bent his head and bit into her flesh in one swift movement. Ariana tried to break free, but she couldn't even begin to budge him. She just hung there, feet dangling above the floor as Ash's teeth burned through her flesh and pain shot down her arm. She had a mental picture of a hunting dog with a bird in its mouth. She'd seen it often in childhood, never imagining that one day she'd be the bird.

As the pain lessened, Ariana knew she was going to die, but she found she didn't care. Warm contentment had replaced the swirling conflict of her passion and fear.

Eventually Ash raised his head and shifted her weight so that he could bring one of his arms to his mouth. He bit into his own flesh, reopening the wound made by the letter opener, and drank. Then he bent to kiss her.

Ariana did not resist. She opened her mouth to him, savoring the taste she knew from their previous kiss and the new, cool flavor his lips now imparted.

Ash broke the kiss and carried her across the room, dropping her roughly on the sofa. Ariana looked at him through lowered lids.

"Prepare yourself," he said dryly. "This may hurt a bit."

For a long moment she just looked at him, still drugged from the feeding and the kiss. Then things began to change.

The room went out of focus, and a blinding pain shot between her left eye and ear. She winced and tried to sit up, but the pain only got worse. She put a hand to her head to try to contain it, but her brain burned, and strange images swam before her closed eyes. Try as she might, she couldn't recognize any of them. It was like watching a masquerade ball. She turned her head back and forth, trying to escape, but the images kept coming.

Soon they began to feel more familiar, like a movie she'd seen a hundred times. A young girl, unseen by all the guests, watching a wedding feast she wasn't allowed to attend. Ariana shook her head. She didn't want to see more. She knew how this one ended.

It had begun in the usual way, of course. Samson had admired her sister and arranged with their father to marry her. Everyone had said they made a beautiful match—Samson's large, dark figure a striking contrast to the pale, quiet beauty that was her sister, Anora. They might have had beautiful children had Anora lived more than a week past her wedding day.

But she hadn't. Instead of a happy, full life, Anora had been burned alive, along with their father. Delilah and her mother had barely escaped with their lives.

She remembered hearing her sister's screams as they ran, her mother's hand pulling her along through the cool night air, as flames and screams clawed at her back.

Even as the years passed, she was trailed by the horrific screams of her sister as she was consumed by fire. Sometimes those screams drowned out everything else. Sometimes they were faint, far away echoes from a half-forgotten life. But they were always there, always reminding her that Samson had taken everything from her and the people she loved. All her life Delilah had hated the man responsible, and she had vowed to make him pay.

CHAPTER 29

Ariana opened her eyes and glared at Ash. "What did you do to me?" she demanded, spitting the words at him. Her eyes widened. "You!" she shouted, getting shakily but quickly to her feet.

Ash was gratified that she recognized him. Vampire blood released past-life memories in humans, but the results were not always predictable. He couldn't give her much more of his blood without risking turning her, but he needed her to remember everything. If she remembered, he could finally get back to the business of hating her.

"Why aren't you dead?" she asked, the hatred in her voice unmistakable, but somewhat unexpected.

Ash welcomed it, though, and gave her a cold, leering smile. "You'd like that wouldn't you, Delilah?"

"Yes!" she shouted back.

"After all, you did your best to kill me before," he said. "You almost succeeded."

"You deserved everything you got, you miserable, selfish, arrogant bastard!"

The force of her fury took Ash aback. "What are you talking about?" he cried, crossing the short distance to stare down at her in disbelief. Her black eyes burned with fury and Ash hated himself for remembering how they'd once burned with other emotions. "You turned me over to the Philistines," he reminded her, "to have my eyes burned out and be left to rot in a prison cell." He grabbed her shoulder. "You sold me to them!"

Ariana lowered her voice, but it was no less virulent. Her gaze cut into him, making him aware that she didn't seem to fear his superior size or strength. Ash knew a moment of relief that she wasn't a vampire. She looked like she wanted to tear him to ribbons.

"It wasn't for the silver, you ignorant lout." The words seemed pulled from her against her will. "It was for my sister and my father."

Ash's brow furrowed. He tried to recall if he'd ever met her family. He didn't think so. "Del, I think you're confused," he said. Maybe the sudden onslaught of all the memories of her past lives had been too much for her.

She stopped talking and looked him up and down. "You still look the same," she said, her voice now reflecting the puzzlement Ash had expected.

Ash saw her eyes widen as she put a hand to her neck. There was no bleeding, but the two wounds were still there. She fingered them gingerly.

"What are you, Samson?" she asked.

"You were always a smart girl, Del," he said, "too smart for your own good." His voice was smooth, sinister. "You figure it out."

He took a long stride and grabbed her by both arms this time. "And while you're at it, maybe you can figure out why I've been looking for you all this time, and why I'd bother to give you your memories back before I killed you."

Ariana looked at him through baleful eyes and laughed. "Please don't tell me that you've been trying to track me down for 3,000 years just to kill me," she said. "For heaven's sake, I've died," she paused, trying to count, "at least 20 times since then. What terror can death hold for me now? If you wanted to terrify me, you should have killed me over there in that chair." Again she raised her black gaze to meet his. "Why didn't you?"

When he said nothing, she struggled in his grasp. "Put me down!" she commanded.

Ash set her on her feet. She wasn't afraid of him. He hadn't expected that. He'd needed her to be Delilah so he could hate her enough to do what he needed to do.

"More importantly, how did you give me my memories back?" she snapped.

Ash frowned down at her. "Our blood has that effect on humans," he explained. "Even the smallest drop will unlock the memories a person's mind carries from their former lives."

A glimmer of fear returned as Ariana looked at him questioningly. "But I'm not—"

Ash shook his head. "Like me?" he asked. "No, you're still quite human. I didn't take enough of your blood, or give you enough of mine, to turn you into a vampire."

Ariana shook her head. "How did you find me—in this body after all this time?" Ariana gave him a scathing glance. "Or was it just chance? Have you not learned any more in 3,000 years than you did in the first 40?"

The hard mask returned to his face. "So now you can show your true colors, eh, Del?" he said. "Well, I was hoping to see the real you one last time." He grabbed her face hard with one hand. "Tell me, where was this vicious tongue all those years ago, if you hated me so?"

"Not hated, Ash." She spoke through gritted teeth. "Hate—present tense." At his puzzled look, she pulled his hand free and continued. "You were much easier to trap with honey," she explained. "Your weakness for women, after all, was well known."

He couldn't argue with that.

"And yet, the Israelites loved you, no matter how many times you fell off the wagon." She moved closer to him, all traces of anger gone from her face. "If you had resisted me…" She ran her hands up the plane of his chest, and Ash drew a startled breath at the bolt of desire that shot through him. "If you had lived up to those pious principles of yours," she continued sweetly, her body melting against his, "I might have had second thoughts."

But he hadn't. He hadn't been able to resist her any more then than he could now. Her teasing had already made his body go tight. He remembered what it had been like between them, and his muscles grew harder.

"You're taking this whole vampire thing rather well," he commented.

Ariana withdrew from him, and gave a hard laugh. "Vampire, schmampire," she said. "If Buffy can kill a dozen of you a week, what's to be scared of? You'll have to do better than that to terrify a girl these days."

Ash sighed and sank down onto the couch. "You know," he said, "getting revenge on you has sometimes been the only thing keeping me awake and alive all these years."

"And so what now?" she asked "You think to get back in some divine good graces by killing me?"

"No," Ash said, shaking his head, "no, I gave up on that a long time ago." He looked up at her. "Killing you will just make me feel better."

For a moment Ariana didn't speak, seeming to consider the options. "And what if it doesn't?" she asked. "What if revenge doesn't make you whole?"

Ash smiled at her with all the cruelty he could muster. "That's a chance I'll have to take," he said.

Ariana moved quickly toward him, clearly wanting to argue the point, but staggered before she'd taken the second step. She tried to catch herself, but grasped at empty air. Ash stood and put out an arm to steady her.

"What do you care if I fall on my face?" she asked. "I thought you wanted me dead..." Her voice trailed off as she fainted.

Ash caught her, all the while asking himself the same question.

"Somehow it just doesn't seem a fair fight to kill you while you're in a dead faint," he said to her unconscious form. "But I can wait."

Ash carried the limp body of his sworn enemy down the long hallway of the manor's south wing. At the end of the hall, he kicked open his bedroom door and walked straight toward the large fireplace. It hadn't seen a fire in centuries.

He pressed one of the large gray stones with his full strength. It gave, and the back wall of the fireplace retreated several feet into a previously hidden space. Ash clasped Ariana tighter against his chest, ducked and walked into the inky blackness. He knew where the stairs began.

Down they went, one flight, two, three. This part of the manor was his own creation, and it had saved his life many times. Tiny rooms were carved into stone tens of feet below the south wing with no apparent plan. If anyone ever found the stairs, they'd still have to navigate the maze below. And only Ash could do that. No one else could get in. Or out.

He found the room he sought. The room he'd had made especially for her. His chest tightened as he entered. He hadn't been in here in centuries, not since he'd had it built to be an exact replica of the room where the Philistines had held him after his capture. He remembered the agony of those days. Chained to the wall like a dog. Unable to see. He shuddered and dropped his burden on the cold floor.

She murmured, but didn't wake.

Ash dragged her effortlessly over to the far wall. Manacles hung there, waiting. They had gone long unused, and he had to pry the first one open.

He clamped the large metal ring around her wrist. It still had his blood on it. He'd taken them soon after he'd brought the temple down, planning to have his revenge on Delilah in short order. But by the time he'd returned to Sorek, she had disappeared.

He tightened the screw to fit her smaller frame. The other followed, pinning her arms to the wall above her head.

Ash stood looking down at her for some time, relishing the sight he'd waited so long to see. It wasn't exactly as he'd imagined. Her hair was golden now, whereas in his mind it was always dark. But it still fell in thick waves around her slumped form. He stepped outside and lit a torch, leaving it in its place on the wall.

Silently he moved to a shelf carved into the wall on the other side of the room. No torchlight reached this place, but he knew every detail. He could see it engraved upon his memory.

He reached out and picked up a dagger. The wood on the handle crumbled under his touch, but the blade itself was hard and sharp. Like a shark's tooth, it was somewhat triangular, designed to slice all the way into its target.

Ash turned toward Ariana. She was the reason it was here.

He lowered the blade as he approached. It wasn't ideal for the task he had in mind, but it would do. He squatted in front of her and winged the blade across the space between them.

One golden lock fell into his outstretched hand. He twirled it between his fingers for a moment before slipping it into his pocket.

CHAPTER 30

The street in front of her stepfather's house was hardly less crowded than the square. Word must have gotten out that Samson and his party would be dining with them.

Delilah avoided the front door and most of the crowd by going up the side staircase. The wooden door at the top swung open and she ducked into the dark upstairs hallway. Her own room was two doors down, past the one shared by the female servants.

Her quarters were quite opulent for Sorek. She had a window and a wooden floor strewn with expensive rugs. Her stepfather was very generous to her.

After her father and sister were killed in the fire, her mother had returned with Delilah to the city where she was born. They had lived with Delilah's grandparents for a time, but her mother was never more than a shadow of her former self. She lived in constant fear that some awful thing would befall her youngest child. Perhaps that fear was what drove her to seek out Lilith.

In the lore of their homeland, Lilith was something between a god and a demon. Her aid was often sought by women in need of help or protection, but the price of her assistance was rumored to be high.

They had been living with her grandparents for a little more than a year when Delilah first began to notice her mother's strange absences in the evening. She wanted to ask about them, but hushed whispers among the adults made her feel that her questions would not be welcomed.

Worried about her fragile mother, she finally screwed up the courage to follow her one night as she left the house. Delilah had worried how she would pass unescorted through town, but her mother didn't go into the town. Rather, she left the house and went up into the mountains.

Delilah followed her, keeping an eye on her mother's light as it bobbed in the distance. She'd brought no light of her own, and she struggled over rocks and low brush to keep that little speck of light in view.

When they'd ascended to a point where even the town looked small down below, her mother's light disappeared. Delilah panicked and ran up the steep slope as fast as her young legs would carry her.

Luckily, her mother had not gone far. She had merely slipped around a large rock and into a cave that reached back into the mountain farther than Delilah could see. As she watched, a robed figure met her mother and led her into the cavern and out of sight. Delilah had been too scared to follow any farther that night, and her mother's mysterious absences stopped soon after.

In time, her mother married a wealthy merchant, securing both their futures. For a long time, her stepfather, Demos, had seemed not to care for Delilah. He wasn't a bad man, just uninterested in children.

When her mother died in childbirth several years later, along with her little brother, Delilah was bereft. Demos hadn't seemed upset himself, but her utter desolation piqued some feeling in him. He was never fatherly, but he was friendly to her after that, and he had continued to care for her as his own child.

As she got older, Delilah came to understand that Demos, in fact, preferred the company of men to that of women, and she had used that knowledge and her own skills to create a role for herself. She took over the running of the household, and Demos was more than content to have Delilah serve the social functions of a wife for him.

After a time, Demos began to converse with her about his business. Delilah would often take the nuggets of information he passed along and convert them into useful predictions about how people could be manipulated into doing what Demos wanted. It only took a few successes before Demos began to brief her daily on what was going on with his suppliers and customers.

Gradually, she learned his business and she learned that her beauty gave her power over men. She used them both—her looks and her mind—to cement strategic relationships for her stepfather. In time, she became almost a partner in his affairs.

Demos never commented on the nature of her tactics, and Delilah did not know if he disapproved or was grateful. He had become much more successful since she had gotten involved. He might not like her methods, but they were all she had, and they worked. And they would work on Samson.

CHAPTER 31

A riana woke slowly and opened her eyes. It was very dark, and she couldn't remember where she was. Dreams and memories swirled around in her head.

After a time, her eyes adjusted to the gloom. Where had Ash taken her? She wondered if she was even still at the manor; instinct told her she was. There was nowhere safer for him to go.

She looked around, but could only make out a dirt floor and rough-hewn stone walls. What part of the manor looked like this? None. None that she had seen, anyway. Ergo she was in a part of the manor she hadn't seen. Probably underground.

She tried to sit up and heard the chilling rattle of chains. Her chains. The bastard had chained her in a dungeon.

Ariana pulled hard against the metal bonds. They didn't budge, which made her furious even as her mind told her she should be afraid.

As Delilah she had bested Samson, but Ash was a different creature. He was still Samson, but only barely. She'd seen his human façade slip in the library, and instinctively she knew how hard he worked to maintain it. It must be lonely being the most powerful animal on the planet, but that's certainly what he was. Delilah couldn't hope to win against this creature.

But she wasn't Delilah, she told herself. Rather, she wasn't *just* Delilah. Memories, like amphibian children finding their way back into the sea, kept slipping into her consciousness. Once there, they swirled and became part of the whole that she'd thought was herself. Herself had suddenly gotten much bigger.

Her life was a mere snapshot in the timeline of her existence, the variety of which astonished her. She'd been a part of every race imaginable, always female, always with the same powerful core of will and intellect. She looked back in awe of the things she'd managed to accomplish. She'd known poverty, grief, crime, and war, but she'd always succeeded in her goals. She had protected her children, saved kingdoms, and won lovers. Sometimes her goals were questionable, like getting revenge on Samson, but she had never failed in them. That knowledge calmed her when she might have given in to panic.

If Ash had grown more powerful over the millennia, she, too, had changed. Now that she had her memories back, she had a wealth of wisdom and experience to draw on. She'd always been the smarter one. Now she just had to figure a way out.

Her thoughts heartened her, but inky blackness stole the legs from her good intentions. Loss of blood had made her weak. She would rest for just a minute. She wondered briefly why she could remember nothing before Delilah. Was Delilah her first life, or were her memories somehow limited by the bounds of Ash's lifetime?

⚜

She woke with a start, knowing she'd drifted off, but unaware of how much time had passed. She'd dreamed of James. A smile formed around the corners of her mouth. If things weren't quite so dire, he'd probably laugh at the mess she'd managed to get herself into.

"Rise and shine, heart of mine." Ash's malevolent sing-song greeting told her he was in the room somewhere, but she couldn't see him. How long had he been there, watching her?

She heard movement off to her left and knew he'd intended for her to hear him. He could certainly move silently if he chose.

A light flared in the distance, hurting Ariana's eyes and seemingly illuminating a giant's form. Ariana knew he was no giant, but from her vantage point on the floor, he might well have been.

She pulled again at the chains. Did she imagine one of them gave slightly? It was hard to tell. Her arms were totally asleep. If she ever got out of here they were going to hurt like hell.

"Are you finding everything to your liking, Del?" His tone mocked her.

"Not quite what I'm used to," she bit back.

"Believe it or not, you do get used to it." Ash knelt in front of her. She could barely see his face, but she knew it was hard and twisted. "I did."

Her heart ached as he said the words, confirming what she'd already guessed. This was what she'd done to him.

"Ash," she said, sympathy filling her voice.

He reached above her head and gave more length to one of her chains. Her right arm fell lifeless into her lap. For a moment, there was nothing. Then fire started at her shoulder and began a slow, unbearable course down her arm.

She writhed, trying to lessen the pain. "Ash," she pleaded.

Ash smiled, but stood and turned away from her. Ariana suddenly didn't want him to go.

"What, no snack for you this time?" she taunted.

He returned to stand in front of her and hauled her to her feet. One arm was still tightly tethered and the other she could barely move. Ash smiled, his fangs just visible.

Ariana sucked in her breath and tried to back away, but there was nowhere to go except up against the hard wall. Ash dropped his head, and she felt his firm lips nuzzle the side of her neck.

"Damn it, Ash" she said, hissing the words through gritted teeth.

"What's the matter, sweetheart?" he asked softly. "You don't like being in chains?" He reached up and cupped his hand lightly over her breast. "You don't like me touching you?"

Yes, she liked it; she couldn't stop the thought. Oh God, she had always liked it, but it didn't change anything. She needed to stop this.

"You still haven't remembered me, have you?" she asked.

Ash's removed his hand and drew back to look at her. She could see the furrows in his brow.

"We met before Sorek," she explained, swallowing hard. "My father tried to offer me to you as a consolation prize, but you wouldn't take me." She couldn't keep the ire from her voice. "Instead, you had to set the village on fire."

Finally, realization dawned for Ash, realization that she was the much younger sister of his wife. The wife he'd married as a young man and left at their wedding feast in a fit of ego.

He had returned for her months later only to learn she'd been given to his best man. Her father offered to let him take her younger sister instead, but she was only a child. In his rage, he'd set fire to the village and crops—and the villagers had retaliated by burning his wife and her father in their beds. Then he retaliated again by slaughtering them all to the last man.

About 20 years later, in another city, he'd seen the woman Delilah. Her dark beauty and frightening intellect had bewitched him from the first. How could he have known?

"I was not the same man the second time we met, Delilah," he whispered. "Could you not see that?" His voice was heavy with stale regret.

"Me?" Ariana scoffed. "How many times were you in my bed?"

Ash tried to remember. *A lot.*

"Did you ever ask about my childhood? Ever inquire about my feelings, my thoughts?"

Her words damned him, even in his own mind. "No, I suppose not." He thought for another moment and offered up a quiet defense. "It's no excuse, I know, but I was so ecstatic just to be with you that nothing else really seemed to matter."

Ariana hesitated, but then shook her head. "You mean you were so certain that I had no further thought other than how I would pleasure the great Samson next, that you just didn't feel the need to bother with the niceties."

The silence between them stretched taut, holding back a myriad of unkempt emotions.

"What's the matter, Ash?" Ariana taunted. "Things not turning out like you planned?"

That is the understatement of the millennia, Ash thought as he turned on his heel and left the little cell. He needed to think.

CHAPTER 32

She was surprised she even remembered the way to the cavern. She'd only followed her mother here the one time.

Delilah once again pondered whether she was making a mistake. She thought not. She had finally reached a station in life where she had connections and influence, at least in Sorek. If she could get Samson here, she could find a way to avenge her family.

Getting him here was the problem. Her influence didn't extend so far or so high as the circles Samson usually traveled, and she couldn't count on mere chance to come to her aid. She needed assistance of another kind.

Surely *she* would help avenge a sister's death at the hands of a philanderer who held himself out as a man of God and a servant of the law.

Darkness was all Delilah could see before her as she moved past the entrance to the cavern. Her gait slowed as fear bloomed within her. Echoes of whispers and a memory from long ago had brought her to this place. She really had no idea what she would find.

A cold breeze passed over her and, as the goose bumps began to form, she was forced to her knees by an invisible presence.

What do you seek, Delilah?

The words were not spoken aloud, but she heard them clearly in her mind, intoned in a strange voice, distinctly feminine, yet hard and cold. She wanted desperately to raise her head and look at the creature that now stood before her. All she could see was a robe, but every instinct told her it was not being worn by a person.

"I seek the aid of Lilith," Delilah said, "as one woman to another, in the cause of the unjust death of my sister, Anora."

"You want the death of Samson."

It was jarring to hear it spoken by another. "Yes," Delilah admitted. "I need Samson to come to Sorek."

There was a long pause before the creature spoke again. "He will come. After he arrives, one of my acolytes will come to collect my payment."

Delilah nodded. "I will pay," she whispered.

Chapter 33

Ariana leaned her head back on the hard wall of her cell and concentrated on the past. She needed to remember more about her bargain with Lilith, but when she was awake, no new memories would come. She decided to put the past out of her mind and focus on finding a way out of her current predicament.

Unfortunately, both her arms were asleep again. She tilted her body to the right, allowing more blood to flow into that arm. The pain went on for what seemed like hours, but she knew it was less.

When she could move her fingers, she reached her right arm over to her left and pulled with all her might. It hadn't been just her imagination. The left manacle was a little loose.

After another hour of pulling and straining, the pin holding her left manacle to its chain slipped free. The heavy links clattered against the stones behind her head, and her arm fell forward. She waited for the inevitable burning pain.

When it came, it sent her crumpling into a ball, but she used the time to figure out how to get her other arm free. She'd never be able to pull the manacle loose now that Ash had put so much length between her hand and the point where the chain was anchored to the wall.

She'd seen the knife sitting on the rock when Ash lit the torch earlier. With her left hand free, she thought she could reach it. She systematically inched her fingers over each rock in the wall around where she thought it should be. The manacle, its few links of chain and the dangling pin all clanked noisily along the bricks as she searched. Ariana gritted her teeth. Finally, she found the little outcropping and then the knife. Now, for the hard part.

A little light would be a big help, she thought, trying to take her mind off the pain of the first cut. She took a deep breath and made a second vertical cut in the back of her hand.

Blood poured out of the dual incisions, and Ariana spun her hand around in the manacle. Fire coursed through her arm, but her hand slipped in the metal ring.

She forced herself to flex her fingers, keeping the blood flowing. She relaxed her hand and pulled harder. Her knuckles slipped down inside the ring. One more pull, and her butchered hand was free.

She fell over onto her side, clutching her hand between her thighs. The pressure would help stop the bleeding, and the pain was so raw that the fetal position was all she could manage for a quarter of an hour.

As her brain and hand adjusted, she found she was able to stand. She took off her tee shirt and wrapped it tightly around the wound.

She thought two long steps should bring her to the door. Her first step had to be finding the torch. Hand outstretched, she found the doorway easily enough. The torch wasn't hard to find either, but lighting it was another story.

Where were the matches? Maybe Ash brought them with him when he came down. No, she thought, that didn't make sense.

She ran her good hand, still dangling its manacle, over the wall all around the torch, and finally found what she was seeking. Between two stones there was a slight gap, and in the gap were four matches.

She pulled one out and awkwardly managed to strike it on the handle of the torch. Quickly she lifted it. Light flared and the scent of burning oil filled her nose. She blew out the match, put the rest of them in her pocket, and picked up the torch.

Turning to her left and right, Ariana strained to see anything that would indicate an exit. In both directions, the passageway curved quickly into darkness. And she'd never heard Ash coming or going, so she didn't even know which way to start.

Shit, she thought. What good was getting out of her chains if she was going to bleed to death in a rat maze? *Wait.* Maze. What had Eric told her? Pick a wall and follow it without fail in any direction. Eventually it would lead her to the exit.

Ariana held the torch with her left hand and raised her right hand close to the wall opposite her. Surely she didn't need to actually touch the wall, she thought. It was filthy and her hand was killing her.

She took two steps and then turned back to the doorway of her cell. With the end of the torch she scratched a triangle into the hard dirt floor as a marker. Then she turned to her left and stepped forward into the darkness.

The corridor went on, twisting and turning for what seemed like miles, connecting a series of rooms whose purposes Ariana didn't even want to guess. She tried to keep her eyes only on the few feet of path the torch illuminated in front of her. At one juncture, she traded her fading torch for a fresh one, using her dying flame to ignite the replacement. Who stocked torches in a vampire's dungeon? she wondered absently. Talk about a thankless job.

Finally, she came to the exit. It had to be the way out. Stairs led her up two or three stories. She lost count.

Unfortunately, when she got to the top, it looked like a dead end. A stone wall blocked any farther progress. She sat down, carefully balancing the torch against the wall beside her, and considered where she had gone wrong.

Finally, realization dawned. She hadn't gone wrong. This was the door. It had to be. It was just camouflaged as a wall. Ariana dropped her head into her uninjured hand. She was so tired. How long would it take her to figure out the mechanism to open the door? Could she get it open before Ash came back?

She unwrapped the blood-soaked tee shirt from her hand and wiggled all her fingers, glad to see that she could, even though it was painful. The movement set one of the cuts to bleeding again, so she rewrapped it as tightly as she could manage.

Leaving the torch where it sat, Ariana stood and examined the wall. *Of course there couldn't just be a big "PUSH" sign*, she thought. Nevertheless, she tried leaning hard against the wall, first slightly to her left and then to her right. *No Scooby-Doo spinning-wall action here*, she thought, smiling slightly despite the dire circumstances. Then, remembering the matches, she set about pushing and poking at every stone and every crevice between them, but nothing worked. Exhausted and out of ideas, she slumped against the wall and sank into any uneasy sleep.

CHAPTER 34

Delilah studied the woman before her for a moment, wondering how she had come to be in the service of the demon Lilith.

"A life for a life," the woman said.

Now that Delilah had heard the price, she had no doubt of Lilith's true nature—but this servant was another matter. She was younger than Delilah and quite pretty, at least the half of her face that could be seen under the hood of her cloak.

Delilah nodded. "Lilith has kept her word and brought Samson to me," she replied. "My sister will have her vengeance and the Philistines will have his life. My life is hers in payment if she wishes it."

The strange young woman shook her head. "Not *your* life," she said. "The life of your child."

At Delilah's confused look, the woman pulled a water skein from the basket she had set at her feet and handed it to Delilah. "You and Samson must each drink half," she said, "and you must lay with him this night."

Delilah took the proffered skein. "What does it contain?" she asked.

"The blood of Lilith," was the surprising response. "Lilith's current form has served her well," the woman explained, "but it is not long for this world. When her blood combines with flesh in your womb, her soul will be drawn into it and she will be born anew."

Delilah couldn't hide her surprise. Her mouth dropped open, and she stared wide-eyed at the girl in front of her.

"You will be the mother of a goddess, Delilah," the girl said. "It is a great honor."

Delilah turned and laid the skein on the table across from her bed. She supposed she could object, but, strange as it was, it was not a higher price than she was willing to pay. She suspected her mother and baby brother had paid a dearer price.

"It must be tonight, then?" she asked.

"Tonight," the woman repeated. She picked up the basket and turned toward the door. "And when it is time for the child to be delivered, you must again return to us. It will not be long."

CHAPTER 35

Nancy waited until the lights from Samson's car had dis-appeared up the manor's long driveway before making her way to his room.

Once there, she crossed over to the large stone fireplace, pulled the small lever hidden between two stones and sighed. After 3,000 years, she'd hoped for something more.

She'd made a promise to Lilith, and when this woman appeared, with the right lineage, the right soul, she'd thought it was too good to be true. Perhaps it was. Perhaps she was a fool for hoping.

❧

Ariana winced as the beam of light hit her eyes. "Ash?" she called out, using her uninjured hand to shield her face.

A smaller form moved inside.

"No, child," a familiar voice said, "it's me, Nancy."

Ariana's breath came out in a rush. "Oh, thank God, Nancy. How did you find me? I thought I might be stuck in here for good."

Nancy helped her to her feet.

"I know most of what goes on here," Nancy explained.

Ariana stepped forward and peered cautiously into Ash's empty room.

"Don't worry," the housekeeper said. "Mr. Samson has gone to take Mr. Justin back to the city. You should be able to make it to the airport before he returns and finds you gone."

Ariana turned to study the small woman at her side. Clearly there was more to the unflappable Nancy than met the eye. Again something teased her from the fog of her memories.

She shook her head. "Thank you."

"Come with me," Nancy said. "We'll get something for your hand, and then I'll call a car to drive you to the airport."

Ariana followed the woman upstairs and down and then into the kitchen she had visited briefly several days ago. Nancy crossed the expansive tiled floor and selected a brown bottle, some ointment and a roll of gauze from inside a low cabinet. Ariana took a seat on one of the stools on the other side of the butcher block island that fronted the stove.

When she approached, Ariana held out her hand and winced as the peroxide flowed over her open cuts. Tears came to her eyes, and she stared at a spot on the wall over Nancy's shoulder and tried to think of anything else.

Keys. An entire rack of them just inside the door caught her attention because each one had a distinctive key chain attached. She could make out the Statue of Liberty from where she sat, and the Eiffel Tower, and—she squinted and let out a breath as the pain in her hand eased—was that one a palm tree?

"There," Nancy said as she taped down the end of the gauze. "You'll need to have that checked when you get home, but it should be okay if you take care."

Ariana smiled through watery eyes. "Thanks, Nancy. I don't know..." Her voice trailed off because she didn't know what Nancy knew or how to thank someone appropriately for freeing her from a dungeon.

Nancy turned and began replacing the first aid components back in their cabinet. "You should go change and pack a few things," she said turning back to Ariana. "Nothing heavy with that hand. I can send the rest of your belongings later. I'll go call the car. It should be here within the hour."

Back in her room, Ariana took a quick, one-handed shower and threw on a loose top and a long skirt.

She had just dropped her cell phone into her bag when it began to ring.

"Ariana Chambers," she said, not sure why she'd bothered to answer it. She wasn't feeling up to talking about work right now.

"Miss Chambers, hi. It's Detective Simmons. How are you?"

Ariana thought for a minute. There was no honest answer to give, so she settled for "I'm doing well, Detective. And you?"

"Fine, thanks. Listen, I probably shouldn't even have called, but you did ask to be informed about anything relating to your husband's case."

"That's right," Ariana said. "What's happened?" She was hit by a sudden bought of dread. "Did you find... him?" Was he going to tell her they'd found a body?

"No, miss, we haven't found him."

Ariana breathed a sigh of relief.

"But, we did have a kid come in yesterday and file a complaint. He says he saw your husband a couple of weeks ago in mid-town and that James attacked him."

"What?" Ariana exclaimed. "That's ridiculous. James wouldn't attack anyone."

"I told you it was against my better judgment to call you," he explained. "At first I thought it might be a real lead. The kid was real specific about how he recognized James from the news coverage of his disappearance."

Ariana waited. "But something changed your mind?"

The detective hesitated. "Yeah, when we got into the details, the kid started saying James had put him in some sort of trance and, well," there was a heavy pause, "basically that he was a vampire."

Ariana sagged against the bed as she felt the room start to spin out from under her.

"But it's nothing for you to worry about," Detective Simmons hurried on. "We found the body of the kid's friend a week before. He'd been murdered and we think this kid must have killed him and is now trying to cover his tracks, or set up an insanity defense."

He tried to reassure her. "I don't think there's really any connection here to your husband at all, except that this kid happened to remember seeing his face on television."

"I'm sure you're right, Detective." Ariana's mind was numb. "Thank you for the call."

"No problem. I'm sorry I don't have a real lead for you, but I didn't want you to see this in the tabloids. You have a nice night."

"Thank you."

Ariana powered the phone off, grabbed her bag, and made her way back to the kitchen.

CHAPTER 36

In the back seat of the fast-moving sedan, Ariana looked at the painted metal key chain in her palm and forced herself to relax. She had circled back to the kitchen and stolen the Statue of Liberty, but she would be halfway to New York before Ash knew either of them was gone.

Hopefully, some time and space would cool his anger and give her a chance to discover what he knew about James. After that, if Ash still wanted her dead, there wasn't much she could do about it, but at least she would know what had happened to her husband.

The motion of the car rocked her tired body, and she closed her eyes, wondering at all that had happened in so short a time. Her body floated, but her mind still raced. She brought her undamaged hand up to touch the side of her neck. The two holes were still there, but they had shrunk to mere pinpricks. What to make of all this?

She wanted to hate Ash, but how could she? Assuming he was telling the truth about not taking enough blood to make her a vampire, she had put him through far worse than he had done to her. For heaven's sake, she had made a bargain with a demon to get revenge on him. A bargain she had never fulfilled because the Philistine soldiers had come too early.

She had filled both their glasses that night with spiced wine and the blood Lilith's handmaiden had delivered. Samson came up behind her and reached around her to grab one of the brimming cups.

"A toast, my love," he announced, his dark eyes glittering at her over the ornate goblet.

Delilah reluctantly took the other cup from the tray and turned to face him. "What are we celebrating?" she asked.

He grinned and licked his lips. "The unbelievably erotic things I'm going to do to you tonight?"

Delilah picked up his wicked tone. "I think we're a little late," she said. "You can't possibly have anything new with which to dazzle me at this point." They had already done things she'd never even imagined. Though she'd had other lovers, none of them possessed Samson's gifts. He took loving women to an art.

He returned both their glasses to the tray, swept her off her feet, and proved her wrong.

Once she'd caught her breath, she left Samson sleeping and went down to the kitchen. If this night held true to form, he'd awake in a few minutes, ravenous in more ways than one.

The earthen kitchen was still warm from the heat of the oven. She was slicing a loaf of fresh bread to accompany their wine when she heard the din of the approaching soldiers.

Her heart began to race and her head pounded. They had come too early. And she was too late. Too late! The rhythm of booted feet hammered the message into her brain. Too late to stop them. Too late to keep her promise to Lilith. Too late.

She heard the struggle start upstairs and carry over into the street. Delilah returned to her room and looked out the window at her handiwork. Samson lay in the dirt, surrounded by a cadre of soldiers. His arm was bent awkwardly beneath his body, and blood was staining the ground in a wide radius all around him.

Their success assured, yet unexpected, the soldiers appeared to be momentarily at a loss. Delilah felt much the same way. She'd planned this for years and dreamed of it for even longer, yet the sight of it did not quiet the turmoil in her soul.

She turned to look at the wine glasses she had prepared. To her surprise, one of the goblets was empty. Samson must have gotten up and drunk his while she slept. Knowing him, he had polished it off in one gulp and never noticed its slightly metallic scent.

She walked over to the little table and picked up her own glass. The untimely arrival of the soldiers meant there would be no godchild from this night. She drained the contents of the cup anyway and closed her eyes. Lilith would likely kill her, but she could do no more. *Perhaps it's just as well,* she thought. She had done enough already.

Chapter 37

Deciding she had skulked around the front door long enough, Toria gave in to her impatience and followed one of Council House's carpeted halls down to a library on the ground floor. There, she scooted inside and picked up a phone from a small, intricately carved wooden table just inside the door and dialed the number on the back of Luc's business card.

Really. Who ever heard of a vampire with a business card? Well, except for Ash, but he was different.

Luc answered on the fourth ring. He must have been down at the cages.

"Luc Benson here," he said.

"Luc, it's Toria. Where is James? You said he was coming early."

"What do you mean?" Luc asked, sounding genuinely concerned. "He's not there?"

"No," Toria said. "He never showed."

"Well, he's not here, and he's not at the apartment either. I just came from there. I assumed he had already gone to Council House."

If Toria knew one thing, it was that James wasn't the type to run off. "Luc, was anything out of place at your apartment?" she asked. "Was there any indication that something might have happened to him?"

Luc grunted. "Of course not. I'd have called you if I'd known anything was wrong."

"Okay," Toria said, rubbing her temple with her hand, "but I'm going to go have a look around anyway."

"Be my guest," Luc agreed. "The key is under the mat. Just don't steal anything."

The line clicked dead before Toria could retort that he hardly had anything worth stealing.

"He's no good, that one."

Toria turned, surprised that Keller had managed to get behind her. As usual, he was wearing the horrid brown robe of his former order. Her mouth twisted in contempt. "Been praying for your soul?" she asked.

Keller smiled serenely at her, his green eyes glittering from beneath impossibly long lashes. "And yours," he said.

"How nice," Toria replied with a sneer. "Now get out of my way. I don't have time for any more of your riddles."

Keller shook his head. "'Tis no riddle. It's simply a fact. Lucas is part human, not a pure child of Lilith. The mixing of the lines of Lilith and Adam will bring the children of Lilith out of the shadows and the end of days will be upon us."

Toria had no patience for this. She reached out with lightning speed and grabbed Keller around the throat, forcing him back against the far wall. Her fangs protruded in a hiss. "Luc can't walk in daylight any more than you or I. If you ever utter any more of this drivel in my presence I'll put an end to *your* days, do you hear me?"

Keller's serene visage remained. He smiled at her and said nothing. Toria dropped him and shoved him to one side. He stood, and Toria saw him reach for a book as she left the room.

Halfway to the front door, she turned around and headed for the elevator. On the third floor, she followed the hall around to the other side of the grand house, to the room Keller had occupied since his sudden arrival here almost a year ago.

She looked both ways to make sure her entrance was not observed. Privacy was closely guarded at Council House, and they did not rely on locks to ensure it. Anyone caught trespassing was subject to expulsion or worse. As an Elder, she had some leeway, but her visit here was not on Council orders. She didn't even have any real suspicions, just a bad feeling.

She opened the heavy wooden door. The smell of incense hit her as she stepped over the threshold. At first glance, the room was small and Spartan, with just a bed, a desk with a chair, two lamps and stacks of books and papers. A strip of leather on the bed caught her eye, and she knew immediately what it was. The monks of Keller's order had put it between their teeth when they whipped themselves into bloody messes trying to achieve some sort of higher state. She'd seen them do it hundreds of years before.

For an instant, pity welled within her. How Keller must loathe himself now. It was hard to make a vampire body suffer. She imagined him in here, kneeling on the floor, lashing his own flesh, biting through the leather strip.

When she'd turned him, he'd gone straight back to his order and told them the truth. The other monks of course tried to kill him then and there, and they had continued to try to kill him periodically over the years. Yet he kept in touch with them—ever trying to do enough penance to get back into their good graces.

She crossed over to the desk, trying to get the image of Keller's bleeding torso out of her mind. She'd feel guilty if he hadn't been just as crazy before she turned him. She'd wanted to break him, break his faith, but she'd failed, and now she had a lunatic living under her roof for all eternity.

Toria shook her head and looked down at the books of medieval and ancient demon lore covering his desktop. She would never understand why he wasted his time with this stuff. Ash was the first, and he didn't know how he'd been made. She didn't have the patience to hunt for clues to a mystery she already knew couldn't be solved.

That, however, was exactly what Keller appeared to be doing. Toria picked up a newspaper clipping. It was from ten years ago when Ash had made a big donation to some charity. He rarely allowed himself to be photographed, but there he was in black and white, smiling and shaking hands, making all the other tuxedo-clad party goers look small and weak and lifeless.

She put the picture back and lifted two of the books off the desk. Underneath were more news clippings and what looked like a portion of someone's family tree.

Toria replaced everything carefully. There was nothing here she didn't already know, and it was no crime to read the paper. Still, she should probably tell Ash.

Keller watched Toria's sleek figure as she pulled shut the door to his room. He was not worried. When she'd gone, he opened the door and took a quick look around. He smiled, noting how nothing looked out of place. She was good at her job.

But now *he* had a job to do. Toria had made him into an unholy monster, and he had to be cleansed. He dropped to his knees and unhooked the stays at the collar of his robe. It fell to the floor around him, leaving his chest bare.

Reaching under the bed, he wrapped his hand around the hilt of a whip. He slid it out and looked at its vicious ends. Once they had been just knotted horsehair, but horsehair could no longer do him harm.

After his transformation, he'd had special blades fashioned with a hole at one pointed end that flared out into two slightly curved sharp edges so each blade resembled a tiny scythe. Three were knotted into the end of each tassel of the whip.

He forced his arm up and back, felt the blades slice and hook into his flesh, and then he pulled up, ripping them free. The pain was intense, but guilt still ate at him because he knew it wouldn't last. He could carve himself into ribbons, but his traitorous flesh would still be whole by the next evening. He could not be a proper servant in this body. None of them could.

CHAPTER 38

Delilah tried not to scream as another contraction ripped through her. Her hand gripped maniacally at the bed-clothes as Samson's child made its way into the world. Barely seven months had passed since Samson's capture, and so much had happened so quickly, it hadn't even occurred to her that she could be pregnant until a few months ago.

She'd known, of course, that Samson was beloved, even in Sorek, but she hadn't counted on being run out of town. Demos had protected her for a time, but when his business began to suffer and the animosity toward her showed no sign of blowing over, even he turned on her. In the end, he'd helped her get established in Gaza, but he had made it clear that there would be no future contact. He couldn't afford it. There was no explicit mention of how she would support herself.

No matter. She had enough money to delay the inevitable for quite some time—at least long enough to bring her child into the world and see to its future.

Delilah didn't know what effect her drink of demon blood would have on the child. Hopefully none. Whatever Lilith's plan had been, this child had been conceived before the night of Samson's capture, before he had drunk of her blood. That should be enough to ensure her child would have its own soul.

An astonishing pain roared forth from between her legs and drenched her whole body in sweat. She almost lost consciousness, hanging on only because she heard a faint cry. Her baby daughter.

She hated that she would never get to know her, but the servants of Lilith would inevitably seek her out and kill her once they discovered they'd been betrayed. Neither she nor the child would be safe in any Philistine city, and the child would be much safer separated from her.

Her maid, Morah, washed and wrapped the babe while Delilah regained her breath. When Morah laid the babe on her chest, Delilah stared in surprise at a tiny pair of blue eyes, more vivid than she had ever seen. *Perhaps this was Lilith's contribution,* she thought.

The maid pulled the child away, as she had been instructed. She and her young husband would take the girl to a new city and raise her as their own. Delilah had sold most of her jewels to get them enough money to get established anywhere they chose. They just weren't to tell her their destination. She could never know what had become of them or the child, nor could anyone else. Their lives depended on it.

⁕

When the plane hit the runway at John F. Kennedy Airport, Ariana jerked awake. She held her breath as the flaps went up to slow the winged beast, and her mind reeled from the latest dream.

Delilah… she… had borne Samson's child. Not the demon host Lilith had intended, but his real child. And she'd given their daughter away to keep her safe. She wondered what had become of her. And she wondered how she had suddenly come to have so many secrets.

CHAPTER 39

Outside the terminal in New York, the sky was almost dark. She gave the dispatcher at the cab stand the address for Ash's townhouse and slid into the backseat of the next waiting taxi.

As the cab crossed the Queensboro Bridge onto Manhattan Island, Ariana leaned closer to the plastic divider. The city glittered through the front window, and she realized she'd missed it.

At the townhouse, the cab sped away, leaving Ariana on the sidewalk fumbling for a moment with the purloined key chain. She considered her choices and opted to try the big brass key on the iron gate that now barred her way.

A mere second of jiggling and the heavy grated door swung inward before her. Ariana's shoulders sagged in relief. *One down, one to go,* she thought.

She wasn't as lucky on the next door, taking three tries to get the right key, but eventually it too succumbed. She pushed it open and stepped inside.

There were no lights, so she dropped the keys into her bag, turned, and searched out a switch with her left hand. Finally, a small table lamp in the foyer flared to life.

She shut the door behind her and headed for Ash's study.

Halfway down the hall, she froze in her tracks when she heard the faint but unmistakable sound of Ash's front door swinging slowly inward on its metal hinges. *Could he have followed me so quickly? No.* She'd barely made it onto the last flight out of Heathrow for the night. He would be at least a few hours behind her, and probably more.

Ariana drew in a sharp breath, and the raised hairs on the back of her neck gave her the split second of warning she needed. As she spun out of the way of her attacker, she let her own fist fly out. It connected with something hard, hurting her already injured hand.

The hard thing was a black-clad woman. Ariana knew instantly she was a vampire. "Ash," she said quickly. "I know Ash. Samson. He'd be very angry if you killed me."

"I doubt that," the woman smirked. Her eyes roved over Ariana from head to toe, and she smiled darkly. "Don't worry," she said. "I promise not to kill you if you tell me who you are."

Ariana said nothing, and the woman moved closer, studying her intently. "I want you to tell me who you are," she said with a voice like a silken razor.

Ariana coughed nervously. "That's the $64,000 question, I'm afraid."

The woman stopped short when she got close enough to look Ariana in the eye. Ariana was surprised to see a flash of recognition.

"Are you her?" the woman asked bitterly. "Is it really Delilah come to grace us with her presence after all this time?"

Ariana understood instantly that this woman wanted Ash for herself. *Tricky.* What would Delilah do?

"I see you've heard of me," she said with a smile. "Good." Ariana raked the woman with her gaze. "Guess you didn't get the other memo. Goth is out this year."

The woman opened her mouth and hissed. Long white fangs glimmered in the darkness.

Okay, no more channeling Delilah, Ariana thought, taking a nervous step back from her rival. She was no match for this woman, but she didn't want her hanging around getting in the way either.

"Do you know James?" Ariana asked.

"Who?" the woman asked, her eyes narrowing.

"My husband, James," Ariana said slowly. "I think he's been turned recently into..." she couldn't say the word, "...one of you."

The woman's tight body relaxed somewhat as she considered Ariana's question. "And if I could bring James back to you?" she queried guardedly.

"That depends," Ariana hedged. "Who are you?"

"Toria," the woman replied. "Ash and I are old friends."

"Hmmm..." Ariana forced herself not to point out that Ash had never mentioned her. "And you know what happened to James?"

"That depends," Toria replied, giving her a knowing glare.

Ariana shook her head. "I don't have designs on Ash, if that's what you're asking," she said. "Can you take me to James?"

"But does Ash have designs on *you*?" Toria asked.

Ariana hesitated before answering, but that was all the answer Toria seemed to need.

"That's too bad," she muttered as she drew back her fist and let fly.

Ariana hit the floor at Toria's feet with a muffled thud.

CHAPTER 40

He just had to be patient, Ash told himself again as he stared at the wall in his study. He still couldn't figure out how she'd escaped, but it didn't matter. He would get her back.

The electronic jangling of his cell phone startled him, but the brief flash of hope in his eyes died when he saw that it was Justin's number.

"What?" he barked into the tiny device.

"Hi to you, too, Ash," Justin said, sounding offended. "What's got you in such a foul mood? Is Ariana okay?"

"Yes."

"Well, you'll forgive my concern," Justin insisted. "You did kick me out of the manor rather abruptly, and I never saw her before I left."

"She's fine," Ash said, hoping it was true. "Look, is this important? I really need to go."

"Well, I don't know. Is finding out who broke into your company important?"

Ash sat back in his chair and forced himself to focus on the matter at hand. "Okay, what did you find out?"

"Thomas really came through," Justin began. "He took all the surveillance video and matched each entry to the electronic access logs. There was an unauthorized entry a few weeks ago."

Ash was pleased to have a result so soon. "So who was it? Do we know?"

"Well, the access logs say it was you."

Ash wasn't sure he'd heard him right. "Me? That can't be."

"I know," Justin said, "but I saw them myself. Someone swiped your keycard at the gate, but it definitely wasn't you."

"We got a picture?" Ash asked eagerly.

"Yes, I'm e-mailing it to you right now."

Ash jiggled his mouse and waited for his laptop screen to come back on. After an impatient few seconds, he opened the file and watched a tall, dark, green-eyed vampire walk through the access doors at Hemogen.

"I'll be damned," Ash said softly. "Keller."

"So you do know him?" Justin asked. "How do you want to proceed?"

"Don't worry about it," Ash said. "I'll get the next plane to New York and find out first hand what Keller's up to."

"Okay," Justin said hesitantly. "But let me know if you need anything."

Ash laughed. "I said not to worry. Whatever Keller's twisted brain has come up with, he's no threat."

Justin said goodbye and hung up, still sounding to Ash's ears a little too motherly.

Ash pressed the intercom call button and within moments, Nancy appeared at his study door.

"What can I bring you, sir?"

"Nothing, Nancy. I will be leaving for New York immediately. Can you get packed and come over on a flight tomorrow?"

Nancy's eyes lit up. "Yes, sir. I'd be delighted."

Ash gave her a puzzled glance. "Really? You normally aren't any more pleased than Ben to have to leave here."

Nancy smiled. "Well, it's getting to be that time of year, sir. I can start my Christmas shopping in the city."

Ash frowned. *What was it about shopping that turned women into totally different people? And who Christmas-shopped in June?*

CHAPTER 41

Unlike Ash, Luc liked to live amidst the bustle. He kept an apartment down in the East Village, but Toria wasn't headed for his apartment.

Across the park, on the west side of the city, Luc rented some warehouse space behind a string of car dealerships. Not many others knew what he did there, but Toria had found him out when she'd first gone searching for James several weeks ago.

Luc's little setup was disgusting, but harmless enough. And the holding facility would be the perfect place to store this kitten out of sight for a while.

At this hour, there weren't many people out on the streets Toria chose to traverse. The few people she did pass couldn't be bothered to inquire about one unconscious woman—and if they could, a scalding glance from Toria made them think twice about interfering.

The heavy door to the warehouse was locked and, from all appearances, long unused. Toria flipped open the door of what looked like a fuse box. Inside a tiny screen flickered. A face appeared on it, a chiseled, masculine face surrounded by hair the color of desert sand.

"Toria. Did you find James?"

As Toria watched his lips move, she wished she'd been the one to make this fabulous creature into a vampire. She wondered who had. They certainly did have an eye for it. She thought briefly about Keller's pronouncement that Luc was part human, but dismissed it as so much gibberish.

"No," she answered into the speaker, "but I have a present for you."

"A present?" Luc's suspicion was evident. "What's the occasion?"

"I need a small favor," Toria answered honestly. "But it's an opportunity for the right male. I immediately thought of you."

"Don't bullshit me, Toria."

"Look," she said, patience wearing thin, "I need a favor. I figured if it was also a chance to stick a finger in Ash's eye, you wouldn't exactly mind. Was I wrong?"

Luc grinned, lighting up the little screen. "Hell no. Why didn't you say so?" A buzz sounded from behind the door. "Come on in."

Toria closed the video phone and grabbed the large handle of the warehouse door. She gave it a quick upward push and pulled it open with a grunt. The door was weighted so no human could open it, and with her precarious package still draped over one shoulder, even Toria found it a little difficult.

She opened it just enough to slip through and walked to the back of the cavernous space. The heavy door rolled shut behind her, cutting off the beam of light from outside. She didn't need it to see, of course, but she, like most vampires, preferred some light. Lack of light meant lack of color.

Not that there was much color to this place, Toria thought as she pressed the button on the far wall. A whirring sound started somewhere below as the freight elevator rose.

Toria shifted Delilah's weight on her shoulder once more before yanking open the grated metal door and stepping in. The woman moaned.

"Not much farther now," Toria murmured.

Light began pouring in around her feet as the elevator made its way to the lower level. With all the lights he kept burning, Toria half suspected Luc was afraid of the dark.

"So, to what do I owe the pleasure?" Luc said by way of greeting as he opened the grated door. "I thought you were looking for James."

He, like Toria, was clad all in black. He sported no leather, though, just jeans, a button up shirt, and cowboy boots.

Toria stepped out of the elevator and shoved the still-unconscious Delilah into his arms. "Thought the place could use a woman's touch," she mocked.

Luc laughed out loud, as his eyes roved over the unexpected delivery. *Not bad. Not bad at all.* "Who is she?"

"Who isn't she," Toria grumbled. "She's James' wife, for one."

Luc frowned. James had never mentioned a wife. "I thought you said this had something to do with Ash."

"She's also Delilah," Toria muttered.

"Delilah who?"

Toria shot him a dark look, and Luc's eyes got wide. "Oh, *that* Delilah," he said. *This is very cool,* he thought. And potentially very bad. Ash could probably kill with just a thought, if he ever really put his mind to it. Or if someone made him mad enough.

Luc looked again at his sleeping captive. What was it about her? She did seem familiar. Something danced at the edge of his consciousness but wouldn't stand still long enough for him to sort it out.

"And just what did you have in mind that I do with her?" he asked, turning to Toria once more.

"Relax, Lucas, you don't have to kill her," Toria said. "Yet. Just keep her out of sight for a while. I need a little time to get Ash back here and talk to him. Plus, we need to find James."

Luc walked over to the couch, knelt, and placed Delilah on it, carefully positioning the cushion under her head. Then he smoothed her hair away from her face and heard Toria give a loud grunt of disgust from somewhere behind him. He didn't care. He wanted her to open her eyes.

"Oh, for pity's sake, Luc, she won't break. Believe me."

Luc turned around. "How long?" he demanded.

"What? Oh. I don't know," Toria shrugged. "As long as it takes, I guess. What's your rush?"

"You obviously intend for me to keep her in one of the cages down below," he said, coming over to where Toria stood with one hand on a precocious hip, "but I'm not running a home for wayward girls here. I use those for business, and I think I should get reimbursed for my troubles."

Toria pursed her lips and grabbed him by the chin. "Careful, Lucas. If you were even a little less gorgeous, I might take offense."

She released him and turned to go. "But I have other matters to see to tonight, so do whatever you want with her for a couple of weeks. I'll have found James by then."

Luc raised a brow. "And if you haven't?"

Toria shrugged. "Well, maybe then I'll consider making an investment in your little operation." She stepped into the elevator and closed the gate. "Just don't let anyone find out who or where she is and don't turn her." She thought about this for a minute, pushed the grate back open and stuck her head out. "I mean it, Luc. If you make her a vampire, I'll kill you both."

With that she was gone as quickly as she had come, and Luc was alone with his new ward.

CHAPTER 42

Luc moved over to the yellow polyester-covered sofa and knelt again beside his sleeping beauty. He smiled at the cliché.

She was beautiful, but this was no fairy princess. This was a flesh and blood woman, the wife of his friend, the obsession of the most powerful vampire alive, and she was asleep on his couch.

He reached out to touch her hair again. This was why light was good, he thought. Not because of color, but because of shine. Nothing shone in the dark. Not the way her hair glimmered and caught the light from the lamp on the desk. Or the way her skin warmed and radiated back the light from overhead.

"Open your eyes, darlin'," Luc whispered. "Let's see what all the fuss is about."

Not even a whimper.

Luc reached for her left arm and pushed up the loose sleeve of her shirt. He began to rub his hands vigorously back and forth over her skin.

As he did so, he caught a whiff of something, a scent he recalled from long ago, and the memory rocked him back on his heels. *Holy Mother of God,* he thought. *A breeder.*

His mother had been a breeder. The Verses said there would be others, but most vampires thought those were just legends. Even he, when he knew it was true, had never thought to find another.

He took a deep breath. Not something he was used to, it sent him into a fit of coughing.

❦

The noise penetrated the fog of Ariana's brain, and she slowly opened her eyes. A bolt of pain rammed through her left temple, causing her to groan. Suddenly a face appeared above hers. For a moment, she thought it must be an angel.

"Hi there," he said.

It registered with Ariana that angels probably wouldn't have Southern drawls. Then again... She smiled even though it hurt. Maybe in her heaven they would. She struggled to sit up.

A hand reached for her upper arm, but never made contact. She righted herself and stared down at the man in front of her.

He returned her smile, and Ariana sucked in her breath. Whoever he was, he was easily the most beautiful person she'd ever seen, with his chiseled cheek bones and blue eyes. *Men shouldn't have eyes like that,* she thought dazedly. They looked back at her, clear as an afternoon sky on the Fourth of July. And just as bright. She wondered at their intensity and why she felt like she had seen them before.

And God help her, she'd always had a thing for blonds.

"Good to know," the man said, his smile growing a notch brighter.

"Oh shit," Ariana blurted. "You can do that too." She tore her gaze away from his lovely, but too-perceptive face and made a show of studying her surroundings. The couch on which she sat occupied most of one wall of what appeared to be an office. The rest of the room had the usual office trappings—two wooden desks, several cheap office chairs, a couple of metal file cabinets—but the floor was cement, partially covered with a ragged piece of Astroturf. Sitting on the yellow sofa, she felt like a guest at a lawn party.

"Where are we?" Ariana asked, puzzled. "And who are you?"

She raised her hand to her throbbing temple as memory came rushing back. Toria.

She eyed Luc warily. "I guess Toria is responsible for me being here?"

"That's right," he said.

"And 'here' would be...?"

"You're in my office, in my warehouse."

"And you are...?" *This is like pulling teeth,* Ariana thought wryly. Or maybe it was more like pulling fangs.

Luc chuckled. "Maybe having you around won't be a total bore. My name is Lucas." He rose from his squatting position and went to lean against the desk to her left. "But you can call me Luc."

"I'm Ariana Chambers. I—I work for Ash."

Luc laughed again. "Oh, I bet you do." Luc's eyes roved over her from head to toe and back again. "And just what 'work' do you perform?" he asked.

Ariana frowned. "I'm a money-manager, to put it in the simplest terms," she said. "Are you a friend of Ash's?"

Luc snorted. "Not exactly. Other vampires are beneath him. Especially us young ones."

"But you are a friend of Toria's?"

He twirled a yellow pencil between his fingers. "Friend is a strong word among vampires," he said.

Ariana raised one eyebrow.

Luc put the pencil down and crossed his arms over his chest. "Let's just say that keeping you away from Ash serves both our purposes for the moment."

"I can guess what her purpose is," Ariana replied dryly, "but what's yours?"

"Let's just say I owe Ash one."

"Great," Ariana said with a long sigh. "So I'm stuck here while you play games with Ash?"

Luc grew still. "Don't mistake common courtesy for me owing you an explanation," he warned. "In case you haven't put it together yet, you're a prisoner here until I decide otherwise." He made a fleeting motion with his tongue and allowed sharp white fangs to intrude onto his smile. "I can do whatever I like with you," he continued, pushing off the desk and coming to join her on the sofa, "except kill you or turn you." He ran a smooth hand along her cheek. "And even those aren't hard and fast rules."

Ariana drew in a deep breath. For a moment she thought he was going to kiss her. Her disappointment when he rose and went back to leaning on his desk shamed her. What was the matter with her? For years there had been only one man in her life. Now they were coming out of the woodwork.

She looked at the wedding ring on her left hand. She'd taken off her engagement ring some time ago, but the wedding band she'd not yet parted with. The platinum circlet was still there.

"James never mentioned having a wife," Luc said.

Ariana's eyes widened. "You know James?"

"I do." Luc's face was enigmatic.

Ariana wanted to scream. "This is really not funny," she said, her voice going thick with emotion. "Look, you can do whatever you want with me. Kill me, I don't care. But please, I need to know if James is okay."

For a long moment, Luc stood, brow furrowed, saying nothing. "I don't know," he admitted finally.

Ariana gave him a confused look. "But you do know him?"

Luc stared at her intently. "That's right. He's been working with me. He was supposed to meet up with Toria just after sundown a few days ago, but he never made it, and no one's seen him since."

Ariana's eyebrow shot up at the mention of Toria's name.

"It's possible he'll be back later," Luc explained. "Toria's looking for him. It's just odd because there have been a lot of disappearances lately, and James was helping Toria investigate them."

"Why was James helping her?" Ariana asked, unable to hide her distaste.

Luc shrugged. "Toria's not so bad, really. Once you accept what you are, it's hard not to accept what she is."

Ariana thought about that, but the ramifications were too painful, so she resorted to pretending once more to study her surroundings. Finally, her eyes came to rest on Luc. He was casually dressed, but the boots he was wearing were new and probably expensive. "What exactly do you do here?" she asked. "What was James helping you with?"

Luc opened his mouth and closed it again. He turned and flicked the yellow pencil he'd abandoned earlier and watched it spin on his desk. "Beauty products," he answered.

Ariana wasn't sure she'd heard him correctly. "I'm sorry, did you say beauty products?"

"That's right," he said. "So what? Turns out vampire blood, when mixed with a little lotion and rubbed onto your face beats the hell out of anything else on the market for minimizing lines and wrinkles. I'm actually starting to make kind of a killing with the stuff."

He must have seen the disbelief on her face. "Vampires have to make ends meet too, you know," he continued, "especially since his majesty got me kicked out of the Council. It costs a small fortune to live in this city, in case you hadn't noticed."

"What?" Ariana couldn't hide her confusion. Was a vampire really lecturing her about the high cost of housing?

Luc smiled. "Sorry. The Council is basically a social club. Mostly a bunch of self-important wannabes, but it controls a lot of money and administers a sort of vampire welfare system. Every vampire who's anybody is 'registered' and on the dole. That way the Elders can keep track of everyone and keep us all nice and grateful."

"And you want back in?" she queried, not sure she was getting the picture. "What did you do to get kicked out?"

Luc rolled his eyes and threw his arms in the air. "Nothing!" He clapped his arms back down to his sides. "Well, Ash and I got into it a little," he muttered. "Thinks he's better than everybody else." He looked back at Ariana. "Two days later the Council cancelled my registration."

"And that's when you started your... cosmetics business?" she asked.

Luc tossed the pencil into the air and caught it between two fingers. "Basically, yes."

"So, what's a killing?" Ariana asked. She couldn't help it. Bargain hunting was in her blood. If anybody anywhere was making a killing in business, it was her business to know about it.

Luc shot her a puzzled look. "What?"

Too late, Ariana realized her question might have several meanings for a vampire. "I meant, what's your profit-margin like?" she clarified.

Luc shook his head. "I don't know. I just keep a notebook with a record of what comes in and try not to spend it all in one place."

"Well." Ariana couldn't believe she was even thinking it, but really, she had to do something. Unless she gained Luc's trust, she was trapped again just as surely as she had been in Ash's dungeon. And maybe being stuck with Luc wasn't so bad. Wasn't staying away from Ash what she wanted? If Toria, for whatever reason, had instructed this vampire not to harm her, perhaps she could make Toria's plan her own. Plus, he could be the last person to have seen James.

She decided to bite the bullet. "So, maybe while I'm hanging around being a prisoner, I can help you get your finances a little more organized," she offered.

Luc looked at her in confusion, but she just shrugged. "It's what I do," she explained. "Did you have something different in mind?" Much would depend on Luc's intentions.

He didn't take long to make a decision. "You're hired," he said on a laugh after only a moment's hesitation. He stuck out his hand to seal the deal. "I will keep your whereabouts to myself until Toria gets over her little snit, and you can help me turn this into a real money-making operation."

Ariana took his hand, not sure what she was getting herself into. Of course, it didn't matter. She'd lucked into a hiding place in the last place Ash would ever look, and she had a place to start looking for James.

"What happened to your hand?" Luc asked as he spotted the bandage Nancy had fashioned.

Ariana watched as he turned her hand over and started to remove the bandage. "Um, just a workplace accident," she said. The truth was just too complicated right now. "I don't think that's ready to come off," she said.

Luc gave one more pull and the gauze parted to reveal perfect, unmarked skin. "Looks okay to me," he said.

Ariana shook her head. "I don't understand," she murmured. "Those were deep cuts. It's barely been twelve hours since Nancy put the bandage on."

Luc pulled off a last piece of tape and tossed the whole bandage into the small garbage can beside his desk. "Who is Nancy?" he asked.

"She's just Ash's maid," Ariana said.

"I'd say it's a safe bet she's a little more than that," Luc replied.

Again Ariana felt answers floating around in her brain, still just beyond her grasp. She returned to sit on Luc's awful yellow sofa and tried to relax. If she didn't think about it, she knew the answers would eventually come.

"So how old are you?" she asked Luc, purposely changing the subject. "You said you were young."

Luc smiled, and Ariana felt her pulse quicken. *It's a good thing Roger doesn't look like that*, she thought crazily. Poor Roger. He would worry about her. She would have to think of something to tell him.

"I was born in 1911," Luc was saying, "the youngest of nine children. At 21, I turned into this." He spread his arms and looked down at himself.

"What about your family?" Ariana asked. "Did you just let them think you were dead?"

Luc shook his head. "My mother died just before I turned, and my brothers and sisters were all grown, so I just sort of wandered off into the dark and never came back." Luc hesitated. "I did see one of my sisters much later, just before she died," he said. "But really," he shook his head, "you can never go back."

Ariana wanted to know more, but Luc cut off her question before she could form it.

"All I knew up to then, of course," he continued, "was being a farmer—when to plant crops, how to slaughter hogs. Not much use when you can't go out in the daylight anymore."

Ariana could not for the life of her picture him as a farmer. She'd grown up on a farm. This was not what farmers looked like.

Luc smiled and continued on. "One of the first things I did was track down the vampire who fathered me. He was a nobody. Just some young kid really." Luc met her gaze. "I killed him, of course."

Ariana looked up at Luc and yawned completely inappropriately. She couldn't help it. The travel, the stress, and the blow to the head were catching up with her.

Luc frowned. "I'm sorry to bore you with my life story," he said.

"That's not it." Ariana shook her head. "It's just been a really long week. Believe me, I want to hear everything you have to say. *Especially* from the point where you meet James."

Luc took a step toward her, sympathy lending a soft warmth to his blue eyes. Tired and confused as she was, her nostrils flared at his nearness.

"I sometimes forget about humans," he said. "That you need to eat and sleep and all that." He strode around the desk and pushed the button to call the elevator back down. "I don't quite know what to do with you yet, but you can't stay here."

"I thought that's why Toria brought me here," Ariana said, "for you to be my jailor."

"It is, but there are vampires downstairs."

Ariana stood, unable to keep the fear and surprise from showing on her face.

"Don't worry," Luc said. "They're in cages, but it's still not safe to keep you down there. You'll just have to come with me for now."

"And it's safe to be with you?" she asked.

Luc gave no indication that he heard her, and Ariana followed him into the elevator and out into the night.

CHAPTER 43

A brand new Harley Davidson was parked around the side of the building.

"Wow—a black VRod. Nice."

"You know bikes?" Luc was stunned.

"One of my old boyfriends was rebuilding a WWII-era Harley while we were going out," Ariana said on a laugh. "Probably still is. But that got me interested in the company. They have quite a brand."

She ran her hand down the bike's long sleek lines. "I'd love to have a bike like this, but James never approved. He thought they were too dangerous." She shook her head at the thought. *So much irony, so little time.*

"So, why do you think James never mentioned you?" Luc asked.

The question took Ariana aback. "I don't know," she answered after a moment. "Probably he wanted to keep me safe. We were getting divorced, but it wasn't acrimonious."

Luc gave her a puzzled look. "Does that mean you were still gonna be friends?"

"We *were* friends," Ariana insisted, hating herself for sounding shrill. "Actually, that's about all we were," she added honestly. "I have such strong memories of our marriage," she explained, "but they are memories from years, not months ago. I still care about him, though, and he's still my husband," she said. *What does it mean to be married to a vampire anyway?*

Luc laughed out loud. "I think the 'till death do us part' thing lets you off the hook," he said.

Still laughing, he threw one leg over the bike and slid forward on the seat. It wasn't built for two, but there was enough room for Ariana to climb on behind him.

She hiked up the hem of her skirt. She liked it for traveling, but with its long slits, it wasn't really motorcycle attire. She tucked the soft cotton around her legs as best she could and wrapped her arms around Luc's lean torso.

The close contact sent a jolt of desire through her that she wasn't prepared for. For a moment, Luc, too, seemed to freeze; then he gunned the engine, sending the bike hurtling downtown at breakneck speed. Ariana could do little more than hang on as the city flew by on either side of her. Before she knew it, they were pulling into a dark garage under a nondescript apartment building.

Luc dropped the kick stand, and Ariana removed her arms from his waist and climbed gingerly off the big machine.

"Quite a ride," she commented, still trying to catch her breath. She watched with far too much interest as his long, jean-clad leg swung over the end of the bike. Good lord, what was the matter with her?

Luc laughed, rewarding her with another of his devastating smiles. Her insides did a flip-flop, and she forced her eyes to look somewhere else. Anywhere else.

"I'm glad you like it," he said.

Ariana returned her attention to his face, noticing that his mega-watt smile had taken on a more predatory glint. He cocked his head to one side, and a few strands of soft, white-gold hair fell across his forehead.

Ariana felt her insides start to melt and realized that, for all his boyish charm, this man knew the effect he had on women. She looked longingly at his bright eyes and sculpted cheekbones. *It isn't right for a man to be that beautiful,* she thought, a little annoyed. But then, on a woman those eyes would be just pretty. On him, they were stunning. It didn't help that he was now looking at her like he wanted to lick her all over. Ariana felt her skin flush at the thought.

"We should get upstairs," he said softly, his voice washing over her from the darkness like an ancient incantation.

Ariana's heart quickened, and she took a step toward him even though, for the life of her, she couldn't have explained why. All she knew was that suddenly his breathtaking smile made everything else seem dark. The weight of her empty life, haunted by the ghost of her lost child and failed marriage, lifted as he looked at her. The dark secrets of her past receded, and she allowed herself to move one step closer to his beautiful form. *God help me,* she thought. She knew it was wrong, knew it was dangerous, but she couldn't help it. She needed to stand in the light.

CHAPTER 44

Luc knew he shouldn't. He knew he should turn and go, or scare her off, but he did neither. The little bit of blood in his body had left his brain and was rushing to places he'd long forgotten. Indeed, he'd been a vampire for so long, he barely remembered what human attraction was like. But as he looked at Ariana, only one thought crossed his mind. He wanted to make love to her.

The absence of bloodlust had him a little at a loss. She drew closer to him, and again he breathed in her scent. Taking her hand, he took two long steps back into the darkness, pulling her with him.

He turned and pushed her gently against the concrete wall of the garage. A few overhead lights dotted garage's center lane, but no light reached them where they now stood.

Luc looked down at her and caressed her face, the unnatural fire of his blue eyes pouring into the bottomless pools of Ariana's darker ones. Luc had never seen eyes as black as hers. He could read the pain in them, the heartache, the hardness. This was a complicated lady, he thought. She turned her face into his palm and closed her eyes.

A complicated lady in need of solace. A little of his guilt dissipated, and he dropped his lips to hers. The first soft touch of skin to skin astonished him. Luc momentarily pulled back, surprised by the force of it. Ariana, too, sucked in her breath.

Luc lowered his lips to hers once more and when she returned his kiss, he wanted to do everything and nothing. He wanted it all and never wanted it to end.

They stood entwined kissing for a long time. Fire like he'd never felt rushed through Luc. His insides screamed to life, but he didn't push. He just ravaged her mouth over and over again until finally, he felt her hands reach underneath his shirt to touch his bare skin. He took his cue from her and moved to explore more of her with his hungry mouth.

He pulled aside the material of her shirt. His touch was rougher than he would have liked, but he couldn't help it. He slid his hand inside her bra, his smooth palm grazing her skin. The weight of her breast filled his hand, and he bent his head to it. Her nipple was like a ripe raspberry against his tongue. He took more of her into his mouth, eager to know all her flavors.

***

Ariana arched back, giving herself over to the erotic delirium that seemed to have taken hold of her the moment she laid eyes on this man. She ran one hand through his hair and down across his shoulders. She could feel the heat of him through his shirt.

Her instinct was to close her eyes against the torrent of desire threatening to engulf her. Instead, she kept them open, watching Luc's gorgeous mouth as it teased and suckled her breast.

Finally, he raised his head and brought his lips almost to hers. "We should go somewhere else," he whispered.

His voice seemed strained, and his eyes burned brighter than should have been possible. Ariana could almost see their heat. Even in the dark, the air around them shimmered like a highway in the hot sun. She shook her head side to side and pulled his mouth back down to hers.

As they plundered each other's mouths once more, Luc pushed her hips back against the wall and pressed fully against her. The feel of his taut erection, the crush of his jeans against the thin fabric of her skirt made her mouth go dry. She moaned into him.

Without breaking the kiss, Luc sent his hand underneath her skirt and up along her naked thigh. His fingers stroked her through slick lace. Ariana opened her legs wider, and her skirt rode up her hips.

***

Luc needed no further encouragement. This moment had been inevitable since he'd first caught her scent. He had a twinge of guilt about not telling her what she was, but he put it out of his mind. They both needed this. In more ways than one.

He stripped her of her panties in short order and moved between her legs. One arm went all the way around her waist. He tore his eyes away from hers to bend his head, and his mouth again engulfed her nipple.

⚜

Once more, the heat of him surprised her. Burned her. Ariana clung to his hard shoulders. Luc brought his mouth back to hers, and Ariana welcomed him greedily. His kisses were like martinis, she thought dazedly. Three of them and the room was spinning.

Luc's hands roamed over her flesh, spreading fire wherever they went. She welcomed the heat. For the moment, it seemed to sear away her pain. Luc unfastened his jeans and let them slide slightly down his hips. Holding her hips with both hands, he lifted her effortlessly several inches off the ground. Ariana put a hand against the brick wall behind her to steady herself. With her other hand, she gripped his shoulder and urged him forward.

Luc entered her so slowly, Ariana thought she would faint. Just when she was about to beg for mercy, he pulled her slightly down so her weight rested on his pelvic bone and he was completely sheathed inside her. Luc buried his head against her neck and, with a groan, began to rock his hips back and forth.

Ariana gave a strangled cry. She was weightless, and yet her weight was being borne back and forth against him in a salty tango that threatened her sanity. She wrapped her legs around him as he moved under her more frantically. She arched her head back, giving herself over, but Luc drew her forward for another bruising kiss. Within seconds, the urgent rhythm of his tongue and hips had her flexing around him in a paroxysm of pleasure. She heard herself cry out.

As the waves receded, she was dimly aware of Luc murmuring something in her ear. She felt him stiffen, felt his muscles go rock hard, and then a warm gushing deep within her.

They both remained still and quiet as their breathing returned to normal. Luc shifted her weight and moved to put some distance between them. Ariana pretended a calm she didn't feel as she straightened her clothes.

Luc pulled up his jeans and turned to flash her a wicked grin. "Come on," he said, taking her hand. "Now, let's go upstairs."

CHAPTER 45

Ariana awoke the next afternoon wondering how the little bed had made it through the last twelve hours. *Hell,* she thought, she didn't even know how *she'd* made it through the last twelve hours. Vampire stamina was not something to be taken lightly.

She looked over at Luc. His lips were parted in a soft smile. Even in his sleep, it was disarming. Once he opened his eyes, it would be devastating. Fearing for her health if that happened, she threw her legs over the side of the bed and put her bare feet down onto the carpeted floor.

The shower was only across the hall, but to her sore body, it seemed like miles. When the hot spray finally hit her, she closed her eyes and turned her mind to the problem of James. His image swam for a long moment before her eyes, and a wave of guilt threatened to overcome her.

"Don't do that," Luc said, as the shower curtain opened, and he stepped in behind her.

Ariana didn't turn around, but in a moment she felt soapy hands on her shoulders. They kneaded her sore muscles, and she began to relax.

"I believe James is a good man," Luc said softly, "but you don't owe him your life. He can no longer be with you, and even when he could have been, you two were getting divorced."

Ariana looked down at the water swirling into the silver drain. "I know," she replied.

"Then don't beat yourself up about taking comfort from me," he said. "And don't do anything foolish to try to find him. Let me and Toria handle that."

Luc's hands left her shoulders and moved to her hair, gently shampooing her long locks. He turned her around to rinse and planted a soft kiss on her forehead.

"I forgot to say thank you," he said, his incredible smile making a welcome return. "I don't guess it's possible to make up for a hundred years in one day, but it'll be a long time before I feel cheated again."

Ariana looked up into his shocking blue eyes and wondered if time had given him the ability to know the right thing to say or whether it just came naturally.

Luc laughed as his strong hands turned her around to slather conditioner into her hair. Then he grabbed the soap and began to thoroughly wash her whole body. It was in many ways even more intimate than the acts of the night before.

Again he rinsed her hair and body. He switched places with her, turned the shower head, and wrapped her in a towel.

"Go get dressed," he ordered gently. "We have things to do today."

Ariana stepped onto the bath mat, a little addled by the sudden gentlemanliness. She toweled off, thinking briefly that if she didn't get some new clothes soon, she could just stop showering altogether.

Luc laughed from the shower. "Sorry about that. I probably have some tee shirts in the closet somewhere. You can see if anything fits."

Ariana went into the next room and perused her choices. Most of the shirts looked way too big. She finally found a few tee shirts at the back of a shelf. Van Halen, no less. She smiled. She had actually liked them back in their day.

She turned to the dresser in hope of finding a pair of jeans. She and Luc actually weren't far apart in size, except that he was taller. She found the shortest pair of jeans she could and rolled up the cuffs. Staring down at herself, she gave a heavy sigh. She looked like a reject from the cast of *Grease*.

⁂

In the shower, Luc put his forehead against the tile. He would forever be a wretch for what he'd done, but he couldn't tame the grin that came to his face. He'd never known passion before, and it was a wondrous sensation, totally distinct from the bloodlust that normally drove him.

Bloodlust was a hunger. It could only be sated by another, but the price for satisfaction was high. The only creature vampires satiated were themselves.

Human passion celebrated the existence and beauty of another person. And now, the fact that the uncontrollable sexual lust between them was gone told him he was going to be a father.

A funny feeling in his chest reminded him of something that might have been happiness. Ignoring the possibility that Ariana would never forgive him or that Ash might kill him, Luc reached for the faucet.

⚜

Ariana heard Luc turn the water off, so she scurried into the living room. She gave the room a quick once over, hating to admit that she'd not even noticed the place last night. Luckily, there was nothing macabre. Just a decent sized, kind of shabby apartment. The furniture looked like it had been purchased from the same store where he'd purchased his office furnishings and was probably second-hand.

The drapes, however, were stunning. Very heavy, embroidered, probably handmade, they hung over the single window in the tiny living room. When Luc joined her, he was back in his regular attire, even down to the boots. He looked at her outfit, smiled, but wisely didn't say anything.

Ariana stared at him for a long moment, then walked over and cradled his face in her hand, gently forcing him to look down at her so she could get a better look. "You have very unusual eyes," she said finally.

"So I've been told," he said with a smirk.

Ariana couldn't help laughing. "I bet," she said, "but that wasn't what I was getting at. I've seen those eyes before."

She dropped her hand and moved away. "3,000 years before, to be precise, they were the eyes of my new baby daughter."

⚜

Luc gave himself a shake. He'd momentarily forgotten about her being Delilah.

Ariana settled into the couch and began to study him anew. "What can you tell me about your family, Luc? Your human family."

Luc shrugged and leaned against the tiny computer desk. "There's not much more than I've already told you. The blue eyes are from my mother, though they got more intense once I became a vampire."

Ariana bit her bottom lip and for a moment said nothing, just continued her close scrutiny of him.

"You said 'fathered' yesterday," she noted finally, "when you were talking about the vampire that made you."

No place to hide, Luc thought. "That's right," he answered, picking up an ink pen from the desk and beginning to toy with it. "A vampire did father me. I wasn't turned in the usual fashion. A vampire mated with my human mother, and I was the improbable result."

Ariana exhaled loudly, but didn't speak, waiting for him to continue.

"It's not totally unheard of," he explained. "Supposedly there have been similar births on occasion, off and on throughout history."

Ariana shook her head. "Improbable indeed," she said. "Even more improbable, I think you're probably my great-great-great—" she stretched her hands wide—"grandson."

Luc's jaw dropped. "You mean from Delilah?"

Ariana nodded. "And Samson."

That floated around between them until Luc grinned his trade-mark grin. "I can't wait to call him Grandpa," he announced.

Ariana's smile quickly evaporated. "You can't say anything," she insisted. "Don't even think it. Not yet. He doesn't know, and I don't want him finding out from you."

Luc put up his hands at the insistence in her voice. "Okay, I won't say anything." *As long as I'm not provoked,* he added silently.

"Are you hungry?" he asked, getting up and heading for the kitchen. He opened and closed a few cabinets and peered into the fridge. "I've got beer," he announced.

"Beer for breakfast—great," Ariana muttered. "Why would a vampire drink beer?"

Luc looked over at her and shrugged. "Same reason as anybody else, I guess. It's not easy for us to get drunk, but I always say if you can't get drunk, you're just not trying."

Ariana shook her head and moved over to the tiny desk. She powered on the computer, watching its screen go from black to blue. "What's your logon?" she asked when it prompted her for a password.

Luc shrugged. "I don't know. Never used it. James set it up. He was getting me on the Internet."

❧

Ariana leaned forward and, on a hunch, typed in James' ID and password. James might be a creature of darkness now, but she'd wager he was still a creature of habit. He had used the same password for everything since before she met him.

"Do you know how?" she asked, turning to look at Luc over her shoulder. "How James came to be turned, I mean?"

"Not by me," Luc said hurriedly. "You have your precious Ash to thank for that."

"Ash." Why was she not surprised?

Luc came around the counter. "Yeah, at least that's what James said, but I never got the details."

A moment passed, and the desktop became visible on the screen. Ariana started at the top and clicked methodically through the folder tree. James had partitioned the hard drive, devoting part of it to Luc's business. That part held lists of customers, lists of vampire "donors," and price information for web hosting companies.

Ariana backed out and went into the other partition. "Here we go," she said, sliding into the red plastic chair in front of the machine.

Luc came around to stand behind her. He put a hand on her shoulder and leaned down. "What did you find?"

Ariana briefly wondered how their passion from last night seemed to have disappeared into thin air. "I don't know," she replied, vowing not to look a gift horse in the mouth.

She opened a file called "cpw." It was a list of strange words.

"Hey," Luc pointed at the screen. "Those on the left are vampires." He seemed very pleased with himself.

Ariana studied the other side of the list. "These look like passwords," she noted after a moment. She turned to look at Luc over her shoulder. "Passwords to what?"

Luc shrugged. "How would I know?"

"You've been around for a hundred years, right?" Ariana couldn't hide her impatience. "You know some of these" —she almost called them people— "vampires." She pointed to the screen. "What do they have in common?"

Luc bent and studied the first page of the list. "Well," he said finally, "they're all fairly active Council members, I think. Or they were. Some of them have disappeared."

"Disappeared?" Ariana asked. "Like James?"

"That's right. It's been happening periodically for some months now."

Ariana pursed her lips. "Does the Council have a network?" she asked, turning again to look over her shoulder at Luc.

"There is some sort of computer system," he confirmed. "All the members get passwords."

"All right," Ariana said. "I need to find out what James was up to, and that's going to take some time. Why don't you go—be a vampire for a while—and I'll fill you in on my progress when you get back?"

⚜

It was phrased as a question, but Luc noted her tone was more suggestive of an order. He shrugged. He needed to finish up at the warehouse anyway. Grabbing the leather jacket hanging on the door handle of his front closet, he got up, but hesitated to leave. "You'll be here when I get back?" he asked.

"I'm not going anywhere," Ariana replied, already immersed in the task she'd set herself.

CHAPTER 46

L uc left the apartment and headed back to the warehouse. The kiddies down below needed to be fed, and so did he.

Tonight it was synthetic blood all around. James had scored a case of the stuff from Council House last week, and Luc now tore into the unopened box.

He carried half a dozen bags over to the cutting table and poured their contents into the drain along with the required sedative and set the timer to release the cage doors at midnight.

This group hadn't been here long, but with everything else that was going on, Luc suddenly didn't want to also be responsible for their care and feeding.

If he was putting his business on hiatus, though, he needed to let a few others know. He left the warehouse, started his bike, and made the familiar run down to a club a few blocks off Times Square.

The aptly named establishment, Vamp, was a multi-level dance club on the above ground floors. The underground floors were where Aleksander Solotnik ran his business. Solotnik had been a Russian mafia hit man until he'd faked his death back in the 1970s and came to the U.S.

Luc didn't know the extent of Solotnik's business interests, but for the vampires who found Council House a bit too upper crust, he provided equivalent entertainments. He also coordinated the supply of synthetic blood to this particular segment of the vampire populace.

Since getting kicked out of Council House, Luc had found out about Solotnik's underground and occasionally availed himself of some of the services. Cash only, of course. Unlike the Council, Solotnik wasn't giving anything away for free, but he didn't require registration either. Luc found it a most convenient arrangement.

Not to mention, now that he had cash, he had some standing among the lower orders. He'd made fast friends with the vampire bouncers at the upstairs club. They knew about his little operation and, for a fee, informed him about likely candidates. Not too old, not too strong, not too well-connected.

They even occasionally delivered.

The pounding bass assaulted Luc when he was still half a block away. He parked his bike around back between two cars.

The line started in front of the next building. Luc kept walking until he saw the two massive vampires standing guard at the entrance. Not your typical vampires, Luc could only assume Aleksander had made them especially for this purpose.

"Hey, Luc," the slightly smaller one called out to him. "Long time no see, man."

Luc extended his hand. "Hey, Willie," he greeted him. Willie had worked construction in the city before getting this particular gig. He was pleasant enough and had no conscience whatsoever. Really, perfect for the job. And for Luc. "What can I say, Willie?" he replied. "The warehouse has been keeping me busy."

Willie nodded approvingly. "So we should be expecting a raise soon? An increase in our investment, so to speak?"

The other bouncer had now turned his attention to them.

"Derek," Luc greeted, looking him over. Derek was a giant of a man. Luc didn't know where Aleksander had found him. "You're looking well," he joked.

Derek growled.

"Okay, then," Luc said, taking a step back. A group of giggling twenty-somethings slid past him as Derek motioned for them to enter the club. One of them grabbed Luc's hand.

"Hey, come with us," ruby lips coaxed. "We can get you in."

Smooth skin under a shimmering tank top. Luc pulled her close, away from her gaggle of friends. "I think I might like that," he said, flashing her a smile.

Her lips parted, and she smiled back at him, pulling him toward the door.

Derek's arm flew out, cutting across Luc's path. "He'll have to join you later, miss," Derek said.

Luc let go of the girl's hand.

"He's right, sweetheart," Luc said. "Business before pleasure. You go on in."

A pretty pout and she was gone, pushed along by the impatient throng still clamoring for their turn at the door.

"Have you taken anyone recently without us telling you it was okay?" Derek asked.

"No," Luc lied. "Why do you ask?"

Derek's eyes narrowed. "One of Mr. Solotnik's daughters is missing. No one has seen her for a couple of weeks."

Oh shit.

"If you have her..."

"I don't," Luc interrupted, shaking his head vigorously.

"Then keep an eye out for her, will you?" Willie asked, putting an end to the interrogation.

"Absolutely." Luc nodded. "What's she look like?"

Maybe he didn't really have her at all.

"Straight dark hair, tall, thin..." Willie's voice trailed off, and Luc tried to keep his expression blank.

"I'll let you know if I hear anything," Luc promised, realizing this probably wasn't the best time to tell them he wouldn't be needing their services for a while.

"So what's going on tonight?" he asked, changing the subject. "Is it worth 20 bucks to follow my little tidbit in or should I just pick one who is already on her way out?"

Willie grinned. "Well, the tournaments are starting up," he said, "but I'd save your money. The good matches don't start until tomorrow." Willie glanced at his still scowling friend. "I'm trying to talk Derek here into entering."

"What kind of tournament?" Luc asked, though, if Derek was a potential contestant, he could well enough guess.

"Combat," Willie whispered. "Good, old fashioned, full fanged battle. Aleksander's had a giant ring built on the bottom floor. Should be a hell of a show, right Derek?"

"I'm not entering, Willie. That's not my job," Derek said, stone-faced.

"Come on, man," Willie entreated. "Tell him, Luc. No one would have a chance against him. Not even the new guy."

"New guy?" Luc asked.

Willie shook his head. "You don't want this one, Luc, trust me. Too old. None of us really even knows what he's doing here, but he's been kicking ass in the ring, so Aleksander's letting him stay."

Oh well. "Maybe I'll come by tomorrow then," Luc said, "and take a look for myself."

He spied another bevy of beauties coming out of the side exit door.

"You two have a nice night," Luc called out, already turning toward the departing flesh. One of them had caught his eye.

He looked back briefly before he rounded the corner.

Derek was still scowling.

Luc picked up his pace and crossed the street. He retrieved his bike from its spot, spun it around, and headed back the way he had come.

At the group of girls, he slowed the bike and rested his booted foot on the pavement. The black-dyed snakeskin shone under the street lights as the girls turned to check him out.

He knew which one he wanted, so he let his blue gaze bore into her. "Need a ride?" he asked, wondering briefly why women never rejected that line.

The girl smiled nervously, looking at her friends. "Sure," she said finally, coming over to him. "We were going to another club downtown. You can drop me there."

Luc smiled. "Sure thing, sweetheart. I'm headed that way myself." Luc helped the girl onto the bike in front of him. Her skirt was impossibly short. "Hang on," he whispered, putting his hands over hers on the handle bars.

He gunned the engine, drowning out the titters and warnings from her friends.

They needn't have worried. Luc delivered her to the club as promised, just a few pints lighter than she was before. The girl stared dazedly up at him as he helped her off the bike.

"You aren't coming in?" she asked, looking hurt.

Luc shook his head. "Not this time, sweetheart." He spied her friends getting out of a cab not far up the street. "Look, your friends are already here."

The girl turned, waved to her friends, and started up the sidewalk toward them as fast as her ridiculously high heels would carry her.

Spirits considerably lifted, Luc turned the bike around and headed for home.

CHAPTER 47

*B*eing a vampire is really starting to suck, James thought, too scared even to notice his own pun. When Memnon had dropped him off at a downtown club, he'd immediately been given an audience with Aleksander, the apparent patriarch of the place. Aleksander wasn't a particularly impressive vampire, not very old or strong or beautiful. Quite the contrary, in fact; one side of his face was hideously scarred, as if at some point he'd been too close to a serious explosion.

Aleksander told him how precious his blood was, because he'd been made by the oldest known vampire. He took a small knife to his own wrist and invited a young female vampire to drink from him.

Suitably weakened, he motioned for the vampire who'd been holding James to bring him forward. Derek, with the chest as wide as an oil drum, did as he was told, and Aleksander refilled his drained body with James' blood. As soon as he could speak, Aleksander licked his lips and told Derek to put James to work.

After that, Aleksander had taken no notice of him, nor had anyone else except Derek, his seemingly self-appointed guardian, and James was relegated to mopping the dance floor night after night. He had looked for a means of escape, but the club was too well guarded.

And now James found himself bare-chested in a boxing ring, staring down a tattoo-covered freak. *At least he isn't huge,* James thought. And he didn't seem to be old.

A voice from behind James announced his name and the name of his opponent, Ringo, to the smattering of vampires who stood, mostly disinterested, around the room. A few cheers went up for Ringo, and he stepped into the middle of the ring, making a show of trying to egg James on. He hopped about for a few minutes, looking to James rather foolish.

"Out of your corner, James," Willie's voice teased from behind the microphone. "We've only got until sun-up."

Maybe not, James thought, moving slightly forward, but so far he'd managed to get his ass kicked by almost every vampire he'd met.

He saw a flash as the other vampire took a swing at him, the silver rings on his fingers reflecting the arena's dangling overhead lights. James ducked and aimed a blow of his own at the guy's midsection.

His fist landed in soft flesh, sending the boy flying backward into the stone post that demarcated one of the corners of the ring.

James wasn't sure which of them was more surprised.

The other vampire got unsteadily to his feet and dusted off his black tee shirt.

"Lucky shot," he mumbled, beginning another advance.

James didn't wait for him this time. He took two quick steps forward and landed several blows on Ringo's head and chest.

Ringo staggered again, but didn't fall. He raised his head and showed his fangs in a spit-drenched snarl. This time his fist went plowing into the side of James' face.

James took the punch and fell backwards, but got to his feet quickly enough to block the next blow and waited for the moment when his opponent would let his guard down.

It didn't take long. They were amateurs after all, but James was far stronger. He supposed he had Ash's blood to thank for that.

He landed two more solid blows to Ringo's head, knocking him unconscious long enough for Willie to declare James the winner.

There wasn't exactly an uproar from the crowd, but James stood there smiling nonetheless. He'd never won a fight before, vampire or otherwise, and was more than a little pleased with himself.

"Nice moves, hot shot," Willie said, covering the mic. "You just won yourself a place in tomorrow's death match."

James felt the blood drain from his face. No doubt about it, being a vampire was definitely starting to suck.

CHAPTER 48

Ash tightened his grip on the cell phone. "I'll kill him," he said, turning to pace the floor of his study. "And you," he exclaimed, piercing the air in front of him as if Toria could see him through the receiver. "What were you thinking?"

He'd caught Ariana's scent the moment he'd opened his front door. Too strong to have been weeks old, he'd known right away that she'd come here. But then he'd detected Toria's scent too, so he'd called her to get an explanation, never guessing that she would have given Ariana to another vampire.

"Why would you do such a thing?" he asked her now, genuinely puzzled. "How could you? When you know how long I've searched for her?"

"What do you care?" Toria said finally. "The Ash I knew swore to kill that woman in the most painful way possible. He wanted revenge on her, not to trail after her like a lovesick fool."

Ash stopped pacing. "Plans change, Toria," he barked, clenching his free hand at his side. "People change."

She scoffed. "We're not people, Ash. We're killers, and you were supposed to kill her."

He could picture her on the other end, eyes narrowed, hand on her hip. But he still couldn't figure out why she'd taken Ariana from him. "Why, Toria?" he asked.

"Because you don't belong with her!" she shouted, forcing him to jerk the phone away from his ear. "You swore to kill her, and now you're concerned that her mattress might not be soft enough." She lowered her voice slightly, and he replaced the ear piece. "That woman has bewitched you a second time, Ash. I don't know how, but you have to snap out of it."

"This is not a goddamn joke, Toria," he said. "If Lucas harms her..."

"Don't worry," she interrupted. "I told him not to kill her—or turn her."

Ash's eyes grew hard. "That's it?" he asked, grinding his teeth. He took an unneeded breath and tried to steady his voice. "I need you to tell me where she is."

For a long moment she said nothing, and he began to think she would acquiesce. "All those years we were together," Toria began finally, as if the words were being dragged from her, "you never stopped loving her, did you?"

It was the last thing he'd expected her to say, and he stared openmouthed at the phone for several seconds, seeing for the first time all the way to the rotten core of Toria's actions. Some of his anger dissipated. She had been a friend to him, and it wasn't entirely her fault. "Toria," he began.

"Don't," she said, cutting him off. "Don't you dare pity me. The only thing sadder than me carrying a torch for you all these years is you carrying one for her."

"Toria," Ash tried again.

"She doesn't love you, you know."

Before Ash could form a response, dead air told him that Toria thought their conversation was over. Ash flipped his phone shut and headed for the door. He wasn't nearly through with her.

CHAPTER 49

Luc flipped the light switch, relieving the room of the solitary blue glow from Ariana's computer screen. "Honey, I'm home," Luc said lightly.

Ariana chuckled in spite of herself. "How was work?" she asked, playing along.

"Bloody," Luc replied.

Ariana looked up, unable to hide her disgust. "Do I even want to know?"

"Probably not." Luc set two bags down on the kitchen counter. "I brought dinner," he said.

"Don't you want to wash up?"

Luc got a beer out of the fridge and took a long gulp. "Sure." He started unbuttoning his shirt on the way to the shower.

When he returned, he was wearing a pair of old jeans and a gray shirt that looked like he'd stolen it from a plumber. He went back into the kitchen and picked up his beer.

Ariana got up and came closer. The smell of French fries made her stomach rumble. "McDonalds," she said with glee. "I love McDonalds."

"Yeah?" Luc asked. "Me, too. I didn't figure you'd go for it, though. It's not very high brow."

"Which one's mine?" she said, looking at the bags. "Wait a minute." She looked up at him quizzically. "Since when do vampires eat burgers?"

"They don't," Luc said with a laugh. "It's just a fluke. I drank from a kid once in the fifties who was carrying a bag of this stuff." He grabbed a bag from the counter and headed to the couch. "I took a bite out of curiosity and have been hooked ever since."

Luc sat down and plopped his bag on the floor between his feet. He fished around for the burger, unwrapped it halfway from the paper, and took a huge bite. Ariana watched as his eyes closed and he gave a satisfied groan.

Looking away, she scooted up onto one of the chairs at the kitchen counter and shifted her attention to her dinner. At least he'd brought her a soda.

"So what have you found out?" Luc said after two more tremendous bites.

Ariana swallowed a French fry. "Quite a bit, actually," she said. "Looks like there's a particular vampire James was focused on. Does the name Keller mean anything to you?"

Luc nodded. "Yeah, he's a prick," he said, his mouth once more full of hamburger. "Thinks he's some kind of mystic. He took one look at me the day I showed up at Council House and started yammering on about the end of time."

"What?" Ariana halted her hamburger halfway to her mouth.

"You know," Luc said, looking up at her, "frogs, locusts, the four horsemen. I'm telling you, he's off his rocker. And his little tent revival didn't help my social standing any." Luc turned his attention back to his burger. "Nothing like being a sign of the apocalypse to put a damper on your social life," he muttered.

Ariana didn't really care about Luc's social life. "And you don't know why James was looking into him?" she asked.

"I didn't even know James was looking into him," Luc said.

"Well, I think I might." Ariana took her Coke over to the computer and resumed the same pose she'd held for the last few hours.

She clicked open the file and hit print. "This list of passwords that we found came from Keller's computer. It looks like James found a way to hack into the account management functions of the Council's network. The accounts of many of the missing had been accessed by the same user—Keller." She looked up to make sure Luc was following. "James got Keller's password, and when he accessed Keller's account, he found this file and downloaded it to here."

Ariana grabbed the pages from the printer and turned to face Luc. "I think this is a hit list, and this Keller person is behind it somehow," she said.

Luc took the pages from her hand.

"Look at the last page," Ariana instructed.

Luc flipped back and Ariana saw the surprise she'd expected. "What does this mean?" he asked. "Why am I on this list?"

Ariana shook her head. "I don't know. Maybe someone intended to get you, but grabbed James by mistake?"

Luc thought it over. "Maybe," he said, "but Keller knows us. If you're right, then he's not doing the actual taking, which means someone else is involved."

Ariana looked at him. "I think I've done all I can here. Can you talk to this Keller person? It seems like he may have answers to a lot of our questions, including what's happened to James."

"My thoughts exactly," Luc replied, already heading for the door.

CHAPTER 50

L uc parked his bike around the corner from Council House and was standing on the sidewalk contemplating his next move when a black sedan pulled past him and slowed to a stop.

When Ash Samson stepped out of the car, Luc felt his jaw drop. He put up his hands, and began moving in the other direction. "I... I didn't hurt her," he stammered.

Ash advanced slowly toward him, the light breeze fanning his dark gray overcoat and making him look for once like the powerful vampire he was. Luc retreated another step.

"I'm glad to see you, Lucas," Ash responded. "This will save me an unpleasant confrontation with Toria—for the time being." He took another step. "Now, tell me where Ariana is and what you are doing here."

Luc's brow furrowed. "Ariana's at my apartment, safe and sound." He tried a tentative smile. "Like I said, I didn't hurt her."

Ash's eyes narrowed. "Your apartment? You've been keeping her prisoner in your apartment?"

"Umm, no, not exactly." Luc hesitated, searching for the kernel of truth that would save his skin. "Once I figured out who she was and she figured out that I knew James, we decided to work together to figure out what had happened to him. That's the reason I'm here. Ariana came up with a lead."

"Lead? What are you talking about?" Ash demanded. "What's happened to James?" He took a half step forward then froze. "Wait," he said. Luc saw his face fall. "Ariana knows about James?"

Luc nodded. "I'm not sure how she found out, but, yeah, she knows you turned him into a vampire, and now he's missing."

"Shit," Ash exclaimed, glaring. Luc thought he wanted to say more, but held back. Instead he ran a hand through his hair and turned to look up at the dark mansion rising behind the stone wall next to which they stood. "Well, maybe Keller will be able to shed some light on that, too," he said finally. He turned and started toward the mansion.

"You're here to see Keller?" Luc called out. "Wait," he said, running to catch up, "so am I."

Ash turned back to him. "Why?"

"James found some stuff on Keller's computer—passwords, addresses—that belonged to a lot of the ones who've gone missing."

"I... really?" Ash asked, his brow furrowing noticeably. "And now James has disappeared, too?"

"Yeah," Luc said. "He was on his way to tell Toria, but never showed."

Ash frowned again, and Luc held his breath.

"Come on, then," Ash said.

Luc felt relief wash over him as he fell in step.

The Council House mansion was set back from the street, its ornate barriers enough to deter the idly curious. Ordinarily, the place was quiet, but tonight it was ablaze with light.

"It's First Feast Day," Ash said as they approached.

Luc looked at him questioningly.

"You know, vampire Thanksgiving."

"The Donner Party?" Luc had been told of it shortly after his arrival at Council House. Even then, the anticipation had begun among the residents. Luc's eyes widened at the prospect of seeing it firsthand.

Ash's mouth twisted in disgust. "Is that what they're calling it now?" He looked sternly at Luc. "We are here for one reason. If you go off feeding, I won't be responsible for you."

Both Luc's pale brows shot up. "What the hell makes you think I need you to be responsible for me?"

Ash walked faster. "I don't know why I'm even letting you come along," he said. "Don't get in the way."

"Right," Luc said, his drawl dragging the one-syllable word out into three. "You know," he called out, "you may think I'm not as good as you, but your precious Delilah seemed to like my warm body just fine."

Ash spun around. "What?" His hand wrapped around Luc's throat, lifting him off the ground. "Don't you even think of it, you—"

Luc couldn't seem to stop himself. "I don't have to think of it," he squeaked out. "I just have to remember it."

To Luc's surprise, Ash's fury faltered.

"It's not possible," he declared.

Luc raised one eyebrow at him. "Anything's possible, old man. Care for a few pointers?"

"But how?" Ash's other hand clenched into a fist at his side.

"Turn me loose," Luc demanded.

Ash took a step back and reluctantly let go of Luc's throat.

Luc swallowed and moved his jaw from side to side to get the feeling back. Once he did, he looked back up at Ash and took pity on his confusion. "Think about it, man," he said. "What kind of woman arouses real lust instead of bloodlust in vampires? You must have felt it yourself at some point. Or are you too old even for that?"

Comprehension dawned in Ash's eyes. "Ariana is a breeder?" he asked, seeming to test the words.

"That's right," Luc confirmed.

"And you and she...?"

Luc couldn't stop a huge, stupid grin. "Oh, yeah," he said.

Ash turned and resumed his march toward the door.

"That's it?" Luc queried.

"It changes nothing," Ash responded, his face a grim mask. "Come on," he intoned. "We have to finish our business here before sunrise."

Luc debated going for another dig, but the fun seemed to have gone out of it. "So, do you have a plan," he asked, changing the subject, "or are we just going to walk in the front door?"

"Yes," Ash answered.

"Yes?" Luc echoed. "Yes, what?"

Ash turned through the large pair of stone pillars and began striding across the courtyard. Crested double oak doors appeared up ahead.

"Front door it is," Luc said to no one in particular as he fell in step behind Ash. "I'm not sure that's the best..." He stopped talking because Ash was already opening one of the heavy doors.

Luc came to stand behind him and peered over his shoulder. The place was about as he remembered, except tonight it was lit completely by candles.

Lining the floor on each side of the marble foyer, they guided entrants deeper into the mansion toward the evening's promised delights. Gilded mirrors at the end of the passage reflected the light, making the room seem bigger than Luc remembered. A row of Corinthian columns adorned each wall, and between each of those, a young woman, each more beautiful than the last, hung mounted on a rack.

Six on each side, the racks were alternately gold or silver. At the top of each, two spikes poked through the wrists of the victim to hold her in place. The rest of the rack was adjusted so the girl could reach the footrest or a little seat. They weren't supposed to exert themselves. These beauties had been the first course, and all of them now hovered near death.

Ash ignored them, making for the end of the hall. Luc stayed just a step behind. Their scent affected him, made him want to feed properly, with abandon.

"Don't even think about it," Ash growled.

"What's the difference?" Luc asked. "It's not like they're going to get better and walk out of here." He kept walking anyway.

The entryway opened onto a larger room. Here some vampires still lingered. The young men always lasted longer.

A few young vampires were clamped onto one particularly hardy fellow in the corner. One sucked from his wrist, one from his neck and a third from the large vein in his inner thigh. He couldn't have much blood left. Still, his eyes implored Luc and Ash for help.

They kept walking, crossing the room and rounding a corner into a long hallway. Luc knew the sets of double doors along the opposite wall all led into the main dining room.

In there, the residents of Council House and all the vampires who were anybody would be gathered at long tables in front of the finest silver and china, all quite civilized. Then a selection of bloody delicacies would issue forth.

The main course was the same every year. A scouting party would have gone out a few nights ago to find several dozen diabetic humans. A cell on one of the floors below the house held them until tonight, when the designated preparer drained them of their already sweet blood and mixed it with wine, warm honey, and fragrant or narcotic herbs.

Luc could hear the metallic scrape of flatware on china. That explained why the halls were empty. The feast had already begun.

He wondered if Keller was in there, but considered it doubtful. Resisting the sultry, metallic scent would provide him a rare opportunity for self-denial.

Ash continued down the hall toward the elevator bay, and Luc followed in his steps.

A tiny bell sounded as the elevator car arrived. Luc and Ash both stepped inside.

CHAPTER 51

It was almost time for the main course. The residents of Council House and a few esteemed guests sat and stood in various states of readiness around long tables.

Each vampire in attendance was clothed in rich, shimmering finery. Some opted for modern dress. Others wore the formal attire of their most beloved era. Toria stood alone, leaning against the wall and watching as the guests engaged each other in more or less interested conversation.

To the average eye, it might have appeared as any formal dinner party, but to Toria's other senses, it was a barely caged bacchanal. In each of them, underneath their pretty faces and polite facades, beat a drumbeat of bloodlust that grew steadier, louder, and faster with each passing moment.

There was a noticeable lull in the symphony of voices as the room's thirteen glass chandeliers began to move into place. Six hung above each long row of tables, with one in the center for the Elders' table. Like glass spiders, the chandeliers silently lowered themselves until they were about six feet off the ground.

Each fixture was a delicate marriage of long, curving glass tubes, dangling crystal ornaments and real candles. The crystals were just for decoration. The glass tubes and candles had real purpose.

The spiced blood that was to be the main course was poured into a heated vat in the upstairs prep room, and from there began an inexorable course down into the chandeliers, slowly filling each tube as it coursed toward their outer openings. The addition of the honey to the blood slowed its course, so you could watch its progress with perfect anticipation, and the lit candles heated it from beneath just before it made the final plunge into waiting glasses or open mouths.

Toria wanted to take her place at the center table with the other Elders. She wanted to forget all about Ash, but a black purpose had taken root in her. His love she could do without; she'd done without it for a thousand years. His trust, in spite of all their differences, she'd always had. Until now. Until *her*. Somehow Delilah had managed to undo in a matter of days the relationship she'd built with Ash over millennia.

She looked once more at the glimmering feast, and then backed out through the dining room doors and into the hall. Giving herself a shake, she took the main staircase up to her own room where she discarded her serpentine silver gown.

Black designer jeans, boots, a silver tank top, and a vintage black leather biker's jacket would be more fitting for the night she had planned. She caressed the smooth leather of her favorite jacket, loving its heavy feel against her skin. She didn't need it, of course. She had her rage to keep her warm.

Her reflection looked back at her from a long mirror. What did Ash see in that woman? The thought made her clench her hands into fists against the old leather. Knowing Ash loved something in that woman made the darkness inside her unfurl its wings.

She would see what it was, she thought, the thing that Ash loved. If it was inside that human woman, she would find it, she would touch it, and she would kill it.

She left the bedroom and followed the hallway back to the main staircase. At the second floor, she gave in to temptation and stuck her head into the prep room.

It was empty. All the work for this night was done, and most of the blood was already winding its way into the chandeliers. Only a small amount remained in the vats.

Toria grabbed a clear plastic measuring cup from a shelf near the door and headed for one of the four large open cylinders on the floor. The dark red liquid bubbled as she dipped her cup in. She raised the warm concoction to her lips and let the fragrant syrup course down her throat.

It had a pleasant burn to it this year. She wiped her mouth with her hand and rose from her crouch, tossing the cup into a large sink on her way out.

CHAPTER 52

They found Keller in his room sitting on his bed. A single lamp burned on the desk, serving little purpose but to cast the rest of the room in shadow.

The former monk was wearing a coarse brown robe over a pair of old blue jeans. He sat very still, hands folded in his lap, but Luc had the impression he was waiting for something. Or someone.

Whatever he was expecting, it certainly wasn't them, Luc thought. When they entered, Keller looked from Luc to Ash and back again.

"What are you doing here?" he barked.

Ash looked at Luc, offering him the first crack.

Luc turned to Keller. "Why don't you start by explaining why you seem to think I should be elsewhere?" he said. "We know you're involved in the disappearances and that you sent someone to grab me. So just tell us where the missing vampires are."

"I have no idea what you're talking about, but you're not welcome here." Keller turned to Ash. "I'm expecting someone, and he won't be happy to see you. You should go down and join the others."

Ash's eyes narrowed.

"We didn't come here for advice," Luc replied. "Just answer the question."

Keller smiled and closed his eyes. An invisible blow sent Luc crashing into the closed door. He landed on his feet, but couldn't help being stunned.

"What the hell?" he queried, looking blankly at Ash.

Ash never took his eyes off Keller. "It seems someone has been teaching our old monk new tricks," he said.

"My faith has been rewarded with knowledge," Keller explained, "and my actions will be rewarded with redemption."

"What actions?" Ash asked, his voice gritty with suspicion. "Breaking and entering?"

Keller smiled softly at them, his green eyes eerily alight. "Restoring God's natural order."

Luc looked up from dusting himself off. "Maybe you could translate that into not-crazy for us?"

Keller's smile faltered, and for a moment he glared at Luc. "You should not be here."

"What do you mean?" Ash asked. "Who told you they were taking Luc?"

Keller looked confused. "No one. He was banished from Council House."

Luc looked at Ash and wiggled one index finger next to his temple while nodding in Keller's direction. Again, Luc went sailing back into the wall for no apparent reason. He looked up in time to see Ash suppress a grin.

"Will you please make him stop doing that?" Luc complained.

"Oh, all right," Ash said.

Suddenly Keller was hanging in mid-air, arms and legs flailing in every direction. "I apologize for Luc's rude behavior," Ash said, "but we did come here for answers. If you don't start talking in more than riddles and nonsense, I'll embed parts of you in every wall of this room."

Luc raised his brows, thinking he might actually like to see that.

Keller struggled against the invisible grip holding him in the air. Fear showed on his soft features, but it was belied by his strident tone.

"You spewed forth all the horrors of our race," he said to Ash. "You turned us into the demon spawn of she who was cursed by God. I'll not answer to you for what I've done, when I've only attempted to undo your accursed bargain."

Ash sent Keller clattering into the far wall just as Keller had done to Luc a moment ago. Before he could rise, Ash was standing over him. He hauled Keller up over his head as if he were a rag doll, and Keller gave a high-pitched yelp.

"That's just the smallest fraction of what I can do," Ash said through gritted teeth. "I didn't come here to kill you, but I will, and slowly, if you don't tell me what I need to know. Now, where is James? And what were you doing at Hemogen?"

Keller didn't speak, and Ash looked down at his dangling feet. The edge of Keller's robe burst into flames. Keller began to scream. Ash again threw him into the corner of the room. A tower of books toppled over. Keller scrambled out from under it, tore off his flaming robe, and started batting it against the floor.

"I don't know where James is," he gasped, "but I'm sure he's fine."

Ash's eyes flew to the dusty laptop that had been at the bottom of the teetering stack of books. "Keller," he began slowly, waiting for the monk to finish extinguishing his burning robe, "who have you given your password to?"

Keller looked confused for a moment, and then his expression cleared. "My computer password? Just Memnon."

Ash's jaw dropped open. "Memnon?" he repeated.

Keller nodded.

"Who's Memnon?" Luc asked.

"He is the second oldest vampire in the world," Keller replied.

Ash nodded. "He was the first one I ever turned," he confirmed, "but he was buried in the eruption of Vesuvius a thousand years ago."

"So how did he get here?" Luc asked.

"An archeological dig," Keller explained. "Almost a year ago. They freed him."

Ash turned again to Keller. "Are you telling me he's alive and in New York?" Disbelief still lingered in Ash's eyes, but his jaw was set firm.

"Yes," Keller answered. "He is here for the Feast. Not to partake, of course." He hurried to explain. "He was allowed to take the rites and join the brotherhood of my old monastery at Clonfert."

Ash's brows shot up. "Is that so?" he queried. "And who told you this?"

"He did. He has become highly regarded amongst the brethren. He has even promised to get me reinstated there."

Ash sighed. "In return for what, exactly?"

Keller hesitated. "In return for delivering the cure the brothers developed to all of Council House."

Luc's stomach sank into his shoes. He saw Ash's face fall and knew they'd had the same thought.

"Cure?" Ash asked.

"That's right," Keller said, his green eyes brightening with his growing enthusiasm. "They found a way—using the notes I borrowed from your company, I believe—to return us all to our original human state."

Ash stood silent for a moment, but Luc didn't miss the brief look of hope that had flared across his face.

"Oh, good grief!" Luc said, throwing his hands in the air. "This is ridiculous." He marched closer to Keller and poked him in the chest. "What gives you, you babbling fruitcake, the right to decide for us that we should all be human again?"

Keller looked as if he didn't understand the question.

"Never mind that," Ash dismissed. "Do you know what Memnon has been doing with the vampires he's taken?"

"He needed them for testing," Keller replied. "He's only recently perfected the chemistry."

"And have you actually seen this cure work?"

Keller's brow furrowed. "Well, no, but Memnon has, and some of the other monks as well."

The noise from the party down below suddenly grew much louder.

"I'll go check it out," Luc offered, already making for the door of Keller's small room. "You stay here with the crazy man."

"Wait," Ash called out. "You should stay here with Keller. You are banned from Council property, remember?"

"How could I forget?" Luc sniped, turning around. He grabbed the little chair from under the desk and spun it around to face Keller. "And just what am I supposed to do if he hurls me into another wall?" he asked.

"He won't," Ash replied. "I can control him that much from downstairs."

"Must be nice," Luc muttered to Ash's retreating back.

❧

Ash left Luc to the interrogation and went out into the hall, heading for the main staircase instead of back toward the elevator. He wanted to be able to see what he was walking into.

Just as he got to the top of the stairs, he became aware that he wasn't alone. One foot hung suspended for a moment in mid-air before he turned cautiously on his other heel.

A figure stood in the dimly lit corner, and Ash could have sworn it hadn't been there just a moment ago.

"Memnon?" he asked.

Only silence greeted him.

The stranger stepped forward and Ash felt his jaw drop.

"Nancy!" he exclaimed.

CHAPTER 53

L uc waited for the door to close and then turned to Keller. "So, how's it supposed to work?" he asked. "This cure you think you have?"

Keller shook his head. "I don't know how it works, only that it does. Memnon and the other monks developed the actual serum. I was just the deliverer."

"Was?" Luc echoed. "You mean you've already done it?"

"Yes, it has already begun."

Luc flew out of the tiny chair, sending it crashing against the desk, and pulled a short knife from his boot. It wasn't much to look at, but its silver-coated tip would get the job done. He was about to threaten Keller with it, when a piece of paper on the desk caught his eye.

It hadn't been visible before, and Luc stared at it for a minute, frozen, then slowly lowered the knife and pulled the single sheet farther out from under the newspaper that covered it. His mother's name was what had caught his eye, but there were even more worrisome details written there.

The author of this little family tree had started with Luc's mother and worked backward. Luc recognized the names of his seven aunts and one uncle. They were printed in block letters with rectangular boxes around them. Lines connected them to other boxes containing the names of their children. Luc's name was there alongside those of his four brothers and four sisters. On it went until, at the bottom of the page, was written another name he knew.

"What is this, Keller?" he demanded, gesturing with his knife to the newly revealed genealogy project.

"My research," Keller answered.

Luc gripped the knife more firmly. "My family is none of your business."

"Quite the contrary," Keller replied. "It is all of our business. The Verses speak of human women who can bare a vampire's child. Until I saw you, of course, I had nothing to go on, but with enough time and access to the right records, I hope to be able to trace the Lilith gene backward from your mother and perhaps even predict who will be a carrier."

"What Lilith gene?" Luc asked.

Keller shrugged. "That's just what I've been calling it—whatever it is that allows some human women to mate with vampires. I think it must be a genetic mutation of sorts."

Luc eyed Keller suspiciously. "Why are you trying to find breeders?" he asked. "I thought you wanted fewer vampires, not more."

"I am a scholar, Luc," Keller said. "I pursue truth for its own sake. Though, in this case," his brow furrowed, "it was Memnon who asked me to trace the future generations."

"Memnon has seen this?" Luc asked, his voice rising with alarm. He looked again at Ariana's name on the bottom of the page. Her father, Thomas Dupree, was a descendant of one of Luc's aunts.

"I don't know," Keller said.

"What do you mean, you don't know?"

"I haven't shown it to him, but he can see us all any time he wants to. If he concentrates, he can observe any vampire without them ever knowing."

Luc thought about that for a moment and realized he could barely comprehend all the implications of such a power. "So he could have been spying on me for years, and I'd be none the wiser?" Luc asked.

Keller shook his head. "No, not you, actually. When I mentioned you, he was surprised. I think for some reason he can't see you."

"That's a comfort," Luc muttered.

"Maybe you are too human?" Keller offered. "He can't see human beings either."

CHAPTER 54

N ancy smiled for a brief moment, and then her look of alarm dropped firmly back into place.

"Nancy, what are you doing here?" Ash demanded.

"Sir, we don't have much time. You have to stop Memnon. He's planning something terrible. He gave me his word you weren't to be harmed, but when you came back to New York so suddenly, and, well, just the fact that you're here means..." Her speech ground to a halt in a mire of self-imposed anguish.

Ash didn't know what to ask first. "Nancy, how... how do you even know Memnon?" he stammered, shock stealing his normal eloquence.

"I didn't, sir, until recently, but he has known us for quite some time. All those years he was buried at Herculaneum, he was watching us. He knows everything we know."

"Who exactly is 'we'?" Ash asked, thoroughly confused.

"Anyone who has drunk the blood of Lilith," Nancy answered.

"You mean vampires—plus you and Ben?"

Nancy shook her head. "No, sir, I don't think the occasional drinks Ben and I take from you are enough. I don't think he can see Ben. Only me."

Ash's visage grew stormy. He knew he wasn't going to like what he was about to hear.

"Spit it out, Nancy," he ordered.

"Long ago, sir, even before you, I drank the blood of the goddess Lilith. It gave me a very long life, long enough that it kept me alive until I came into your service. Getting some of your blood ever since has helped top off the tank, so to speak."

"Nancy, there is no such thing as Lilith," Ash intoned.

"No, sir, that's where you're wrong," his maid said. "You never knew it, but you drank her blood that night, the night you were captured by the Philistines."

Ash's eyes grew wide, but Nancy continued on in a rush, eyes glued to the tops of her shoes.

"I know because I took it from Lilith's dying hand and delivered it to Delilah. She put it into your wine as she promised, but something went wrong. You were captured too early and you lost too much blood. With no blood of your own, her blood, and her curse, took over." She stopped for a breath and looked up at Ash. "Lilith's blood saved your life, but it drove you into the dark and the hunger, places you were never meant to be."

Ash couldn't believe what he was hearing. *Delilah had made him a vampire?*

"Nancy, I don't understand. Are you saying Lilith was a real person?" Ash asked.

"Not a person, no," Nancy's voice sank to a whisper, "but a flesh-bound creature, yes. I was one of her acolytes at the time Delilah came seeking help. Lilith brought you to Sorek, and part of the price was for Delilah to feed you her blood."

"No one brought me to Sorek," he began. "Wait, do you know what happened to her—after?"

"Lilith?" Nancy asked, her face falling. "She died."

"Not Lilith, what about Delilah?" Ash pleaded.

"Oh," Nancy replied flatly "Well the answer is the same. Having failed to fulfill her promise to Lilith, Delilah could not be allowed to live. She died less than a year after your capture."

Ash's mind was reeling, but his attention was diverted when the din from downstairs turned to howling.

CHAPTER 55

Ariana opened the door on the first knock. "You're back sooner than I—" Her gaze met Toria's.

"Expecting someone else?" Toria asked, her voice a dose of saccharin-coated venom. She pushed her way inside and closed the door behind her, resting her weight on it for a moment.

Ariana backed up as Toria pushed farther into the room. She suddenly wished she'd asked Ash more questions about vampires, like how to kill them. She halted her backwards progress, deciding to put on a brave front. "What are you doing here, Toria?" she demanded. "Does Ash know you're here?"

"Does Ash know you're here?" Toria mocked her in a high-pitched echo. Her face twisted into a cruel smirk. "No one knows I'm here."

"What do you want?"

Toria paused as if considering. Ariana noticed her eyes were slightly glassy.

"Oh, yes," Toria said, taking another step toward Ariana. "I remember now. I want the last thing you see to be my hands rummaging through the bloody pool of your own guts."

Ariana took a step back, and Toria followed.

Ariana's mind raced through every horror movie she'd ever seen. There was precious little chance of being able to set Toria on fire or chop off her head.

The vampiress laughed. "You've got that right." Her voice was loud in the tiny apartment.

"Why don't we talk about this, Toria?" Ariana offered. "I'm not after Ash. I'm married to someone else."

"Ha!" Toria barked. "You think it will make any difference to Ash? He's been searching for you for 3,000 years. I've been his friend for almost a thousand, and tonight he suddenly doesn't trust me anymore." Toria drew closer still, rage lighting her eyes from within. "Do you think he'll let a detail like your husband stand in his way?"

"It's not just about what Ash wants," Ariana pointed out.

Toria laughed again. "Don't fool yourself, kitten. It's *always* about what Ash wants."

She smiled grimly at Ariana's confused face. "Except for right now," she said. "Right now it's about what *I* want, and I want him to suffer." Her face twisted into another cruel grimace. "I want him to be free of you. I don't want to see a beautiful, powerful vampire playing house with some wretched human. It's bad enough he works with them. I hadn't thought it was possible to domesticate such a wild beast, but you might actually succeed." Toria took another step forward. "I won't let that happen."

Ariana saw the leather-clad arm begin its rapid advance toward her chest. She moved, but not in time. Toria's white fingers plunged into her flesh just below her collar bone. Ariana screamed as the force of the blow sent them both skidding into the wall. The impact rammed Toria's hand all the way through Ariana's shoulder and lodged it in the plaster. For a moment they were anchored there, staring at each other. Toria looked surprised to have missed her mark.

"You crafty little bitch," she sneered. A drop of white foam landed at the corner of her mouth.

Toria put a booted foot onto the wall to pry herself free. Blood gushed out of Ariana's shoulder as she pushed off, staggering back into the middle of the living room. Ariana almost passed out from the pain and the sight of it. But fear of dying kept her eyes open and glued to Toria, who seemed to have trouble regaining her balance.

Toria shook her head as if to clear it and then ripped her jacket off. "Hot," she hissed, clawing at her thin tank top. Her sharp nails ripped the slight material to shreds and then started on the white skin underneath. "God, it's burning!" she cried, her fingers never ceasing their horrid movement. She stared wide-eyed at her chest as her fingers pulled the flesh apart, revealing a gleaming sliver of her breast bone. "Something's inside me!" she cried. "It burns! God, help, it burns!" She looked up at Ariana as she screamed the words. Her eyes had turned to saucers; her whole mouth was covered in bloody foam.

Then she stumbled and fell to her knees.

Ariana pushed herself off the wall, leaving a huge dark stain. Each step shot a lightning bolt of pain from her shoulder into her frantic brain. She blocked it out and forced her wrecked body across the small space of Luc's living room. She kicked Toria as she passed, knocking the vampire face-forward onto the floor.

On the opposite wall, an autographed Johnny Cash album hung in a wooden frame. Ariana grabbed the frame off the wall and threw the album aside with one hand. Then she slammed her foot down hard on one corner of the square.

The effort split the frame open at the joist. One more kick and she had a side of the frame completely loose. As soon as she could breathe again, she wiped the tears from her eyes and turned back to Toria.

The vampire had rolled over and was staring blindly at the ceiling. Her body writhed and contorted on the floor, but she no longer said anything. She might have been trying to scream, but her teeth were clamped shut.

Ariana didn't know if this vampire was dying or why, but she knew she couldn't take any chances. She put her right foot down over Toria's naked bicep and raised her makeshift wooden stake up as high as she could.

Hoping her aim was true, she used both hands to slam the wooden point into the vampire's heart. Toria contorted for another few moments before her body dissolved into a foul-smelling green-ish-brown slime.

Tears streamed down Ariana's face as blood soaked the whole left side of her shirt.

CHAPTER 56

At the sudden commotion, Ash left Nancy calling after him and vaulted over the wooden rail of the staircase. He landed softly 30 feet below on the floor of the main hall.

Vampires had already begun spilling out of the dining room, their faces hideous masks of pain. They clutched their sides and tore at their hair and flesh.

One of the Elders burst through a set of the dining room doors. He spied Ash from across the room and ran toward him.

"You!" the large vampire screamed, his fingers digging into the wall of his chest, seemingly out of his control. Huge bloody gashes showed through his white shirt, matching his red robe. "How could you?" he cried. "We are your children." He seemed to want to say more, but his words devolved into a plaintive mewling as his hard body fell writhing onto the floor.

Ash stood rooted in shock.

"We are your children!" the vampire screamed, before blood-speckled foam gurgled up into his throat and choked off any further cries.

"Hey, what's going on?" Luc shouted from the top of the stairs. He started down, taking them two at the time.

"I have no idea," Ash said when Luc reached the main floor. "They're just—"

As Ash spoke, the writhing Elder turned into a steaming glop of green sludge. Luc's jaw dropped.

Ash closed his eyes for a moment, remembering Keller's talk of a cure. "Shit," he muttered. This was no cure. It was mass murder.

He looked up. Luc was backing toward the door. Ash grabbed him by the arm. "Oh, no you don't," he said. "We have to see if we can find Toria." He looked at the bodies falling all around them. "Or anyone who looks like they can be saved. Then I need to get some straight answers from Keller."

Clawing, spitting vampires now poured out of all the dining room doors. Ash and Luc batted them aside and stepped gingerly over what remained of the others.

Inside the dining room, blood still poured from the chandeliers, but no one drank. It slopped out onto white table linens. The whole room was cloaked in its warm, metallic scent, but now the slimy vampire remains were giving off their own competing odor.

There was almost no one left in the dining room. A few vampires lingered, writhing in their chairs, but most of them appeared to have perished here or as they tried to make it outside. There was no sign of Toria.

"Maybe she wasn't here," Luc offered hopefully.

Ash frowned, saying nothing. He pulled a thin black phone from his coat pocket and dialed her number. No answer. He flipped the phone closed and headed back through the double doors. Luc followed, almost running into him when he stopped short.

"Hey," Luc exclaimed. Then he saw what had captured Ash's attention and frozen him in place.

A robed figure floated in mid-air. Luc could see the outlines of a face beneath the hood, but little more.

"Revenge has always been your specialty, Samson," the figure said, "but I think I'm doing pretty well for my first time out, don't you?"

"Memnon," Ash said flatly. He looked at the carnage all around them. "Is that all this has been about, getting revenge on me?"

Memnon threw back his hood and laughed. "As usual, my friend, you flatter yourself."

He looked the same, of course, all golden planes of muscle under a warrior's rough features, but Ash couldn't hide his surprise. He wouldn't have thought a vampire could go without feeding for as long as Memnon had and then be completely restored.

"There are many things you don't know, Samson, even with all your power—power you just squander, masquerading as a human."

Ash's eyes narrowed. "I would have thought you would have approved, Memnon. You were always a big fan of the straight and narrow. No drink, no women, just ever the soldier."

218 — ALICIA BENSON

Memnon glared down at him. "Because we were helping Alexander make over the known world," he said. "We served a great leader, but your service was only half-hearted, Samson. Mine was total. That's why I was the best." He pointed at Ash. "You had no discipline."

He was probably right, Ash thought. "So you've come back from the dead to try to kill all of us?"

Memnon smiled. "No, not all, Ash. Just the ones you care about and any who might be loyal to you. And you, of course."

"Did you kill James?" Luc asked, pushing his way in front of Ash.

"Luc," Ash whispered, "get out of here."

Luc stood his ground as Memnon floated to the floor and walked closer to him. Finally, when he was close enough to reach Luc, he stopped.

"The born vampire," Memnon declared, examining him as if he were considering an important purchase. "I have wanted to meet you," he said, sniffing the air. "You certainly smell human. Tell me, do you have any other human traits or... abilities?" Speculation glowed in warm brown eyes.

Luc shrugged. "I asked you first," he retorted.

Memnon's mouth extended into a hint of a smile. "Ah, yes," he said, looking back at Ash. "James, your newest spawn. I'm afraid he got too close. Ironic, though, that out of all of you, he was the only one who found me out. The others," Memnon continued, "as you've probably already guessed, were test subjects for tonight's little surprise." He looked around the entrails-spattered entryway. "They turned to sludge long ago."

"You're a monster, Memnon," Ash declared. "I don't know what happened to you, but the soldier I knew wouldn't have stooped to such tactics."

"*You* happened to me," Memnon responded darkly. Then his features cleared, and he laughed. "Really, you have no one but yourself to blame," he said. "You made me, and then you started researching blood diseases."

His maniacal smile widened as he saw realization dawn in Ash's eyes. "That's right," he confirmed. "As soon as you turned that first researcher, I was able to start working right alongside. After hundreds of years of looking over shoulders, you'd be amazed what I've learned."

"You've really been able to watch any vampire all this time?" Ash asked.

"That's right," Memnon affirmed. "Not immediately, of course, but eventually, I did figure out how it could be done. Something ties us all together." He smiled at Ash. "If your maid is to be believed, it's the blood of Lilith."

"Is that what you think?" Ash asked.

"I don't know," Memnon replied, "but we couldn't get into Hemogen without her help, so I played along. She had pieced together that the breeders were probably Delilah's descendants, but she had no way to find them. I handed over the names Keller plucked out of Luc's family tree, and Nancy gave me your keycard. I can guess which one caught her eye, of course," Memnon continued. "I was surprised to see Ariana's name on the list myself, but not to worry," he mocked Ash, "she won't be giving birth to any more of your demons anytime soon."

Ash pushed Luc aside. "What are you talking about?" he demanded. "What's Ariana got to do with this?"

"Possibly everything," Memnon said. "In fact, I don't know why you blame me at all. Delilah's the one who called down a demon to get rid of you and somehow turned you into a vampire and your child into a breeder." He paused, clearly enjoying Ash's dismay. "Still think you have a way with women, Samson?" he taunted.

"Are you saying Delilah and I had a child?" Ash repeated.

"So it would seem," Memnon said, "spawning a dynasty the culmination of which is standing before you now."

"What?" Ash looked at Luc. "Luc?" He didn't think it was possible to be more surprised.

"Feel like the proud papa yet?" Memnon laughed. "Your little woman really did a number on you." His laugh died. "On us all. Like you, I hadn't quite figured out what to do with her yet, but your friend Toria has saved us the trouble."

"What do you mean?" Luc interjected.

Memnon's eyes never left Ash's face. "I mean Toria—and presumably Ariana—are both quite dead by now."

At Ash's horrified look, Memnon laughed. "You are truly pathetic, Ash. Look at you. Brought to your knees—again—by a woman."

Ash quickly reached out and grabbed Luc by the collar of his jacket. "Get out of here, now," he ordered.

Luc hesitated.

"Now!" Ash yelled, pushing him backward out of the room.

CHAPTER 57

Luc knew what he had to do. Once out front, he ran to his waiting motorcycle, and blew through every red light between mid-town and his apartment.

His sense of smell told him something was wrong as soon as the elevator doors opened. The same terrible stench that pervaded Council House was noticeable even in the hallway. Panic lodged in his throat.

He reached down and pulled the knife from his boot and stood for a moment outside the door, listening. No sound issued from inside, just the overpowering stench.

He tried the door. It wasn't locked.

Inside, the lights were on, revealing the visible signs of struggle. He saw the blood-stained wall. He saw Ariana lying in a heap on the floor.

He ran over to her still form, fearing the worst. He turned her over, trying to hurry but still be gentle. He shuddered at the huge wound in her shoulder, for once seeing the horror of blood. He felt for her pulse, knowing it was pointless.

To his utter astonishment, he felt a faint rhythm. A mere human would have missed it, but it meant he wasn't too late.

Luc flicked his fangs out and dragged one across his wrist. It stung, and red droplets formed a dark crescent on his pale skin

He hesitated for a moment. If he was wrong... he wasn't wrong. This was the only way. And he didn't know if he could even do it.

He smeared his thumb through the bloody pattern on his arm and spread it on Ariana's lips and over her tongue. Her lips twitched imperceptibly.

He looked again at the hole in her flesh. What if making her a vampire wasn't the only way?

Luc moved his wrist over her wound and squeezed hard with his other hand. Droplets formed again. They trickled downward, collecting at the ball of his hand into a red raindrop. Finally, that raindrop fell onto her broken body, and several more followed in its path.

He moved his wrist back to her mouth. The warm red liquid dropped onto the back of her throat, and Ariana swallowed.

Luc pulled Ash's phone out of his pocket and looked at the most recently dialed numbers. "Car" presented itself as the second item in the list. He pressed the button and dropped it back in his pocket.

Lifting her gently, he settled Ariana's head against his chest and strode out of apartment. As soon as his foot hit the sidewalk, he broke into a flat out run. At the end of the block, a black sedan pulled up and a uniformed driver got out and held open the back door. Luc put Ariana in and yelled an address at the driver as he ran around to the other side of the car. The sleek vehicle was already moving as Luc shut the door behind him.

The ride to the warehouse was too long, and Luc began to panic. He once more drew his teeth across his already healed wrist and squeezed precious drops onto the unconscious woman in his lap.

The car pulled to a hard halt at the warehouse door. Luc licked his wrist and gathered Ariana in his arms. He dismissed the driver and entered the combination to the heavy warehouse door.

Inside, he didn't bother to turn on any lights, just went straight to the elevator and took it down one floor, stopping at his office. There he turned and went out the side door into a narrow hallway. Most of the rooms behind the office were small storage areas, but there was one bathroom. Luc pushed open the seldom-used door.

It wasn't clean, and the fixtures were ancient, but there was a claw-footed porcelain tub. Luc laid Ariana in it and ripped her flimsy tee shirt off with one swift tear.

Her eyelids fluttered.

Luc turned and ran down the hall to the rickety stairs that led down to the third level. He sincerely hoped none of his four friends was still around. He didn't see anyone as he ran to the cooler. He really didn't care. He'd kill them all if he had to.

The bucket of their blood was still in the fridge. Luc grabbed it and ran back up the stairs toward the bathroom, just in time to see a slight, dark figure slip in ahead of him. He set the bucket down carefully, just inside the door of one of the other rooms, and pulled his knife from his boot.

The door to the bathroom where he'd left Ariana was now closed. He crept toward it, refusing to dwell on what the ramifications of killing Solotnik's daughter might be. It didn't matter.

Luc paused outside the bathroom door, but only for a moment. He knew where she would be—kneeling over Ariana. He drew a picture in his mind and hoped his aim was true, then rammed his whole arm through the flimsy wooden door. He felt the knife tip strike home. A high-pitched scream curdled up from inside the tiny room.

Luc pulled his arm back and opened the door. The female vampire he'd had caged below flew at him in a rage. He caught her as she came at him and turned her around. They hit the opposite wall, her back to his chest.

Luc reached around her and plunged his knife into her heart. She struggled as the traitorous organ pumped her now silver-tainted blood into all the cells of her body.

It took a few moments, but when she was still, Luc carried her into the bathroom and slit her throat and wrists. He closed the drain and flopped the top half of her body into the tub at Ariana's feet so her blood would begin to drain.

Luc stripped off the rest of Ariana's clothes, returned with his bucket, and added the blood from it as well. He turned on the warm tap until a pink pool covered Ariana up to her neck and then bit into his own wrist again.

He dragged his fangs through several inches of tissue this time and drained his own blood into the swirling water. It wasn't long before he felt himself losing consciousness. Still he pressed his wrist. He wanted her to fight, to live. He wanted their child to live. Soon he felt his arm slip, saw the bathroom floor rise up to meet him, and then the room went dark.

CHAPTER 58

Ash turned back to Memnon and launched himself full force at his robed figure.

Their two bodies collided in mid-air. Memnon laughed, and Ash thought it was the emptiest sound he'd ever heard. *Had Memnon been this soulless as a human?*

He shook his head, clearing the momentary fog. Memnon had thrown him back down to the marble floor, and a great crack was spreading across its ringed design.

"You can't defeat me," Memnon rasped. "You were a great warrior once, Ash, but you've gone soft. You've forgotten the reason we fight, if you ever even knew."

"What reason is that, Memnon?" Ash scanned the room as he spoke. He needed a weapon.

Memnon sneered. "I left Pompeii out of disgust for what the Romans had done to the world. Now, after all this time, nothing has changed. The world has gone to hell. Its leaders and its people are corrupt. It begs to be conquered by a force that can unite it and turn it to a better purpose."

Ash remembered this. Conquer, assimilate, and repeat. It had been Alexander's way and his father's before him. The Romans had been expert at it as well before becoming too bloated to maintain their empire.

Alexander and his fighting force were always light, nimble, and mobile. That was the only way to rule an empire. To be everywhere at once.

Ash hadn't much cared for that time. Alexander preached piety and restraint, yet repeatedly ordered them to slaughter soldiers who had surrendered.

"And you plan to fill Alexander's shoes and try to conquer the world?" Ash asked.

Memnon laughed. "I would never try to fill Alexander's shoes, but I serve one who can. He will bring the world to heel."

Ash snorted. "You're a fool, Memnon. An anachronistic fool."

"Who will stop us?" Memnon asked. "Certainly not you. You have power, but you lack the discipline for a long war. Already I have taken your friends and loved ones from you, and you do nothing. You sit there like a coward."

Memnon rose once more into the air and hung near the third floor banister. He ripped off the tattered cloak and threw it to the floor, revealing a warrior's physique to rival Ash's own.

"No more pretending then, Memnon," Ash called out. "No more running around in robes, co-opting maids and monks, spying on the rest of us from across the globe—all rather makes *you* sound like the coward, wouldn't you say?"

Memnon growled, clearly not seeing things Ash's way. "It's just a matter of time before I crush everything you treasure," he continued, ignoring Ash's baiting. "Before this world and these humans you love are no more recognizable to you than that bit of your friend there." He pointed at the glob of goo that had been a Council Elder and laughed once more.

Finally, Ash had found his weapon.

He launched himself off the ground and straight up into the air. He hovered opposite Memnon for a moment, his eyes ablaze.

The banister behind Memnon began to shake, and Memnon looked on in shock as it exploded into thousands of flying splinters. Shrinking back from the flying wood, he used his mind to divert most of the tiny torpedoes to the floor.

Several dozen, however, managed to lodge themselves in his white flesh. Memnon looked down at them and laughed.

He concentrated for a moment and the pieces began to wriggle free of his skin. Drops of blood pooled where they exited.

When Memnon looked up, Ash flung a handful of the goo that had once been the Elder at him. It hit dead on, and splattered across Memnon's blood-speckled torso.

Memnon hissed and sucked in a breath. "No!" he screeched, frantically wiping the sludge from his skin.

Ash rose higher and pulled another pole loose from the banister. This one he aimed himself. It flew toward Memnon, puncturing his goo-covered side and pinning him to the wall.

Memnon screeched again. This time it was an audible howl. Ash didn't gloat. Memnon sounded more angry than hurt, but he was hurt.

"That's what we call tasting your own medicine, my friend," Ash said.

At that moment, Ash heard a faint cry from upstairs. Nancy. He left Memnon pinned in his own goo and soared up to the third floor landing.

He started running as soon as his feet touched the carpet. "Nancy," he called out, "where are you?"

He kicked open the door of Keller's room and found Keller draining the helpless Nancy like there was no tomorrow. Ash belted him across the forehead, sending him flying, and caught Nancy's limp body before she hit the floor. Keller hissed and snarled at him from across the room.

Finally, Ash saw the bleeding wound in his gut. Luc must have stabbed him with something before coming down stairs. It wasn't a life-threatening wound, but Keller was losing blood. He needed to feed, and poor Nancy must have walked right into the lion's den.

"Shit," he said, knowing what he had to do.

"Get up, Keller," he ordered. The monk, though still snarling, did as instructed.

Ash wanted desperately to finish Memnon off, but he couldn't risk it. Not at the cost of Nancy's life. Not even at the cost of Keller's. Enough lives had been extinguished this night. Memnon would wait.

CHAPTER 59

A riana didn't want to open her eyes. She moved her arm and realized she was wet. More than that, she was under water. Her eyes flew open.

The first thing she saw was a lifeless head hanging over the edge of a bathtub looking at her with accusing eyes. She screamed and tried to back up, but it was no use. Everything was wet and slippery. Realizing she was sitting in a pool of blood, she screamed again. Her hand flew out and somehow found a perch against the white tile. She levered herself up to a standing position. Her body was stiff and weak, and she couldn't raise her other arm.

She saw Luc on the floor, and called out to him, but he didn't move. Then she remembered. *Toria.* She looked down at her body. It looked no different than it had yesterday. She remembered Toria's hand going all the way through her and into the wall of Luc's apartment. Where was the wound, the gaping hole that her shoulder should have been? Why was she even alive?

Ariana looked down at the bloody pool in which she stood. Quickly she put her right hand to her mouth. She didn't feel any fangs, but the only one who might know for sure was on the floor, possibly dead. Ariana stepped cautiously out of the tub and bent to look at Luc. *How do you tell if a vampire is dead?*

She put both hands under him and rolled him over onto his back. His head thudded on the tile floor, and Ariana winced. She moved his head, gingerly this time, and seeing no apparent damage, she stepped over him and knelt down. The floor was cold on her knees. She grabbed Luc's face with one hand and shook his head back and forth, calling his name. When that didn't work, Ariana began to panic. Weakness clawed at her bones. She hung her head low over Luc's carved features. He might have been made of stone, she thought. She began to pound on his hard chest with her fist.

Her wet hair dropped rivulets of blood onto his face. When the first drop hit his mouth, Luc's eyes snapped open. He grabbed her hand in mid-air, and Ariana straightened to a sitting position.

⋙⋘

Luc had to get out of there. He knew it, but for a moment he didn't move, allowing his eyes to drink in the naked, blood-soaked beauty straddling his hips.

A great smile cut across his features.

"Ariana, you can get up now," he said softly.

She rose shakily to her feet.

Luc opened the cabinet under the sink, but there were no towels. He gave Ariana his shirt and her own somewhat bloody jeans.

Ignoring her protests, he carried her back up to the street level, where he again dialed for Ash's car service. He'd have to thank the arrogant bastard if he ever saw him again.

Dawn was breaking, but Luc didn't care. They'd be in his apartment long before the sun got high enough to harm him.

Ariana fell asleep in his arms in the car and slept all the way back. When they reached his apartment door, she opened her eyes. "What happened?" she asked.

Her brown eyes were warm and trusting. Luc's guts twisted under the weight of all he had to tell her. He gave her what he hoped was a comforting smile. "Let's get you cleaned up first, okay? Then I promise I'll tell you everything."

He gently carried Ariana to the shower and stood her under the warm spray. Dried blood liquefied and ran off her flesh and into the drain. Luc clenched his teeth and began to bathe her.

Finally, it was over. Luc wrapped her in the biggest towel he could find and carried her into the bedroom. He laid her on top of the covers and watched her tired eyes close.

Then he turned on his heel, telling himself he was giving her time to get her strength back, not just postponing the inevitable.

He spent a few moments cleaning up the mess that had been made of his living room. His eyes were drawn to the comfy cushions of his well-worn sofa, and he couldn't stop his body from following. It was fully light outside now, and his every cell screamed for sleep. He closed the curtain and stretched out his long frame. As soon as it was dark he'd explain everything to her.

Luc smiled in spite of his weariness. He'd saved her. He'd saved her and his child.

⁂

Hours later, Ariana's gentle shaking roused him.

He swung to a sitting position, and she moved to take a seat in the desk chair across the room. She wore another pair of his faded jeans and one of his old tee shirts.

Luc rubbed his eyes and stared at her for longer than was really necessary. Her complexion was still pale, but he marveled at her rapid recovery.

"What's going on, Luc?" she asked softly.

Luc shook his head. "I hardly know where to start," he said. "What happened here?"

"Toria," Ariana replied, confirming Memnon's version of events. "She tried to kill me, but..." she grimaced at the recollection, "something happened to her." Ariana closed her eyes. "I mean, I stabbed her. I didn't think I had any choice, but before that... she... she was crazed, rabid almost." She looked earnestly at Luc. "I can't explain, but there was something wrong with her."

Luc nodded. "Don't worry about Toria," he said. "You didn't kill her. She was poisoned. Someone spiked the blood supply at Council House, and almost all the vampires there wound up just like Toria."

Ariana sighed, before her eyes flew open in alarm.

"Ash?" she asked.

Luc cocked a golden brow at her. "I don't know about Ash," he said. "When I left, he was fine." He leaned back into the sofa cushions. "I'll try to find him tonight, but it's important you don't talk to him until I tell you it's safe."

Ariana's confusion was visible on her pale features. "Why not?" she asked.

"Memnon, the vampire responsible for last night's carnage, can apparently tune in to any vampire he wants and see whatever they see. He saw Toria attack you, and thinks you are dead. I don't want him to know that's not the case."

"He can't do the same with you?" she asked.

Luc shook his head, ignoring the note of suspicion in her voice. "Apparently not," he said. "I seem to be a little too human for it to work on me. Who knows," he tried to smile reassuringly, "maybe Ash did away with Memnon last night and there's nothing to worry about."

He stood up and took Ariana by the hand. "Come on," he said. "You need to lie down. You're about ten shades paler than you were when you came out."

Ariana stopped short and Luc quickly turned to face her. "What's wrong?"

"I'm not becoming a vampire, am I?" she asked.

Luc shook his head, silently grateful that he'd thought of another option. "No," he replied, "that isn't what's happening. You had lost a lot of blood, so I did give you some of mine, but not enough to trigger the transformation. The rest of the blood was external and it seems to have only done what it was supposed to do—heal your arm."

She acquiesced to the pressure on her hand and let him lead her into the bedroom. Luc pulled the covers up and sat next to her for a moment, smoothing her hair back. "There's one other thing," he said reluctantly.

Ariana looked up at him. He wished she didn't look so fragile.

"I think Memnon also killed James," he said softly.

For some time, Ariana said nothing, and no expression registered on her features. "What do you mean, you think?" she asked him finally. "Are you sure?"

Luc nodded. "I didn't see it happen, but Memnon is capable of it, and there's no reason I know of for him to lie. Looks like he killed all the other missing vampires as well."

Ariana turned her head into the pillow.

"I know it's a lot to take," Luc murmured. "You should rest here for a while. I'll run out, see if I can find Ash, and maybe pick up some food on the way back. Okay?"

Ariana nodded mutely, and Luc got up and left the room.

CHAPTER 60

Deciding his first stop should be Council House, Luc pulled his bike out of the garage and weaved his way through evening traffic up into mid-town and down the street where the monstrous Gothic mansion should have been. But wasn't.

Only smoke and ruins now rose from its foundations.

Luc didn't even stop. He just gunned the bike and kept heading east toward Ash's townhouse.

At least that was still standing, he thought as he pulled up in the drive. He parked his bike in front of the garage door and bounded up the front steps to the large wrought iron gate.

A buzzer sounded somewhere inside when he pressed the bell, and after a moment, the gate opened of its own volition. Luc passed through it into yet another entryway. He didn't have the patience for this, he thought, trying the handle on the big mahogany door without knocking.

"Make yourself at home," Ash said as Luc crossed his threshold uninvited.

Luc raised his brows when he saw Ash coming to greet him in old jeans and an untucked white shirt. "I thought you had servants for this sort of thing," he remarked.

Ash shrugged and for a moment neither said anything. Luc could see the question in his eyes, but he couldn't go there yet. He wasn't relishing what he had to do.

"So," he asked, "what happened to Memnon? I see you survived."

"Please," Ash said, his face returning to its usual guarded smirk, "try to contain your relief." He motioned for Luc to follow him into the sitting area. There he poured two glasses of Scotch and handed one to Luc before continuing. "I don't know," he said finally. "I can only assume he survived and fled somewhere."

"What happened?" Luc asked, taking a pull of the sharp liquid.

"I wounded him with the sludge left over from the poisoned vampires." Ash absently sampled his own drink. "I got lucky. Apparently, it doesn't have to be ingested to be effective. Even greatly diluted, it just has to come in contact with the bloodstream."

"So why didn't you finish him off?"

"Thanks to your handiwork," Ash said disapprovingly, "I got sidetracked having to rescue Nancy from Keller."

Luc shrugged. "I didn't want him running away," he said by way of explanation. "Stabbing him was all I could come up with at the time."

"At any rate," Ash continued, "I left Memnon hanging on the wall and brought Nancy and Keller back here to nurse them back to health."

"Are they okay?" Luc asked.

Ash nodded. "They're both fine now, though Keller is having a hard time accepting his role in what happened. And Nancy refuses to talk about hers."

Luc nodded, but he didn't really care about Keller's hurt feelings or Ash's domestic problems. "You haven't been back to Council House today then?"

"No," Ash replied, "I was waiting for the sun to get low enough." He studied Luc more closely. "But, judging by your question, you must have."

Luc nodded. "I think it's safe to say that Memnon is still alive," Luc said. "Unless he spontaneously combusted and just happened to burn the place down."

Ash turned to refill his drink; his eyes were full of questions when he looked back at Luc. "What was it Memnon called you, Lucas—a born vampire? Is it true?"

Luc nodded. "Yes, I was the biological child of my vampire father and my human mother."

Ash lowered his glass and stared at Luc, his forgotten drink sloshing perilously close to the edge. "I'll be damned," he said. "That explains a lot." He looked at Luc with new eyes. "You've lasted longer than any of the others. I'll give you that."

"Others?" Luc had assumed there were others, but he'd never known for sure.

Ash nodded. "There haven't been many, but you are not the first." Ash thought for a moment. "You may be the first to survive into full adulthood, though."

"Why?" Luc wanted to know.

Ash shrugged. "No born vampire has had the strengths of both species," he explained. "Vampire genes, though dormant at first, eventually become dominant. All the offspring of human/vampire unions have been perfectly human until about puberty and then began to change into full vampires."

Luc nodded. "That's what happened to me," he said.

"Not quite," Ash said. "You clearly have some lingering human traits—the heat you give off, and apparently an increased tolerance for sunlight." Ash studied him again. "You can't stand full daylight can you?"

Luc shook his head. "No, just the in-between times."

"You should consider how to use that to your advantage," Ash commented.

Luc wondered at the level of arrogance it took to assume he'd never thought of that. "Thanks," he said. Wanting to get back to why he'd come, he asked, "Do you think Memnon really killed James?"

Ash raised his glass and took a long slow pull at the amber liquid circling there. "I don't know," he said. "Probably. Memnon's not one to draw things out."

Luc closed his hand for a second and then finished what he came to do. "He didn't lie about Ariana, either," he said slowly, knowing it was necessary, yet hating the lie. He could see his words twist across Ash's face.

"Toria did go after her," Luc continued. "My apartment was all busted up when I got there. Toria had... dissolved, or whatever it was that happened to the rest, but not before she got in some good licks. It looked like she put her fist through Ariana's chest."

Luc stopped and looked at the man in front of him. He mirrored the sadness he saw there in his own voice to make the lie more believable.

"They were both dead when I got there."

Luc put his glass on the sideboard and turned to look at Ash. "I'm sorry," he said earnestly. "There's nothing else I could do." His drawl blurred the tense of his apology.

He turned and headed back the way he had come, stopping just short of the front door.

"What do you intend to do about Memnon?" he asked.

Ash had his back to him and didn't turn around. "Find him and kill him," he responded, "what else? He's bound to be hiding somewhere in the city."

Luc nodded. "Good luck," he said. "I'll keep an eye out as well."

"Don't try to fight him, Luc," Ash called out to his retreating guest. "You won't win."

That brought Luc up short. He turned back to Ash. "You know," he said, "I just may have an idea of where to look for your missing warrior."

Ash looked surprised. "Really? Where?"

Luc shook his head. "I think I'd prefer if he didn't know everything I was thinking."

Ash opened his mouth, but quickly swallowed his objection.

"Give me a few days to check it out," Luc said. "When I know something, I'll give you a call."

❧

When Luc was gone, Ash sank down onto the settee and put his head in his hands. He had lost Delilah, and he couldn't look for Memnon. In one day, he'd gone from being all-powerful to being Keller's babysitter.

Maybe he had just lived too long, he thought. He had outlived everyone he knew and most of the vampires he'd created. He had even outlived his hatred of Delilah, something he hadn't thought possible. Even with everything he now knew, he couldn't summon any hate. Maybe it had never truly been hate at all.

He shook his head, remembering all she had put him through. Surprisingly, it didn't matter. Hate or love, friend or foe, she was a worthy companion.

Fear reminded him of the creeping nothingness that had begun to color his life before he'd found her again. Without Delilah, without even his hatred of her to keep him warm, how long before he would feel nothing at all?

Ash raised his head. *First things first*, he thought. He was responsible for unleashing Memnon on the world, so he would also be responsible for killing him.

Chapter 61

Luc left Ash's townhouse and made his way back downtown to Vamp. It was early yet; no pounding music greeted him down the block and Derek and Willie weren't even at their posts. Luc opened the large faux-gothic door and went in.

People milled about inside, but most were just sitting at the bar. The music hadn't started up yet, so the dance floor was empty, though the lights underneath it were on and cast an eerie blue pall on the surrounding tables and patrons.

Luc took a seat at the bar.

"Whiskey," he said, raising two fingers when the bartender looked his way.

"Nine dollars," the man said, putting the drink in front of him. "You wanna start a tab?"

"No," Luc said, paying the man. Not for nine bucks a pop he didn't. Plus the bartender was a human, so Luc needed to find someone else to pump for information.

He left the cushy bar stool and took his drink to a booth that faced the door. Finally, people started to trickle in, and then the trickle became a stream.

"Willie," Luc shouted when he saw the bouncer appear. *Not a moment too soon,* he thought. He had almost broken down and bought another nine dollar shot.

"Luc," Willie said when he got closer, "what are you doing here?"

"I couldn't make it the other night, but I thought the Tournament went on for weeks." He looked around at the mostly empty bar. "I guess there's no show tonight?"

Willie shook his head. "No, not for two more days. I guess you haven't heard that someone burned down Council House and killed most everyone inside."

Luc decided to play dumb. "What?"

"Yep," Willie said. "We haven't figured out quite how they did it yet, or who, but Aleksander declared three days of mourning. The Tournament is suspended until then."

"That was nice of him," Luc said, a little surprised.

There was a gleam in Willie's eye. "Not entirely," he said. "Aleksander wants his new warrior to make it to the Tournament's final round. The rumor is that he was injured in the fire and wasn't ready to fight today, so Aleksander put the whole thing on hold."

"Is that right," Luc said dryly. "Lucky break, him not dying in the fire along with all the rest."

Willie grinned. "There's been some talk along those lines, but Aleksander shut it down quick. I'd advise you to keep those thoughts to yourself around here."

"Thanks," Luc said. "So, the fights will be back on in two days then?"

"That's the plan," Willie said. "You thinking of entering or just watching?"

"Definitely just watching," Luc replied.

"That's for the best. You're way too young to tussle with these guys." Willie thought for a moment. "On the other hand," he said speculatively, "getting thrown out of Council House probably saved your life, so maybe lady luck is on your side."

CHAPTER 62

Two blue stars stared down at Ariana like accusing eyes as she turned onto Ash's street. Her steps slowed under the weight of all the secrets she carried and the fear that lurked dangerously close to the edges of her consciousness. Fear of Ash, fear of Memnon, fear of all vampires, in fact.

She reached into her bag and fingered the knife she had stashed there. Luc didn't know she had taken it, but after they'd argued again about her coming here, she'd just wanted to leave quietly. Its silvery length on the nightstand had caught her eye and she'd pocketed it, figuring Luc could get along without it better than she. She and Ash needed to talk, but she wasn't taking chances. She owed him the truth, not her life.

She paused at the stone staircase outside Ash's townhouse. Instinct told her he was here. She pushed the button on the intercom, ignoring the other instinct that bid her stop and consider.

"May I help you?" asked a voice she recognized.

"Nancy," Ariana replied, "it's Ariana Chambers. I'd like to see Mr. Samson."

There was a brief pause, and then a buzzing sound as the heavy metal gate clicked open. Ariana continued up the stairs and pulled the gate shut behind her.

When she turned around, the front door had been opened and replaced by an even more impenetrable barrier. Ash.

Emotions ravaged the hard landscape of his face, coming so fast and varied that Ariana was reminded of time-lapse photography. Before she could tell for sure what he was feeling, he had wrapped his arms around her and pulled her to his broad chest.

"I thought you were dead," he whispered.

She didn't know what to say. "Does this mean you don't still want to kill me?" she asked.

Ash relinquished his hold on her. "Of course not," he said, looking questioningly at her. "How could you think that?"

Ariana's jaw dropped. "You went to an awful lot of trouble to do just that," she pointed out.

"Not really," he said. "I'm not sure I ever *really* wanted to kill you."

She closed her eyes. "Then you should have left well enough alone," she said. "And you should have left James out of it."

Comprehension flickered in his eyes and he stepped back from the entryway. "I think you'd better come in," he said.

Ariana noticed as she stepped over the threshold that his stony mask had slipped back into place.

"I don't know what Lucas told you," he continued when he had shown her upstairs into his study and closed the door, "but it's not as diabolical as you must think."

Ariana swallowed a biting response and looked around the gleaming, masculine room. She tried to remember how many days had passed since she last stood here, kissing him, before she knew how wrong it would all go.

"No?" she queried. "Tell me then," she said, seizing on her last train of thought, "did you know James was alive the last time we were in this room together?"

There was a damning pause, and she sat down on the sofa behind the door and tried to collect her thoughts.

"Yes," he said finally, "but as a new vampire, James couldn't go anywhere near you, for your safety. New vampires are dangerous, Ariana, even if they don't intend to be. Regardless of my involvement, it was essential that he stay away from you and that you believe he was dead."

"And when did your involvement begin?" she wanted to know.

Ash turned from her, but continued talking as he prepared a drink. Ariana noticed he didn't offer her one, and also that his hands seemed to be shaking.

"I did turn James," he admitted, "but only to save his life. Toria had already left him for dead when I found him, purely by chance."

She raised her eyebrows and felt her arm start to ache at the mention of Toria's name. But it was only an ache. For that she had to give Luc credit. As much as she didn't like being bathed in vampire blood, two days later, her arm was completely healed. Well almost completely, but an occasional ache and a little fatigue were a small price to pay to still be among the living.

"It's true," he said, catching her look in a quick glance over his shoulder. "It wasn't until later that I found out James' wife and my—" He stopped and cleared his throat. "And Delilah were one and the same."

"And how did you know that?" she asked, not wanting to leave the subject of James, but indulging her curiosity nonetheless.

Ash came back to lean against his desk and gave the ice cubes in his glass a quick swirl. "I can see traces of the souls of humans," he said, "enough to recognize people I knew well, even in a different body."

"Not to downplay the whole vampire thing," Ariana mused, "but finding out that we get reincarnated has been the most interesting thing I've learned so far."

Ash gave her a pained smile. "Yes," he said, "it does give one hope."

She studied him for a moment before the question dawned. "What about your soul?" she asked. "You said you can see souls in humans, but what about vampires?"

He frowned. "I don't know," he admitted. "I don't see them, but that doesn't mean they aren't there."

Ariana wondered if that wasn't just wishful thinking.

"No more than you were wishful thinking just a moment ago, sitting there assuming *you* had a soul," he argued without waiting for her to make her point out loud.

Perhaps. "But you were supposed to be specially chosen by God when you were Samson," she pointed out. "Do you still think you have a soul?"

He sighed. "You always did know how to turn the knife, Del," he said, running a hand through his hair and taking another long pull on his drink.

Ariana felt a flicker of fear. "If you want to finish what Toria started," she said, "you might as well get it over with."

Ash smiled at her, and her heart did a reluctant flip flop. "Maybe you have a point," he said, seeming to ponder it. "I do still have half a mind to burn your eyes out with a hot poker." His glass landed on the desk with a plunk, and then he was standing in front of her. "And then strangle you." A wicked glint crept into his eyes as he looked down at her. "After all," he said, "I can always apologize profusely in your next life."

"You'd be wiser to stop looking for me," she said, hoping his smile meant his words were all in jest. "You'll get no apology from me and no forgiveness either." She hoped she hadn't misjudged his anger, but reminded herself that she had come here to tell him the truth. All of it.

"Ariana," Ash began, with no hint of a joke this time, "you can't know how sorry I was about what happened to your sister. I only knew her for a short while, of course, but she was sweet and kind. She was everything I thought I needed. When she sided with her family against me, I was hurt." He put up his hands to forestall her protest. "I know I overreacted."

That was the understatement of the millennia. "I didn't mean about that," she said. "I was talking about what you did to James."

"Ariana," he said, dropping to kneel in front of her, "I told you, I didn't set out to do anything but help James."

She shook her head. "I don't think I'd call making him a soulless murderer a big help, Ash."

His face had grown hard while she spoke.

"And even if it were," she continued, "you should never have left him alone. He was new, you said it yourself, and now he's dead, because you were too busy chasing after me to protect him."

For a long moment, Ash said nothing, but then his arms shot out and he stood, hauling her off the small sofa.

"I'm not perfect, Ariana," he said, "especially not where you're concerned. But if we're going to start throwing stones, you don't look so perfect yourself."

She put her hands on his chest to push herself away, but his grip was like iron.

"What are you talking about?" she asked.

"You slept with Luc," he replied, his mouth twisting into something that came very close to a pout.

She opened her eyes wide and began to laugh. "Of all my sins," she asked when she had caught her breath, "That's the worst you could come up with?"

His gaze darkened. "No," he said, removing his hands from her arms and unbuttoning his shirt.

When she would have stepped away, he pulled her back, forcing her to touch the now bare skin of his chest. It was cool under her fingers. Cool and hard and smooth.

"I'm not sure how," he said, "but it seems you turned me into this." He bared his fangs and glared down at her. "If we're casting blame," he growled, "why don't you tell me how you thought I deserved this?"

CHAPTER 63

Ariana's eyes widened in surprise. "It was an accident," she said. "I swear I never planned to turn you into a vampire. I didn't even know it was possible."

"Oh, so you only wanted to kill me and just happened to feed me a little demon blood?" Ash's voice was hard, but his fangs retracted.

She looked at him, and in that instant, it was so clear he wasn't human, she wondered how she'd ever thought otherwise. "I was desperate," she explained. "You had taken everything from me, yet no one would hold you accountable. I asked Lilith to bring you to Sorek, so I could see justice done myself."

His jaw hardened. "I never knew you at all, did I?" he asked. "All that hate you bore me and I never suspected." His eyes bored into her.

She noticed her fingers were nervously working themselves against the skin of his bare chest, but she couldn't seem to stop them. They moved to reacquainting themselves with the strange, familiar territory. She sucked in her breath, and his dark eyes began to glitter.

"Did you really feel nothing for me?" he whispered, his voice again the low rumble that threatened to liquefy her insides. "Not in all the time we were together?"

"Ash," she said, hesitating and bringing her hands up to caress the sharp planes of his face, "I don't know what to tell you."

"Just tell me that you don't hate me."

The naked need in that simple request almost did Ariana in. She wasn't ready for this man, for what they could be together. "How is it that you can read random thoughts," she asked, lighthearted, "but you can't tell whether I hate you or not?"

"It's complicated," he said. "I've never been good at emotions, especially with people I know. It's too hard to tell which are theirs and which are mine."

"Oh." She paused to think for a minute. "No," she said finally, after waiting longer than was truly necessary. "I don't hate you, Ash."

His look begged for more reassurance.

"I remember hating you," she said. "I remember hating a man I didn't know very well. The memory is there, but the actual hate seems to have burned away. And you've changed." She paused, struck by the obvious. "Heck, Ash," she said, "you're not even a man anymore."

He smiled wryly, and Ariana watched the smooth movement across his rugged features. Really, when he was calm, except for the fact that his skin was a little too perfect, he appeared more or less normal.

"Yes," he said, "contrary to popular belief, the older we get, the harder it becomes to distinguish us from humans."

Suddenly a thought struck her. "The other night at dinner, you spoke of your wife. Were you talking about my sister?" she asked.

"Of course," Ash replied. "She's still the only wife I've ever had."

Ariana's eyes got misty. "You're the only person I've ever truly hated, you know."

Ash's mouth dropped open. He started to speak but she continued. "So many lives, so many loves, but you were the only one that made me burn with hate."

She held onto his shoulder when he would have stepped away. "No, you don't understand," she whispered. "You're the only one who ever made me burn at all. Everything about me burned brighter with you." She drew in a breath. "Only with you."

"And I've spent a hundred lifetimes pretending to hate you," he said. "For some of that time, it might even have been real." His gaze warmed as he looked down into her upturned face. "The real question is where that leaves us now."

She couldn't speak. She didn't know what was in her heart for this man. Her feelings were all jumbled up. So she just went with her gut and wrapped her arms around him and pulled him close, this man who'd tried to kill her, this man who'd given her more knowledge in an hour than she could have learned in a lifetime, this man who was not even any longer a man. When she put her head on his bare chest, he finally ringed his arms around her.

"Ash, you're the strongest man I know," she said, her voice filled with longing, "but I won't break."

His lips were on hers the moment he understood her meaning, and the fire she remembered flared between them. She couldn't fight it, even if she'd wanted to. Whatever ghosts separated them, the passion that bound them was a force of nature. She sighed and gave in to the tiny waves of pleasure that his lips and hands had already begun to stir.

Ash deepened the kiss and groaned when she welcomed him farther into her mouth, but he wasn't content with a kiss. In an instant, she was in his arms and he was carrying her to the door.

"Not here," he explained, seeing the confusion in her eyes.

Moments later, he had mounted a narrow staircase, kicked open the door to his bedroom, and was closing it behind them, all without relinquishing his hold on her. Finally, he lowered one arm and allowed her to slide down his body until her feet met the floor.

The friction made her breathless. She turned and the lovely burgundy carpet seemed to rush up to meet her. She staggered and put out a hand to steady herself.

Ash grabbed it. "Ariana, are you all right?" he asked. His eyes, unguarded for a moment, told her how much of his soul was in that question.

"I'm fine," she said, shaking her head. "Just a little tired. I guess I haven't recovered from Toria's butchery as well as I thought."

He led her to the edge of the bed, but didn't join her. Instead he crossed the room and pressed a button on the wall.

Only a moment later, Nancy opened the door.

"That was fast," he remarked. "Can you bring up some food for Ariana? She hasn't been well and needs to get her strength back."

Nancy nodded. "Yes, of course," she said. She looked from Ash to Ariana and back again, seeming to Ariana's eyes unusually hesitant. "I came to tell you there's a car out front for you, sir," Nancy revealed finally.

"I didn't call for a car," Ash said, frowning in confusion.

"The driver says he was sent by someone named Benson. Luc Benson, I believe. Do you know the name?"

"What's going on, Ash?" Ariana asked.

He shook his head. "A little unfinished business, I'm afraid." He turned to Nancy. "Tell the driver I'll be right down," he said.

Nancy scurried back the way she had come and Ash crossed over to where Ariana sat on the edge of the bed. He leaned down, put both his hands into her thick hair, and inhaled deeply of its scent. "I can't believe I'm leaving you here," he said. "In my bed."

Ariana looked up at him. "Will you be long?"

Ash stood and pulled her against him for another kiss. "Say it again," he said raggedly when he'd lifted his head.

"What?" she asked, still a little foggy from the lovely ministrations of his lips.

"Tell me again that you are here because of me," he said, his voice a silken command. "That this has nothing to do with James or Luc or anything else. That you are here with me because you're mine."

She opened her mouth, but had no answer to give.

He waited a moment, and then took advantage of her opened lips to kiss her again. Her mouth melded to his, answering in a way she could not. He raised his head and raked her bottom lip with his teeth. "Say you're mine, Delilah," he whispered.

She gave a half-whimper as her body bid her acquiesce to him, but some more central part of her refused to comply. "Don't call me that," she said, not knowing where she got the strength. "If you're here with me," she ran her hands across his broad chest, "then be here with me. I'm not Delilah anymore."

"Ariana," he said, sucking in a breath. He smiled down at her. "I think I can get used to that."

He stepped back, took a breath she knew he didn't need, and kissed the top of her head. "I have to go," he said. "We'll finish this when I get back." He looked down at her and frowned slightly. "And you're feeling better."

Ariana watched him go and then sank back onto the bed.

CHAPTER 64

The car Luc sent whisked Ash downtown, but not as far as he'd expected. When it slowed to a stop near a club called Vamp, he began to wonder if this was Luc's idea of a joke.

Ash saw him standing at the corner, and he reluctantly got out and closed the car door.

"You found Memnon?" he asked as Luc approached.

"I think so," Luc answered. "I haven't seen him, but I think he'll be in the ring tonight."

"What ring?"

Luc nodded. "This place has an underground tournament going. I don't know exactly how it works, but they're all gaga over some new warrior."

Ash turned toward the door. He knew how it worked. "Let's go check it out then, shall we?"

Luc led the way, greeting Willie and Derek at the door.

"Who's your friend?" Willie asked.

Luc looked at Ash, but got no signal. "Ash Samson," he replied.

Willie's gaze flew back to study Ash anew. "You don't say?"

"I don't care who he is, you both have to wait your turn in line like everybody else," Derek said. "We're expecting a packed house tonight."

Willie turned to his friend with a look of disbelief. "Are you crazy, man? Do you know who this is? If he wants to come watch the tournament, he gets to come watch the tournament."

"Who said anything about watching?" Ash responded as he and Luc passed through the door Willie was now holding open.

"All the way to the back," Willie called out. "Then down to the lower level."

Following Willie's instructions, they pushed their way through the throng of people surrounding the dance floor. Ash wondered what promotion they'd run to fill the place to the rafters on a weeknight. No doubt they needed the noise up here to cover the noise from down below.

Ash led them to a staircase at the back of the room. Down they went, two flights, then three. There the stairs ended.

"What the hell?" Luc asked.

Ash looked over the railing. There was a landing about two stories below. He motioned for Luc to take a look.

"I think it's a type of self-selection," Ash explained. "If you can survive the jump, you're obviously in the right place."

Luc slapped one hand onto the metal rail and vaulted over. Ash followed, landing softly on the concrete floor below.

"Show-off," Luc muttered.

Ash smiled. "Just getting warmed up," he said.

"Do you really plan to get into the ring with him?" Luc asked.

Ash turned a surprised look to him. "Isn't that what you intended?"

Luc shrugged. "I don't know what I intended. I was leaning toward letting him fight himself silly and then you taking him out when it was all over."

Ash frowned. "That's not the way a warrior fights, Lucas."

"Well, he's not a warrior," Luc retorted. "He's a murdering bastard."

Ash started forward down the dark corridor. "Aren't we all?"

⁘

Luc followed in silence. He could smell blood already.

As they entered the arena, Luc noted that an early match was already underway. Not that he could see anything through the crowd, but the cheers, grunts, and cries from farther up told him all he needed to know.

Some of the vampires back near the entrance strained to see the action, but most were engaged in low discussion or casting curious looks at Ash. Whoever was fighting up front, it wasn't Memnon yet. He would have held their attention.

Ash found a spot near the edge of the room. Since he was a head taller than most, he could see the action in the ring fine from there. Luc was left staring at the back of someone's head.

"Are you sure this is a good idea?" he asked Ash.

Ash smiled. Luc wasn't sure why this bothered him, but it did.

"I'm not sure of anything," the first vampire answered, "but it's the only idea I've got at the moment." He looked down at Luc. "Unless you've come up with something better?"

Luc still liked the idea of an ambush, but apparently that was beneath the great Samson. "Well," he said finally, "no, and I can't see a damn thing from here, so I'm going to try to get closer to the ring."

Ash nodded, and Luc began his slow progress toward the center of the room. In many ways, this arena resembled the one at Council House, he realized. It was three stories tall, with a square roped off in the center for the fighters. The ring itself was much smaller, though, looking like it was only built for individual matches.

Nor were there any balconies for spectators. Luc wished there were. As it was, he was making enemies literally right and left, but he did finally manage to get just a few rows from the ring, slightly off to one side.

The ring was elevated a couple of feet off the floor of the arena and demarcated by four poles connected by a single piece of rope. On each of the poles was a large bowl partially filled with warm blood. Warm blood also filled a trough that ran around the base of the ring. Luc supposed it was so the fighters could refresh themselves, but the smell of it suffused the entire room, serving the dual purpose of working the crowd into a frenzy.

The rest of the room was just poured concrete. A few pipes hung from the ceiling far above. The only weapons Luc could see were a few long wooden spears on the floor, leaning against the platform.

Several rounds went by while Luc watched, but none of them were death matches. Finally, a couple of Vamp employees came out to clean up the blood on the floor of the ring. As they finished, the crowd jammed in tighter, and conversations quieted to a minimum.

Apparently the real entertainment was about to start. Luc was startled when Aleksander Solotnik entered the ring.

"Ladies and gentlemen," his deep voice boomed out over the crowd, "we have three excellent fighters scheduled for this evening's elimination rounds." Cheers went up from the crowd. *Obviously the fighters' reputations preceded them*, Luc thought.

"As your host, I promise you a night you won't soon forget and all the cocktails you can wash it down with. And don't forget," Solotnik continued, "tonight there is a wild card slot—available at the end of the last round to anyone who will dare to challenge the winner."

Luc smiled. That was a great gimmick. It would keep people around even if the first matches were blowouts. Being a businessman himself, he had to appreciate great marketing. *And tonight will be the wildcard match of all wildcard matches*, he thought, beginning to relish the spectacle.

"First, my son Viktor Solotnik will take on our guest from L.A., the underground champion from the City of Angels, Roderick, better known to his fans as El Toro!"

Two vampires climbed up onto the edge of the ring. Viktor so plainly resembled Aleksander that Luc could have picked him out easily. Too bad his sister didn't also share the family resemblance, Luc grumbled to himself. And too bad she was clearly the favorite. No father who cared for his son would put him in the ring, especially not if Memnon was the next opponent.

Not that El Toro looked like an easy mark. He was dark-skinned, *probably a mix of black and Hispanic*, Luc thought, and stood almost as tall as Ash. He towered over Viktor and probably outweighed him by a hundred pounds. Being outweighed wouldn't matter to an older, more powerful vampire, but Solotnik himself had only been turned several decades ago. He'd turned his children some time shortly after. There was no way they could be very powerful.

As it turned out, though, the two were pretty evenly matched. Roderick was more powerful, but Viktor was quick and he had the support of the home crowd, which, in the end, made all the difference.

The lack of weapons in the ring, Luc realized, was by design. The crowd had all the weapons. When Viktor looked like he could prevail, swords, knives, maces, and spears appeared from out of the crowd.

Viktor was able to grab a sword tossed up by a spectator and take Roderick's head off with it.

Aleksander rushed into the ring to hold his son's arm up in the air. "The winner!" he shouted. Viktor pulled his arm free and went to drink from one of the four bowls of blood. His father carried on. "Now, in just a few moments, you will see Viktor take on last week's winner, Memnon!"

The crowd cheered and heaved to and fro as the blood was once again mopped from the ring floor in anticipation of the next round. Viktor never left the ring, and when Memnon joined him, the noise from the crowd fell to a murmur.

Aleksander rushed back to center stage. "Viktor versus Memnon!" he cried, arms flung open to indicate the two men in opposite corners.

The room was now so jammed Luc could barely breathe, much less move. He forgot his claustrophobia, however, when the fight began in earnest.

From the first, it was clear Viktor never had a chance. He let Memnon advance first, dodged his initial blow, and landed a hard kick across Memnon's chest.

It was plain to all, however, that Memnon was just toying with him. Luc knew he could fly or send Viktor skewering onto a spear with no more than a thought, but he never did any of those things. He just physically outmatched him. Where Viktor was quick, Memnon could be quicker. Where Viktor sought the element of surprise, Memnon was always a step ahead.

The fight really went on longer than it should. Luc suspected this was solely because Memnon didn't want to offend Aleksander by offing his son too easily.

In the end, the result was as expected. Viktor lay pinned to the floor by Memnon's superior strength, fangs bared and hissing, but losing blood from multiple wounds.

From his kneeling position over Viktor's body, Memnon met Aleksander's gaze for a moment and Aleksander gave a quick nod.

Memnon grabbed one of the long wooden stakes leaning against the ring, twirled it over his head and brought it back down through Viktor's chest and into the solid surface of the ring floor.

Aleksander waited for the cheers to die down and strode back into the ring, this time grabbing Memnon's arm to hold aloft.

"We have a new champion!" he boomed, to fang-filled cheers from the crowd. "Unless, of course, there is someone here who wants to challenge him for the honor?"

Some laughter broke out among the crowd of young vampires. No one expected a challenge tonight.

Aleksander made a show of looking around, and finally his gaze came to rest on a vampire standing near the spot Aleksander had been using as his vantage point during the matches.

James! Luc couldn't believe it.

"Perhaps our winner from the first night's rounds will try his luck!"

The crowd roared its encouragement, but it didn't escape Luc that Aleksander wasn't asking.

Without a sound, Ash floated down into the ring behind Solotnik and his new mascot. The crowd grew silent as Memnon turned around.

For a moment, Solotnik was at a loss as to why the cheering had stopped. Then, he felt Memnon's arm drop away and turned. When he saw Ash, his face split into an evil grin.

"What an honor!" he sang out to the crowd. "Why don't you tell them who you are? Some of them are young and know you only by name." He tried to hand Ash the microphone.

Ash Samson! came the reply, but not in the form of words. Ash broadcast it out to the mind of every single person in the crowd.

Nice, Luc thought. The crowd was impressed, even if Memnon wasn't. A hush descended, and Solotnik pulled back the microphone, his strange grin replaced by an enigmatic sneer.

"You are challenging Memnon?" he asked, once more using the mic.

Ash nodded. "I am."

CHAPTER 65

Solotnik turned once more to the crowd. "Ash Samson to challenge Memnon!" he called out. Then he quickly exited the ring.

Memnon moved to one corner, bare-chested and covered in blood. Ash removed his overcoat and shirt, throwing them over the rope.

"Need a drink before we start, Ash?" Memnon taunted, nodding toward the bowl of blood in Ash's corner. "I know it's been a while since you've fed properly."

Ash smiled grimly. "Your concern is touching," he replied, "but I don't need a blood boost to defeat the likes of you."

He rolled his shoulders and stretched his neck to one side and then the other, feeling his supernatural muscles leap to do his bidding. "Now," he said, "did you come here to talk or did you come to fight?"

There was no more discussion after that. They circled each other for a moment, and the crowd moved with them, waiting for the first blow. Ash soon tired of waiting and let one of his huge fists fly into Memnon's face. Memnon wasn't quick enough to dodge it, and he staggered back, blood pouring out of his mouth.

His fangs shot down into view; he growled and launched himself at Ash, forcing him back into one of the posts at the edge of the ring. The stone slab snapped under their combined weight, and the crowd below scattered to get out of the way of the falling rock.

Ash slid down the post, and Memnon took advantage of his improved position to rain blows down on his opponent's face. For a moment, Ash couldn't move.

Then he reached up, just as Memnon was about to land another punch, and caught the moving fist, holding it suspended as Memnon struggled to complete the blow. The effort made muscles ripple in both their bodies, but Ash, even from his seated position, had the upper hand. He was simply the stronger of the two.

With a mighty heave, he pushed Memnon back across the ring and rose to his feet.

Memnon grabbed one of the remaining bowls of blood and took a long gulp.

⚜

Luc started yelling when it was apparent Ash was just going to wait for him to finish. There was no way Ash could hear him over the rest of the crowd, but it made Luc feel a little better.

Finally, Luc realized he could do more than yell. He reached down into his boot, but his hand found only empty air where his knife should have been. He looked down to confirm with his eyes what his fingers were telling him. Sure enough, the sheath was empty.

A clatter of wood on stone drew his eyes back to the ring. Memnon had dropped the bowl and turned to Ash again, his eyes too bright. He began to circle, waiting for Ash to lose patience and swing.

This time, Memnon knew it was coming. He dodged the heavy blow and landed a vicious uppercut of his own.

Even then, Ash recovered instantly and continued his assault, his superior strength evident as he unleashed blow after blow onto a stunned Memnon, driving him across the ring.

"Kill him!" The cry went up from a few rows behind Luc. Not a sentimental crowd, they clearly favored only whomever looked to be the winner. Memnon fell to his knees, and the cry was picked up by the rest of the crowd.

Ash stopped mid-swing and looked out into the sea of pale faces and blood-stained lips. Luc suddenly knew how they must appear to him—a mob of his own twisted, bloodthirsty offspring. He could see some part of Ash didn't want to give them the satisfaction of a kill.

Memnon could see it too, and he took advantage of Ash's momentary distraction to sink his fangs deep into the flesh on Ash's thigh.

Ash yelled and stepped back in surprise.

Even when he moved, Memnon didn't let go. Blood began to pour down Ash's leg and onto the floor. Memnon sucked harder.

Ash reached down and clamped his hand around Memnon's neck, squeezing his throat closed, forcing him to let go.

Memnon's eyes glittered brighter still.

"You bit me," Ash said in shock and disgust as he held him by the throat. He appeared impervious to the bubbling flow of blood down his leg.

"You know the rules, Ash," Memnon choked out. "There are no rules."

Ash threw him back across the ring. "You were a warrior once," he called out. "Now you're just a murderer."

Memnon swiped at the blood still shimmering on his lips and shook his head. "I play by the rules, Ash," he sneered, "but I play to win."

"Rules?" Ash scoffed. "Whose rules? Whatever honor you had once, Memnon, you lost when you started kidnapping and poisoning other vampires."

Memnon growled and lunged for the wooden stake that still stood embedded in the floor of the ring, surrounded by Viktor's dusty remains. He hurled it across the ring at Samson. Ash neatly side-stepped it, and it sailed out into the crowd, landing with a firm *thunk* in the chest of a spectator.

"Shit," the boy cried out as a dark stain appeared on his faded red tee shirt.

Luc leaned forward to try to see if it had been a fatal wound. The boy was on the other side of the ring, but from the sudden hush and the boos from the crowd, Luc assumed it had been.

An out of place movement on his side of the ring caught Luc's eye. Aleksander had made his way down into the front row and was placing a short knife onto the edge of the ring floor.

Memnon grabbed it and immediately sent it following after his first throw. Ash, still looking out into the crowd, jerked when the blade embedded itself in his back.

He reached a long arm around to pull it out. He turned back to Memnon and held up the tiny blade. "This is what you call playing to win?" he asked contemptuously.

Luc saw him stagger before he even finished the question.

ᴄ✦ᴏ

Ash looked at the knife and wiped his blood from it. The stain of some other fluid was visible underneath, and Ash turned a stunned face to Memnon.

"Poison?" he asked, not really needing an answer. He could feel the unfamiliar heat suffusing his body. Combined with his loss of blood, he knew he didn't have long.

He heard Memnon laugh. "No rules, Ash!" he said, sounding far away. "You never were willing to do what it took to win. That's why you were never made a Shield Bearer back then. It's why you're dying now."

Ash dropped to his knees, and Memnon grabbed another knife from the arena floor. He stalked over to Ash, raised one of his huge arms into the air, and ripped the blade through Ash's forearm, splitting it from elbow to wrist.

He dropped Ash's arm and put the bowl he'd emptied earlier underneath the dripping flesh. "Now the power of your blood won't be wasted," Memnon hissed into his ear. "The poison will dissipate, and with your blood in his veins, Aleksander will be unstoppable."

Memnon's words registered in Ash's mind even as he knew he was dying, and it became clear to him that the massacre at Council House was just a stepping stone on the way to some much grander scheme. Memnon's vision might be limited to getting revenge on Ash, but Ash was now certain this new Aleksander would not be so modest.

He had to protect Ariana. And Luc. And the rest of the world. And so, for the first time in 3,000 years, Samson moved his lips in prayer.

He prayed for forgiveness. He prayed for mercy. And he prayed for a second chance.

CHAPTER 66

Luc shook off the weight of the disbelief that hit him as he watched Ash's body fall to the ring floor. Through the surging crowd, Luc started making his way over to James. Aleksander and Memnon were celebrating their victory. Luc could barely even see them anymore through the circle of vampires gathering to cheer their achievement, but he spied one of Aleksander's lackeys carrying the precious bowl of blood out of the room.

James hadn't joined the crush, Luc noted, finally reaching him and grabbing his arm. "Hey, we've got to get out of here," he said.

James shook his head. "I don't think so," he replied, his voice strangely distant.

Luc looked at him as if he were insane. "Why on earth not?"

"There's no Ash anymore," James said as if that explained everything.

Luc shrugged. "There's no Toria anymore either," he said, "and no Council House, and no Elders. So what? That means you have to stay here and get whacked too?"

James's eyes clouded. "So, it's true then, what happened at Council House?"

"Damn right," Luc said. "Nothing left of them but a funny smell. So let's go," he said, stressing the last syllable.

"Don't you see?" James asked. "That means it's just them."

"What are you talking about? Look," Luc said, taking James' arm and trying again to steer him in the direction of the door, "we have to go, now."

James shook his head. "I don't think so. Memnon and Aleksander aren't out to kill me. They never were. This was all about Ash. Now that he's gone and they got what they were after, I'm just another vampire to them."

"And so you want to stay?" Luc asked, incredulous. "What, you think you have a career as a prize fighter?"

James laughed. "Not exactly. But I'm a pretty useful guy to have around. I can be as useful to these guys as I was to you. And then I'll know what they're up to."

Realization finally dawned on Luc and he backed away. James was going to be a spy.

"Check your e-mail every now and then," James said, smiling at the look of shock and newfound respect that had come over Luc's face.

Luc nodded and turned to go.

"One thing," he said, turning back. "Memnon can see what you see if he chooses to look, so you'll have to be careful."

James looked confused.

"He can tune other vampires in like TV stations," Luc explained. "My advice—stay off his radar."

CHAPTER 67

Nancy sat her petite form on the edge of the mattress. "Don't try to get up."

Get up? Ariana thought. She couldn't even open her eyes. Why was she so tired?

"You're pregnant," Nancy explained.

That got her attention and her eyes popped open. "Pregnant?" she squeaked. Ariana shook her head at the gray little woman who stood beside Ash's giant burgundy bed. "You're letting your imagination run away with you, Nancy."

"I don't think so, dear," she said. "I told you long ago there would be a price."

A price. A price. Oh god. A price long unpaid.

"You cheated us, Delilah," Nancy said, confirming Ariana's worst fears. "You cheated Lilith. Did you really think the debt would never come due?"

Now Ariana recognized the voice. She'd heard it before, younger and without the English accent, of course, but heard it she had.

"It was you," she whispered, staring up at Nancy. She could see in her face the vestiges of the pretty young girl who had come to Delilah's room so long ago

Nancy smiled. "The one who brought you to Lilith? That's right," she confirmed. "I brought you into her home. I brought the blood of the goddess to you as she lay dying, and I watched you cheat her out of her birthright. Yes, that was me."

"Goddess," Ariana choked. "Don't you mean demon? Look what her blood has done to Ash," she said, "to all of them."

"That was never Lilith's intent," Nancy argued. "You bungled that yourself."

"And now?" Ariana asked, sinking back into the pillows and fearing she already knew the answer.

Nancy handed her a cup of tea, which Ariana drank greedily. Anything to give her strength.

"Now," Nancy answered when she was again holding the tiny porcelain cup, "you and the master have fulfilled the promise."

Again Ariana shook her head. "Nancy, I hate to break it to you, but the master and I haven't fulfilled anything. I can't have children. It's impossible."

Nancy smiled gently at her and smoothed her hair the way she might a sick child. "After all you've seen, dear, do you still believe anything is impossible? Lilith has come to claim her bargain."

❧

Luc cleared his throat. "I don't mean to interrupt," he said from the doorway, "but she's at least half right." He nodded toward Nancy, then came in and took a seat in a brocade-covered chair near the door. "I didn't know how to tell you before, Ariana, but you're what we call a breeder."

He waited, trying to gauge Ariana's reaction.

When it came, all she said was "That's flattering," her tone clearly indicating it wasn't.

Luc stiffened. "Hey, my mother was a breeder," he said.

Nancy turned to study Luc.

"What are you talking about?" Ariana asked, pulling herself up on the bed.

"You're a breeder," Luc repeated, "which makes you irresistible to vampires. Something in you causes them to feel sexual desire and, in some cases, allows them to sire natural offspring."

"You mean I give off some kind of vampire pheromone?" Ariana asked, disbelief sending her eyebrows up a notch.

"What's a pheromone?" Luc asked.

Ariana rolled her eyes. "A smell," she replied tartly, "a scent of some kind."

"Well, yeah," he said. "That's pretty much it exactly."

"And how do you know this?" Nancy asked.

"It's like I said," Luc repeated, turning to the older woman. "My mother was one. All I know is what she told me—and Ash—and the little bit of rumor I've picked up here and there, but so far, it's been dead on." Luc rose and came over to the bed. "When Ariana and I first met, we couldn't keep our hands off each other." He sat down on the other side of the mattress from Nancy. "For heaven's sake, Ariana," he said, "we made love in a parking deck."

"You what!" Nancy screeched.

Luc ignored her and continued on, watching Ariana's eyes to be sure she understood. "Vampires don't have sex," he explained, "We don't need it. It's not how we reproduce. Bloodlust is the only lust we feel."

Finally, the first spark of understanding began to dawn in the dark depths of her gaze. "No," she said again, shaking her head from side to side. "It can't be."

Luc leaned forward and kissed her softly on the forehead, then backed away. "I couldn't have done that the day I met you—at least not without ripping your clothes off, and you know it. Didn't you wonder why the attraction between us only lasted a day?"

She was silent for so long, Luc felt compelled to say something else. Anything else. He rested his head in his hands. "I'm sorry about this," he offered, not looking up at her. "I'm sorry about everything."

"So, you think I'm carrying your child?" Ariana asked.

"Children," Luc corrected, a frown marring his ethereal features. "Didn't she tell you? Nancy thinks its twins."

"Twins?"

Luc was startled to realize it was fear he saw on Ariana's face. "Ariana," he asked, "what's the matter?"

She wiped the beginning of a tear from one eye with the back of her hand. "Nothing," she said, "I just hadn't really planned on giving birth to one demon spawn today, that's all, much less two."

"Hey," he said, smarting. "That's a little harsh."

"No," Ariana said, "you don't understand. Long ago, as Delilah, I made a bargain with a demon, and the price for her help was that I was to bear a child—Samson's child. That child was to be a vessel for Lilith to re-enter the world."

Luc leaned forward, still unable to fully grasp what she was telling him.

"Lilith's blood is what turned Ash into a vampire." She looked into Luc's unusual eyes. "I even think it's why certain women can mate with them. Those women—and you—are descendents of the child I was already carrying when I drank her blood. There just haven't been any offspring strong enough for Lilith to enter."

Until now. The words hung unspoken in the air between them.

"Without the infusion of Lilith's blood at the moment of conception, as the ritual required, all the resulting human children were too weak," Nancy explained. "And the vampire traits of the born vampires don't manifest until puberty, which is too late. These children, though," she looked at Ariana's belly, "are something different."

"Whoa, hold on now," Luc demanded. "We don't know that. We don't even know if it will be twins. We just have Nancy's say on that. And they will be my children, mine and yours," he said, taking Ariana's hand, "not Samson's or Delilah's." He turned to Nancy. "Wasn't that also required?"

An enigmatic smile played at Nancy's thin lips. "Perhaps," she said. She smoothed her perfectly pressed gray dress. "But fate has seen her to the same result, and Lilith has deemed the child of the breeder and the born-vampire a worthy vessel."

Ariana sank back down into her pillow, then sat back up. "Where is Ash?" she asked suddenly, looking back and forth between her two bedside chaperones.

Luc took her hand. "Ash fought Memnon last night." She looked blankly at him, forcing him to spell it out. "It was a death match," he said, "and he... lost, Ariana."

"The Master lost a fight?" Nancy asked.

Luc nodded. "Not a fair fight, but, well, it's a no-rules kind of game."

"Does that mean..." Ariana's voice trailed off.

Luc nodded, knowing she needed to hear it outright. "Yes, Ariana, he's dead. I'm sorry, but I saw him disintegrate with my own eyes."

A small gasping squeak came out of her and then nothing else.

"Ariana," Luc laid his other hand on top of hers, "please don't worry. I'm going to take care of you and the twins."

Ariana looked at him coldly. "Really? And just how do you plan to do that? Up your output of vampire beauty lotion? And watch for signs that our children may be demons?"

Luc's jaw dropped, and Ariana was instantly contrite. "I'm sorry," she said, turning her hand to clasp his. "I don't know what I'm going to do yet, but everything will be fine somehow."

"I'm not rich," Luc acknowledged, "but those children will need both of us, and you shouldn't underestimate the value of having some-one around who's only interest is in protecting you. And the twins."

Ariana smiled at him. "I guess you're right," she said. "I know my world, and I've gotten very used to getting my own way in it, but," her gaze drifted from his face to the windowless room behind him, "like it or not, I'm part of this world now, and so are our children. And we'll need your help."

"You'll have it," Luc confirmed. He smiled at her "Besides," he said, "there are two of them. They can't *both* be Lilith." He nodded toward Nancy. "And maybe Nancy's just plain gone senile," he added. "How long can a demon hang around waiting to be born anyway?"

Nancy gave an unattractive harrumph, but Ariana smiled a genu-ine smile this time. "Ever the optimist," she said.

Luc broke out his trademark grin. "That's more like it," he said. "After all, they're just kids. It's not like it's the end of the world."

ALICIA BENSON currently resides in Northern California with her husband, Robert, and their dog, Goldie. She considers herself lucky to have lived and worked in some of the greatest places in the country—Boston, Washington, D.C., New York City, California's Bay Area, and her home in rural North Carolina. For fun, she writes books about vampires, travels and watches sci-fi movies and television. THE FIRST VAMPIRE is her debut novel. You can read more about her work at www.aliciabenson.com.

ALSO IN PRINT FROM VIRTUAL TALES

The Curious Accounts of the Imaginary Friend—P.S. Gifford

Dr. Offig's Lessons from the Dark Side, Vol 1—P.S. Gifford

Dry Rain—B.J. Kibble

Earrings of Ixtumea—Kim Baccellia

Figgy-Dowdy—Frank Minogue

Have Wine, Will Travel—Jacquelynn Luben

Rough Justice—Lee Pierce

COMING SOON FROM VIRTUAL TALES

The Haunting of Melmerby Manor—David Robinson

Portal to Murder—Michele Acker

The Autumn of the Unfortunates—Christopher Treagus

My True Love Sent to Me—Elizabeth Hopkinson

Hero—Dan Rafter

VISIT US ONLINE
WWW.VIRTUALTALES.COM

Printed in the United States
205334BV00005B/1-3/P

9 780980 150681